D0311384

A WILD LIGHT

MARJORIE M. LIU

WITHDRAWN

ACE BOOKS, NEW YORK

THE BERKLEY PUBLISHING GROUP
Published by the Penguin Group
Penguin Group (USA) Inc.
375 Hudson Street, New York, New York 10014, USA
Penguin Group (Canada), 90 Eglinton Avenue East, Suite 700, Toronto, Ontario M4P 2Y3, Canada
(a division of Pearson Penguin Canada Inc.)
Penguin Books Ltd., 80 Strand, London WC2R 0RL, England
Penguin Group Ireland, 25 St. Stephen's Green, Dublin 2, Ireland (a division of Penguin Books Ltd.)
Penguin Group (Australia), 250 Camberwell Road, Camberwell, Victoria 3124, Australia
(a division of Pearson Australia Group Pty. Ltd.)
Penguin Books India Pvt. Ltd., 11 Community Centre, Panchsheel Park, New Delhi—110 017, India
Penguin Group (NZ), 67 Apollo Drive, Rosedale, North Shore 0632, New Zealand
(a division of Pearson New Zealand Ltd.)
Penguin Books (South Africa) (Pty.) Ltd., 24 Sturdee Avenue, Rosebank, Johannesburg 2196,
South Africa

Penguin Books Ltd., Registered Offices: 80 Strand, London WC2R 0RL, England

This is a work of fiction. Names, characters, places, and incidents either are the product of the author's imagination or are used fictitiously, and any resemblance to actual persons, living or dead, business establishments, events, or locales is entirely coincidental. The publisher does not have any control over and does not assume any responsibility for author or third-party websites or their content.

A WILD LIGHT

An Ace Book / published by arrangement with the author

PRINTING HISTORY
Ace mass-market edition / August 2010

Copyright © 2010 by Marjorie M. Liu.
Cover art by Craig White.
Cover design by Judith Lagerman.
Interior text design by Laura K. Corless.

All rights reserved.
No part of this book may be reproduced, scanned, or distributed in any printed or electronic form without permission. Please do not participate in or encourage piracy of copyrighted materials in violation of the author's rights. Purchase only authorized editions.
For information, address: The Berkley Publishing Group,
a division of Penguin Group (USA) Inc.,
375 Hudson Street, New York, New York 10014.

ISBN: 978-0-441-01901-4

ACE
Ace Books are published by The Berkley Publishing Group,
a division of Penguin Group (USA) Inc.,
375 Hudson Street, New York, New York 10014.
ACE and the "A" design are trademarks of Penguin Group (USA) Inc.

PRINTED IN THE UNITED STATES OF AMERICA

10 9 8 7 6 5 4 3 2 1

If you purchased this book without a cover, you should be aware that this book is stolen property. It was reported as "unsold and destroyed" to the publisher, and neither the author nor the publisher has received any payment for this "stripped book."

PRAISE FOR
THE HUNTER KISS NOVELS
BY "RED-HOT LIU"*

DARKNESS CALLS

"[Liu's] ability to deliver kick-butt action and characters whose humanity resonates, even when they're anything but human, is a testament to her outstanding storytelling skills. Liu's imagination is an amazing place to visit."
—*Romantic Times* (Top Pick)

"*Darkness Calls* is one riveting book, and Marjorie Liu is one great writer. The desperation Maxine feels as she deals with her past and unknown future is one that will keep you reading and anxious for the next terror Maxine will have to endure."
—*Fresh Fiction*

"Liu has done an excellent job of developing and expanding the mythos she created in *The Iron Hunt* . . . I look forward to reading the further adventures of Maxine Kiss." —*SFRevu*

THE IRON HUNT

"I adore the Hunter Kiss series! Marjorie Liu's writing is both lyrical and action packed, which is a very rare combination. Heroine Maxine Kiss and her demon friends are wonderful characters who are as likable as they are fierce. You'll want to read this series over and over."
—Angela Knight, *New York Times* bestselling author

"Liu is one of the best new voices in paranormal fiction."
—*Publishers Weekly*

"Marjorie M. Liu writes a gripping supernatural thriller."
—*The Best Reviews*

*Romantic Times

continued . . .

"From the imagination of one of today's most talented authors comes a mesmerizing, darkly disturbing world on the brink of apocalypse. With her new Hunter Kiss series, Liu has created a uniquely tough yet vulnerable heroine in Maxine Kiss . . . Through Maxine's eyes, readers take a heart-stopping ride where buried secrets could change the fate of the world."
—*Romantic Times*

"Readers who love urban fantasies like those of Charlaine Harris or Kim Harrison will relish Marjorie M. Liu's excellent adventure. This is the superb start of a dynamic-looking saga."
—*Midwest Book Review*

"Ms. Liu does a lovely job in . . . preparing us for the high-speed action in her demon-filled adventure. A creative and well-written story line provides a strong backbone for this new urban fantasy series, and the unique characters in *The Iron Hunt* will charm, tempt, and surprise readers into coming back for more."
—*Darque Reviews*

"A stunning new series . . . The mythology is fascinating, the characters complicated, the story lines original. I'm a big fan of Liu's Dirk & Steele series, but this one surpasses even it."
—*Fresh Fiction*

"An incredibly complex, engrossing story that will stretch your imagination and broaden your ideas of what is and what could be."
—*Romance Junkies*

"Marjorie Liu seems to have an endless imagination for creating new and interesting characters and stories. I can't wait to see how this story develops and the world of Maxine Kiss evolves. This is a character and a story that has potential to keep the reader interested for an extensive series of books."
—*Affaire de Coeur*

MORE PRAISE FOR THE NOVELS OF
MARJORIE M. LIU

"Raises the bar for all others competing in its league . . . Liu's screenplay-worthy dialogue, vivid action, and gift for the punchy, unexpected metaphor rocket her tale high above the pack. Readers of early Laurell K. Hamilton, Charlaine Harris, and the best thrillers out there should try Liu now and catch a rising star." —*Publishers Weekly* (starred review)

"The boundlessness of Liu's imagination never ceases to amaze; her ability to translate that imagination into a lyrical work of art never ceases to impress."
—*Booklist* (starred review)

"Red-hot Liu . . . packs her stories with immensely intriguing characters, making the high-stakes plotlines even more mesmerizing." —*Romantic Times* (Top Pick, 4½ stars)

"Nonstop adventure . . . a rich world with paranormal elements." —*SFRevu*

"A wonderful voice." —*Romance at Heart Magazine*

"Liu is masterful in merging espionage, romance, and the supernatural into fiction that goes beyond the boundaries of action-adventure romance or romantic suspense." —*Booklist*

"Fabulous romantic suspense fantasy that will hook the audience from the first note to the incredible climatic coda."
—*Midwest Book Review*

Ace Books by Marjorie M. Liu

THE IRON HUNT
DARKNESS CALLS
A WILD LIGHT

eSpecials

HUNTER KISS

Anthologies

WILD THING
(with Maggie Shayne, Alyssa Day, and Meljean Brook)

NEVER AFTER
(with Laurell K. Hamilton, Yasmine Galenorn, and Sharon Shinn)

INKED
(with Karen Chance, Yasmine Galenorn, and Eileen Wilks)

To the families we love, whether born to or made

ACKNOWLEDGMENTS

Many thanks to: my lovely editor, Kate Seaver; my fantastic agent, Lucienne Diver; all the wonderful people at Berkley; and my great copy editors, Bob and Sara Schwager.

And hail their queen, fair regent of the night.

—ERASMUS DARWIN

I will vanish in the morning light;
I was only an invention of darkness.

—ANGELA CARTER

CHAPTER 1

I T was my birthday, the anniversary of my mother's murder, and on the way to the party, I made a special point to stop and kill a zombie.

I did it every year. My secret. Only Zee and the boys knew. Our gift to each other.

Sun had been down for only an hour, but this was Seattle, the skies were black as midnight, and the rain pounded the windshield like each drop was trying to break the glass. Cyndi Lauper played on the radio, softly, because I wanted to hear Dek and Mal sing along. "True Colors," one of my mother's favorites.

The little demons were coiled around my shoulders, heavy and warm, their breath hot against my ears as they hummed the song in their high, sweet voices. Aaz and Raw sat in the backseat, uncharacteristically quiet, their little legs dangling over the floor as they clutched half-eaten teddy bears against their scaled, muscular chests.

Zee crouched in the passenger seat. Razor-sharp spines of black hair flexed against his chiseled skull, and his eyes glinted red. His claws flexed, in and out, in and out, and every few minutes, he raked his arms in quiet agitation. He was difficult to see, even seated beside me. All of them were. Blending with the shadows, falling into shadows, except for the silver glint of veins and their burning eyes.

"Left," Zee rasped. I didn't question his instincts. I turned at the intersection. We were in the south end of Lake Union, near the park. I pulled into the lot near the armory. The boys were gone before I turned off the engine, disappearing into the shadows like ghosts. Only Dek and Mal stayed, heavy and reassuring around my throat. Little bodyguards.

The downpour did not ease. I didn't worry about it. Less visibility was a good thing.

I only had to wait ten minutes. Zee poked his head out from beneath the dashboard. He didn't have to say a word. I got out, hunching down, as the rain slammed me. Cold as ice. My gloves were already off. I looked down, once, at the armor hugging my right hand: organic metal, quicksilver as mercury, embedded in the skin of my fingers and wrist, connected by threads that traveled over the back of my pale hand.

Magic. Or close enough not to matter. It certainly didn't matter tonight.

Zee loped ahead on all fours. We moved amongst trees planted in concrete beds, my bootheels clicking sharp. Rain slid down the back of my neck into my clothes. My hair plastered against my skull. My nose began to run.

Aaz and Raw waited beneath a tree, near the jogging path. A zombie lay between them. A woman. She wore sweatpants and a lightweight rain jacket. Blond, young, possessed by a demonic parasite. Her aura was old, fluttering with a darkness deeper than the night.

She bared her teeth when she saw me, but it was the beginning of a scream, and Zee clamped his small hand over her mouth. She bucked upward, but Raw had a firm hold on her legs, and Aaz had already pulled her arms over her head. All of them, touching her as gently as they could. Hosts were innocent. I always assumed so, anyway.

I crouched. Stared long and hard at the zombie, memorizing her face and the thunder of her aura. I didn't ask questions, I didn't care about crimes. I didn't think too hard about the last two years and how some demons could be reformed, converted. I didn't think about the possibility of innocence. Tonight, I didn't accept innocence.

Instead, I thought about my mother carrying my birthday cake across the kitchen, and the window exploding, and her head doing the same. I thought about her blood, and the boys weeping, and my screaming. I thought about the possessed men and women—the zombies—who slaughtered her.

I had lost count of all the demons I'd exorcised over the years, but the ones I took on my birthday were always special.

I was gentle. I pressed my palm against her brow. I said the words, and the demon stretched and stretched, the parasite holding on for dear life. It had been a deep possession. Years, maybe—even decades. Controlling this woman, using her as a puppet to feed on the suffering the demon certainly had caused around her. Growing fat on pain.

The parasite snapped free. Aaz caught it first, and then Raw and Zee took hold. Dek and Mal purred. I looked away, trying not to listen to the high screams of the creature as it was eaten. I focused on the woman. Checked her pulse. Found her ID. She lived nearby. A jogger. Bad night for exercise. Those parasites and their fun.

Zee glided close, running his long black tongue over his teeth. I smelled sulfur and ash.

"Maxine," he whispered. "Happy birthday."

I wiped rain from my eyes and walked back to the car.

⟞⟐⟝

I had started keeping a box of prepaid disposable phones in the car. Public pay phones were becoming a rarity.

I dug one out, made a call. Told 911 that a woman was unconscious in the park. An amnesiac, too, I didn't add. It was an old routine. Aaz ate the phone after I was done.

We didn't talk as I drove to the party. Dek and Mal blew on my hair, trying to dry it. I jacked up the volume on the radio. Aaz and Raw yanked whole steaming pizzas from the shadows and ate them, along with two gallons of paint, a box of plant fertilizer, and several canisters of whipping cream. Zee sat in the passenger seat, held his sharp knobby knees to his chest, and rocked back and forth in silence.

Grant waited for me just inside the entrance of the art gallery. Tall, broad, leaning hard on his cane. His brown hair was damp, like he had been poking his head into the rain, searching for me. Inside, the lights were dim. I heard music upstairs: Tchaikovsky. *The Sleeping Beauty.*

I tried to smile, but I was wet and cold, cold beneath my skin. My heart hurt. Grant took one look and pulled me inside, into his arms. He held me a long time. I listened to the rain, and Dek and Mal as they purred, and the scratch of claws on the hardwood floors. I listened to my heartbeat, and I listened to Grant's. Perfectly matched.

Slowly, slowly, I relaxed.

"I don't like having birthdays," I whispered.

He didn't try to reassure me. He didn't tell me it would get better. All he did was hold me, and kiss the top of my head, my closed eyes, my mouth, his rough cheek rubbing against mine. He was so warm.

"Come on," he breathed finally, in my ear. "Dance me to the stairs."

I smiled and kissed his throat. "It's your life."

"I trust you." Grant leaned hard on his cane and offered me his arm. "I'll even let you lead."

"Oh, wow," I replied, wiping my sleeve across my nose. "That's love."

"Eh," he said, but with a grin and cocky shrug. Aaz and Raw giggled. Zee, crouched nearby, pulled jasmine petals from the shadows and tossed them at our feet.

I helped Grant climb the stairs. Neither of us said so, but I knew his leg hurt him. I was his shoulder, and we moved with the rise and fall of the "Sarabande" portion of the ballet. Near the landing, I glimpsed a shadow move across the golden light spilling from the door into the stairwell.

"Need help?" Byron asked. He was young, no older than fifteen, pale and dark-haired, wearing jeans and a soft white T-shirt that had SHAKESPEARE HATES YOUR EMO POEMS written across the chest.

I flashed him a smile. So did Grant. "Almost there. But thanks."

The boy nodded but didn't move until we were on the landing. I ruffled his hair. He smiled, just a little—but that might as well have been a grin, with nothing guarded in his eyes. Good kid. Smart, honest. He'd come a long way from living inside a cardboard box.

I heard pots banging from the apartment. Grant squeezed my hand. "Jack's been busy."

"Is that a warning or a threat?"

Byron had already begun picking his way through the books on the other side of the door. "He made pies. Grant said you hate cake."

I stared at the boy's back. Grant leaned a little harder on the cane, his hand tightening around mine.

"I didn't tell you I hated cake," I said.

"You also didn't tell me when your birthday was. But you *did* tell me how your mother died." Grant kissed my ear, and lingered. "My brain, it works sometimes."

"You're going to make me sentimental."

"Jack has you beat. In all his thousand million years of being alive, I'm not certain he's ever celebrated a grand-daughter's birthday."

"In all his thousand million years, I'm sure he had other children, tons of grandchildren."

"Maybe. But he has *you* now." Grant patted my ass. "Go on, Wonder Woman. He's wearing an apron just for you."

The apartment had been cleaned. Or rather, the aisle between Jack's stacked books had been widened, just a little. The walls were lined with shelves, sagging with books and pottery, masks, stones—but those were just the walls, and the walls were a good ten feet away from the center of the room, which was the only place a person could stand and walk without tripping. Everywhere else, towers of books, half-opened crates, papers and journals tipping sideways—some lamps perched precariously on boxes, cords disappearing into the maze—along with used coffee cups, chocolate-bar wrappers, and the occasional glass eye, which I pretended did not watch me as I passed.

I smelled pie. I heard mumbling, the screech of the oven door opening. I heard Jack say, "Put down the knife," and an older woman reply, "Bad lines, Wolf."

I walked free of the maze into the kitchen. My grandfather stood at the table. He was, indeed, wearing an apron—white, with cherries and frills—tied over his khakis and dress shirt. Somehow, it looked entirely proper. Mary stood on the other side of the table, white hair wild and hanging loose over the shoulders of a navy housedress covered in embroidered shooting stars. Her large, sinewy hands clutched a knife that was digging point first into a pie, one of several on the table—which was otherwise barely visible beneath boards, rolling pins, mixing bowls, and about a ton of spilled flour.

"Got skills to cut," Mary said to my grandfather, thumping her chest with her fist. "Go lick yourself."

"Charming," replied Jack. "I suggest you stick to growing *marijuana*, Marritine, and leave the pies to me."

The old woman hissed at him. Byron was perched on encyclopedias, watching them, sipping calmly from a cup of what seemed to be hot chocolate. I didn't miss the wariness of his gaze whenever it fell on Jack—an involuntary response, one that I doubted would ever go away.

The boy held up the cup to me, but I said no. Dek and Mal, however, poked their heads free of my hair, staring at his drink. Byron pretended not to notice. He was good at not noticing the boys.

Grant tapped his cane on the floor. Mary's scowl melted into a sweet smile that almost made me forget she was a trained killer. She left the knife standing straight up in the pie and danced on the tips of her toes to Grant. He kissed her cheek. The old woman melted, just a little.

I joined Jack at the table. He was trying to yank the knife out of the pie and having no luck. I nudged him aside. Mary had stabbed the blade tip right through the pan into the table. Kooky broad.

"You didn't have to do all this," I said to my grandfather, jerking the knife loose with a grunt.

"How could I not?" Jack dipped his finger into the pie hole left by the knife and licked it. "Apple. And that one over there is peach. The pecan is self-evident. All of them fresh, I assure you. I walked down to Pike Place Market this morning for the ingredients, and battled zombies and young women with grabby hands—just for you."

"My hero. I didn't even know you could bake."

"My dear," he said, resting his hand on my shoulder, "before the Spanish Influenza killed me, I lived briefly as the son of a baker in New York City. Early twentieth century. I still have the knack."

"And how many lives have you lived? I'm surprised you remember anything at all."

"I don't." He rolled up his sleeve to show me his tattoos: words and symbols, even numbers. "Old men need help, sometimes."

I smiled to myself and began slicing pie. "You're trouble, Old Wolf."

"Of course." He leaned on the table, watching me, and it felt comfortable, easy. My grandfather. I had a grandfather. I could say that again and again, and never grow tired of hearing it.

"What was your name when you were a baker's son?"

"Michael," he said. "I found him in the womb when he was just a little ball of cells. Quite darling. And then I simply embedded myself and dreamed a little, and the next thing I knew, I was born. My mother was Hannah, my father was Robert, and they were good people. Stern, rather too serious for a couple who sold sweets to children, but I liked them well enough."

"Why did you allow the flu to take your life? Couldn't you have fought it off?"

"I was done in that body. Other adventures awaited. And, experiencing mortality in all its different forms can be . . . illuminating." Jack's smile faded. "Is something wrong?"

I thought about the zombie I had exorcised less than an hour earlier. "You make it sound so easy. But I still have trouble reconciling the idea that you possess humans. You're not demon, but you and your kind still use human bodies. Some, more so than others. I suppose . . . I wondered what my mother thought about that."

"I don't know," Jack said, and fumbled for a small box of candles. "We talked very little the few times we met."

I was sorry I said anything. I patted his hand. "Thank you for the pies, and for . . . for all of the rest. It's wonderful."

"You're loved," he said simply, then busied himself with setting candles into the pie, ignoring me as I leaned on the table, drawing circles in the spilled flour while suffering a peculiar weight in my chest that was hot and good, and heartbreaking.

I looked around the room. Byron had opened up one of the books and was reading—studiously ignoring Raw, who perched several stacks behind him, peering over his shoulder while picking slime from his nose with his claw. Mary was also seated on books, eating fresh marijuana leaves directly from a plastic bag—tapping her feet, humming to herself. Grant watched her, shaking his head—and then he looked away, at me.

I always felt a jolt when our eyes met. Always. My man. My good man. I was a mess, I was dangerous. I was the last living Warden of a failing prison that would one day release a demonic army on this world—and I had always expected to be alone, except for the boys. Never homebound, just road-bound, rootless, without a single person in the world knowing or caring whether I lived or died.

That had been the future. That was the way things were done in my family.

Except I'd made a different choice.

Claws touched my knee. Zee, beneath the table. I crouched and drew him into a brief hug. He didn't let go.

"Bad dreams coming," he whispered, for my ears only. "Can hear the whispers, singing in the storm."

I got chills, followed by a sinking feeling in my gut. I took a deep breath, steadying myself. "And?"

"Won't be the same." Zee glanced over his shoulder at

Aaz, who was sitting nearby; then Raw, who crawled from the shadows beneath the table to join his brothers. Dek and Mal slithered free of my hair, roping down my arms. "Will never be the same."

A strong hand touched my shoulder. Grant, looking down at me with concern. I couldn't pretend there was nothing wrong. Never mind I was a terrible liar. There wasn't anything in a person that Grant couldn't see—and what he could see, he could change—with nothing but his voice. Made him almost as dangerous as me. More so, maybe. I could kill. But I couldn't alter souls.

"Later," I mouthed to him, and he nodded faintly. I glanced at Jack, but the old man was still fussing with candles. Pretending, maybe. Hard to tell. Mary had stopped eating her marijuana leaves and held Byron by the hand, drawing him to the table while singing softly to herself.

I looked at them all. My family. My random, mismatched family. None of us was entirely human—not human like the rest of this world was human—but we belonged together. I'd found home.

The candles were lit. Twenty-seven, burning. Years, burning.

I blew them out in one breath, and made my wish.

❦

I woke only minutes before dawn, on the edge of a nightmare.

Coiled in darkness, in my dream. Made of darkness, stitched from a vast oubliette of forgotten things, endless worlds of bone and blood and skins, stretched upon a canopy of stars. I felt the stars in my veins, glittering as my heart pumped light into the darkness, waiting, and in my dream I ate that light, every burning morsel, and swallowed it down a throat that curved, and twisted, and knotted itself into a mighty, unending circle. I *was* the circle, and the twist, and the knot, and there was no end to the hunger that filled me. No end, ever.

We tried to warn you, my mother's voice echoed in the darkness, each word caught in the stars flowing inside that doomed river in my blood. *Gave you signs and riddles, and scars. Fed you dreams. These dreams.*

But you did not understand. And so it comes.

So you come.

Be strong, baby. Be strong.

I opened my eyes.

I was not in bed. I was curled in a ball on the floor, shivering. It was cold. So cold, there was a moment I imagined myself lost in snow, ice, pinned to frozen ground. But there was no snowdrift or black sky. Just a room filled with books and soft chairs, a grand piano in the corner and a red motorcycle parked by the couch.

Home.

Sweet home, part of me thought, but I felt inexplicably uneasy at the idea. It didn't feel right that I had a home. I was a nomad. I lived out of my car and hotel rooms. No roots.

But I recognized this place. I knew it was home. I belonged. I lay very still, soaking in that sensation, and felt small tongues lick my ears. Heavy bodies coiled through my hair, long as snakes. Twin purrs rumbled low, soft, against my scalp.

"Maxine," rasped a low voice. "Sweet Maxine."

I did not move. Remaining still seemed like the safest thing I could do—still and quiet, like a mouse.

"You sound afraid," I whispered. "Zee."

The little demon shuffled into sight, dragging his claws against the hardwood floor. Graceful, even so—as though his muscles were water and wind, flowing beneath his taut skin. A silver vein pulsed against his throat, but the beat of his heart was not slow, or steady. Fluttering, instead. Shuddering.

He could not meet my gaze, and the unease I had felt since opening my eyes—that growing sense of *wrong*—bloomed hard and wide through my gut. Chased, too, by emptiness: a vast hole centered in my heart. It felt like it should be grief, but I didn't know why.

I heard sniffling, and tried finally to sit up. I needed help. My muscles were inexplicably weak, joints rubbery, as though I had been running all night, swinging a baseball bat. Every inch of me felt used. My head hurt. Made me want to lie back down.

Slender clawed hands reached under my elbows. Raw and Aaz, spiked hair slicked tight against dark skulls, red eyes wide, glistening. Oversized baseball jerseys covered their bodies, the hems dragging, tangling in clawed feet as the two demons clung close, falling into my lap. I felt them tremble. Listened as they started sucking their claws, like babies. In my hair, Dek and Mal coiled even tighter against my scalp, their purrs ending in terrible silence.

I tried to speak, but my voice broke. I tried again, more slowly, feeling as though I were having a stroke as I struggled to say each small word.

"What is it?" I managed. "What happened?"

No one spoke. No one looked at me. Raw and Aaz pushed harder against my body, as though trying to burrow through my stomach. Zee stayed where he was, claws digging into the floor, cracking wood. I braced myself, trying to stay upright, and looked down.

Blood. Drying blood, glistening in spots.

Took me a moment to understand what I was looking at. I hadn't seen that much blood in a long time. It covered the floor from me to the kitchen, dull and rusty as poison. My hands, I realized numbly, were soaked in it. Left hand, nothing but red. Right hand, also stained, except for the armor. I knew instantly what the armor was and wasn't— *magic, a key, growing in your body until you die*—but it seemed as unreal as the blood, or the floor beneath me, or the breath in my lungs.

My right hand balled into a fist. I could smell the blood now, as though seeing it released its scent: metallic and warm, gushing through my nose and down my throat until I thought I would choke.

And I did choke, when I looked over my shoulder and saw who lay behind me.

"Jack." I knocked aside demons, scrabbling on my hands and knees to reach the old man. I slipped in blood. His blood. So much blood, sticky and thick, surrounding him like some terrible red sea.

He faced away from me, clad in a light gray sweater, dark slacks. His white hair, wild. So proper. So eccentric. My grandfather was—

I touched him and knew.

I knew. Stared, unable to breathe. Watching, as though from a great distance as my fingers closed around his arm and shoulder, tugging gently, rolling him over. He was still warm, and it was difficult. I was weak. I was terrified.

But then it was done, he lay on his back—and I froze, staring. Punched in the heart so hard, everything stopped: my pulse, my blood, my life.

His throat had been cut. Ear to ear. Flesh gaped like an ugly smile.

Jack Meddle. My grandfather.

And the knife on the other side of him, in his blood, was mine.

CHAPTER 2

I did not scream, but only because I clapped a shaking hand over my mouth. I might have screamed a little, after that. I don't know.

I turned boneless. I turned blind, except for Jack. I couldn't make sense of what I was seeing. His body seemed obscene, a waxen shell made of clay and incantations, held together by threads of fingernails, hair. He horrified me.

Never mind it was impossible for Jack to die—not with any lasting permanence. I didn't care about technicalities. My grandfather had been murdered. I was sitting in his blood—blood draining from a body that had loved my grandmother, that had made my mother. And, in a fashion, me.

It felt the same as losing him for real.

And I didn't remember how any of it had happened.

I couldn't move. My knees were warm, wet. I tasted the scent of death in my mouth—not just blood, but piss, shit. All the little humiliations. My mother had smelled the same after her murder.

"Zee," I croaked, searching out the little demon, who crouched nearby, spiked hair drooping, red eyes nearly shut as though with pain.

I couldn't say anything else. I watched him share a long look with Aaz and Raw, while in my hair, twin voices began humming the melody to "Highway to Hell."

I was going to vomit. I managed to scrabble backward, smearing blood across the floor. Holding my breath, my mouth. My back hit the couch. Nothing changed with distance. Nothing got easier. No miraculous resurrection.

"Zee," I whispered, again. "What happened?"

He would not look at me. He stared, instead, at his claws—as though he were seeing them for the first time: long, curved, black as pitch. Sharp enough to split hairs. Or cut a man's throat.

Much like my knife, still resting in Jack's blood.

I could see it from where I sat. My knife. My mother's knife, part of a specially crafted set that had been passed down to me. No hilt. Just blade. Made for steel-laced gloves, and hands incapable of being cut. No one used them but me.

My hand, even now, felt the weight of the blade. But when I searched my memories, all I recalled was sharpening a knife on Zee's round stomach. Sitting on the couch, near the bookcase—*after the party, I had been at a party with pie, and laughter, and Sleeping Beauty*—watching old episodes of *Yogi Bear*. Listening to the boys eat bags of iron nails, whole garlic cloves, broken glass, washing it all down with engine oil.

I remembered. I remembered, every sensation and sound: the nubby texture of the couch beneath my palm, scents of garlic and oil burning my nostrils: the giggles of the boys when Yogi tried to steal a picnic basket. *I'm smarter than the average bear* floated through my mind, again and again, along with other memories that would not fade: a silver flash of the blade, the blade on Zee's stomach, its sharp edge turning tricks of sparks and light. Soft as light, sharp as light.

I recalled nothing after that. Just a hole where my memories should be. I could touch the edges, and it felt like the rim of a cup with no bottom and only darkness for water. No Jack. No violence. No clue as to who had left my grandfather dead—and me on the ground, unconscious.

Which should never have happened. The boys protected me. Their lives depended on it as much as mine. Ten thousand years bound to my bloodline, defending mothers and daughters. Keeping us alive until it was our turn to die.

But it was not my turn. Not yet.

"Zee," I said.

"Maxine," he rasped. His expression was terrifying in its emptiness. Blank, dull, as though part of the little demon was locked away from me—just as numb as I was.

He was in shock, I realized. All of them were. Raw and Aaz huddled together, rocking back and forth. Dek and Mal continued to hum the refrain to "Highway to Hell," an unusual tinny quality to their soft voices.

Then they stopped, entirely.

Zee looked at the apartment door. So did Raw and Aaz, their rocking motions slowing to perfect stillness. My skin crawled, watching them—but that was dawn, I told myself. Sunrise was coming, no matter how dark the windows appeared.

I heard a clicking sound. Heavy footsteps on the stairs.

I tried to stand. My legs wouldn't work. I slammed my fist into the couch cushion, hissing at Zee. He ignored me. I snapped my fingers at Raw and Aaz; but except for troubled glances, they remained bolted to the floor, shoulders tense as though bracing themselves for a blow. The tears burning my throat rose into my eyes. This could not be happening. I needed time. I needed to be alone with Jack.

The door burst open. A man limped inside, leaning hard on a wooden cane. His hair was brown, thick, and tousled, and he wore a green flannel shirt that stretched across broad shoulders. His dark eyes were wild. He seemed out of breath, like he had been running. Or trying to run, given the leg that dragged behind him.

Not a demon. Not a zombie. No dark cloud in his aura. But I still froze when I saw him, and not just because his presence was unexpected. More like I suffered a boom inside my heart, a collision, like two mountains striking each other. An impossible sensation. I didn't know what it meant, but it made me flinch.

So did the fact that the man ignored Zee and the boys— so completely they might not have been there at all. He sought me out first instead. Staring with an intensity that left me breathless, cold.

And then he tore his gaze from me and looked at Jack.

"Oh, God," he said, swaying. He took a step, nearly went down, and swerved from the old man to stare at me again with something terrible in his eyes. He leaned on his cane so hard I thought it would break. His face was bloodless, white.

"Maxine," he said, and the sound of his voice, rough and broken, sent chills through my bones. "Maxine, are you hurt?"

I stared at him. Zee had not moved, not one inch, but Raw and Aaz crawled into my lap again, making sounds of distress. I was too numb to hold them, and the man still didn't seem disturbed by their presence—though he clearly looked down at their faces.

"Maxine," he said again, louder. I listened to him say my name, and the hole in my heart, in my mind, grew wider: vast and cold, making me feel small, incredibly lost. I had not felt so lost in years, or alone.

The man lowered himself to the floor with some difficulty, wincing visibly when his bad leg twisted at an awkward angle. His gaze, though, never left mine, not for an instant—nor could I look away. Something bad would happen if I did: death or lightning, or earthquake. Maybe the complete and utter loss of my ability to breathe. I was certain of it.

The man tried to take my hand. I snatched it away. Raw and Aaz shuddered. Del and Mal began humming again, but I barely heard them over the roar of blood in my ears. Behind the man, Zee rubbed his red eyes, dragging his claws directly over the pupils as though he were trying to dig them out and reach inside his head. I understood how he felt.

I looked at the man—looked at the way he looked at me—and trembled with another kind of horror that had nothing to do with my murdered grandfather.

"I'm sorry," I whispered. "But I don't know who you are."

⊰⊱

I did not know his face. I did not know those cheekbones, or that firm mouth. I did not know those eyes, which stared at me, unblinking, edged with an odd light that seemed born from more than the reflection of the lamp on the table beside him.

Nothing about the man was familiar. I had never met him. Never breathed the same air as him.

I had never been stared at so relentlessly, or with such concern.

"Maxine," he whispered.

"No one knows that name," I said, but faces flashed, memories: Jack, Byron, Mary, a handful of others; and it felt as though I floated outside my own mind, listening to echoes of some television program that was a fantasy, only.

I have friends. This is home.

Home. Most elusive word. But I glanced around the room at those brick walls and enormous dark windows, at the piano and books, and—hell, my mother's leather jacket draped over the back of the couch—and again, I suffered the heat of some pure *knowing*. This was home. I had *friends*, impossible as that should have been.

I had a grandfather whose corporeal body was dead. Murdered.

And I had a man sitting in front of me with another kind of *knowing* in his eyes, looking at me like no one ever had. No one I remembered. Paying no mind to the demons surrounding him, as if he didn't care.

I edged away. The man grabbed my wrist, and the contact burned. So did the fact that Zee and the others didn't even twitch. They watched us with hooded eyes, spikes drooping, claws twitching. Anxious. Upset.

"Maxine," said the man, with quiet urgency. "You know me."

I twisted my wrist, breaking his grip—ignoring his hiss of pain. I shoved demons off my lap, scrabbling backward, and somehow managed to stand. Only for a moment, though. My knees buckled. I sat down hard on the couch, aching and brittle.

Jack's corpse haunted the edge of my vision. When I flexed my fingers, his dried blood cracked and pulled my skin. I rubbed my hands, numb inside: numb except for the ache in my throat; numb to death except for the fear in my heart; so numb I wanted to scream, or run.

Dek and Mal pushed free of my hair, slithering down my arms into my lap. Muscles flowed beneath their long, serpentine bodies, and tiny vestigial arms gripped my wrists as they licked the blood off my hands. Their tongues were hot. The man looked at them, then me. Grim, haggard—but unafraid.

"Zee," he croaked. "You know who I am."

Hearing him say the demon's name made my heart stop. Zee closed his eyes. The man twisted, searching him out. "Zee."

"Know you," rasped the demon, after a terrible hesitation. "Grant."

I shoved Dek and Mal off my lap and staggered from the couch. Took two steps toward Jack's body, and stopped, holding my stomach, my throat. This couldn't be happening. We'd had pie last night. He'd sat on books and rambled about the beekeeping practices of the ancient Romans. He'd hugged me good night, kissed my cheek.

I knelt in blood and touched his foot. I had never paid attention to his shoes, but they were sensible and brown, leather cracked with age. Made for walking. The only part of his body that I could look at safely.

"I knew something was wrong," whispered the man behind me, accompanied by the sound of wood scraping against the floor. I envisioned that cane in his hand, and it jarred me like another good blow. "I was in Bellevue. Do you remember that? I left hours ago to deal with one of our morning suppliers. You stayed because Jack called in the middle of the night. He wanted to talk with you. He said it was important."

Important. Everything was important to Jack.

But nothing else the man said rang any bells. Except, perhaps, the word *suppliers*. An image arose: a massive, homey kitchen crawling with volunteers, music from

Oklahoma! blaring from speakers in the ceiling; counters stacked with industrial-sized containers filled with juice and Egg Beaters and frozen sausages. I imagined I smelled sausages; that the scent was drifting through the open apartment door.

From the kitchen, I told myself. The Coop. I lived above a homeless shelter.

I could not recall why.

The cane clicked on the floor. "I felt you, Maxine. I felt . . . something terrible happen. I came back as soon as I could."

Too late. Maxine is gone.

Dek and Mal rolled across the floor toward me, whole bottles of whiskey lodged in their mouths, choked halfway down their throats until all I could see were the glass bottoms, golden liquid sloshing inside. Their eyes rolled back as they swallowed the bottles. I had no idea where the liquor had come from, but the boys were like that. Beside me, Raw and Aaz touched the tips of their long black tongues against the bloody floor. Slowly, thoughtfully, as if tasting stories. The hems of their baseball jerseys were stained red.

My skin tingled. Head to toe, along the edges of my fingernails, and the roots of my hair. Windows were dark, but this was Seattle, and it had rained for the past week. Sunrise was coming. I had minutes at most. Not long enough for all the answers I needed.

I still touched Jack's shoe. "Zee. What happened?"

Still no reply. I heard a shuffling sound. Glanced over my shoulder in time to see the man bend down and grab Zee's arm. I flinched, waiting for him to scream.

He didn't. He should have lost his hand. Fingers, at the very least, or skin. No one touched the boys but me, and that was their choice. Every inch of them was razor-sharp, when they willed it to be. But the man held on, staring at Zee. With fury, I realized. Pure inconsolable rage.

"Answer her," he said.

Zee shook his head. I stood, swaying on my feet. I looked at the knife lying in the blood. I could not bring myself to touch it.

"Zee," I said, hoarse. "Who killed Jack?"

Zee mumbled to himself and glanced away. So did the rest of the boys. None of them would look at me, and that alone chilled me to the bone.

"Don't make me beg," I whispered. "What happened here?"

The demon closed his eyes. "Mystery."

"That's no answer." I stepped toward him, every part of me aching. "Did *I* kill him? Did I murder my own—"

Zee snarled, wrenching away from the man. Blood spurted from his hand. He hissed, clutching it in a fist against his stomach—and stared at Zee, white-lipped, eyes hard as flint.

"There's no way you could have hurt your grandfather," said the man, looking at the demon and not me. "No way, Maxine."

I didn't answer him. Zee stared into my eyes, little chest heaving, the floorboards beneath him cracked and ruined. Smoke rose off his bony back, filling the air with a sulfuric scent that burned my nostrils. He looked angry, but that was a nervous, grieving odor.

I touched my brow, light-headed. "I killed him. Yes or no."

"Don't know," rasped Zee, and a shudder rolled through his body, wracking him until he hunched on the floor in a bony ball. "Can't remember."

"What—" I began, and stopped myself, swallowing hard. *That's impossible,* I wanted to add, but demons never lied. Riddles might be told, or words twisted into knots, but lies were anathema; and so was breaking a promise.

"Can't remember," Zee breathed, staring at his claws as though they were new to him. "Remember nothing. Opened eyes, opened eyes to blood, and nothing, nothing, *nothing*."

"Zee," I whispered, but he shuddered again and banged his head against his knuckles and claws, trying once more to dig out his eyes. All he got for his trouble were sparks in the air, but I fell on my knees in front of him and grabbed his gnarled wrists. He could have broken my bones with a twitch, but he stilled, trembling, chest heaving. I yanked him into my arms.

He had been so quiet before, so emotionless, but when he finally looked at me, there was something broken in his gaze, the closest thing to horror that I had ever seen on his sharp, craggy face.

"Like lightning gone," he whispered. "Our memories, gone."

I felt heat against my shoulder. The man, drawing near. I tilted my head just enough to see Raw and Aaz clinging to his legs, burying their faces against his knees.

I was too numb to feel surprised. But not too numb to acknowledge that there was some deep shit missing from my brain. Deep, intimate shit.

I tried recalling anything of the man—anything, before the last ten minutes—but all I got for my trouble was an aching heart, a heart that felt cut to shreds—and a feeling of loneliness so vast, so terrible, I couldn't breathe.

Blood streamed between the man's fingers, staining his green flannel shirt and dripping on the floor. I couldn't look any higher than his hands. I was afraid to see his eyes, and that fear made me feel so small. I had never been a coward.

Cowards died. Cowards let other people die.

Zee studied the blood, then him. Him, and me.

"Good heart," rasped the demon, with an urgency that made my vision blur with tears—and then spill over as he placed his clawed hand against my chest. "Don't lose the good heart."

I scrubbed my eyes. Dawn was on the edge of my skin, tingling with an echo of the sun rising somewhere beyond the walls and clouds. "Go to sleep. Tonight, answers."

"Maxine," Zee whispered mournfully. "Afraid answers kill."

Dek and Mal ceased humming. Raw and Aaz glanced at Jack. I tried to do the same, but could only look as far as his shoes, his legs, the edge of his pale hand, fingertips dipped in blood.

"Then we better find out why," I breathed, and steeled myself as sunrise arrived.

Happened fast. Less than a second, quicker than a heartbeat, half of a moment and half of that: The boys disappeared. Fading into smoke that reappeared on my skin.

I stared at my arms and hands. My skin had not seen the sun since my mother's murder. Never would again. Pale flesh gone, covered entirely now in tattoos: sinuous, tangled bodies etched in coal and mercury, shimmering with veins of silver fire. Scales, claws, teeth, tongues: pressing upon my skin, covering every inch from toes to scalp, between my thighs. Only my face was free, but that was vanity— easily rectified if threatened. Happened more often than not: bullets, the buses I had been thrown under.

Mortal at night. Immortal by day. Nothing could kill me from now until sunset. Not a nuclear bomb, not water or fire, not the worst monster in this world—or any other.

My bloodline had been made to fight monsters. To protect this world from the very worst creatures no one dreamed existed. There had been others, once. I was all that was left. Just me, standing against a demonic army locked away inside a prison surrounding earth. Me, standing against Jack's own people, Avatars, alien beings who had created my bloodline ten thousand years ago, and who were almost as much of a threat as the demons imprisoned behind the veil.

I rubbed my hands together, dried blood gone, absorbed by the boys. Black nails, hard enough to cut steel, glimmered in the lamplight like an oil stain. Even the armor had changed its appearance, like a chameleon—etched with knots and tangles that resembled roses. I felt heavier. The boys were dense. Red eyes stared from my palms: Dek and Mal, sleeping on each hand. The boys never rested in the same place twice. Just like me.

But that was wrong. I had a home. I had put down roots, lived here for—

—*almost two years,* I told myself. *Two years of living warm.*

I could feel that warmth. Not heat, but something deeper, in my gut—as though I was observing the life of another Maxine Kiss. Another woman with my face and blood, living a life I had never dreamed for myself. A life where I remembered sitting down at a table with strange friends and the boys, all of us together—without secrets, laughing, making happiness beneath the skin. Beneath a roof that was . . . mine?

"Maxine," said the man, quietly.

I sat a moment longer, gathering my resolve. Stood slowly, ignoring his proffered hand, which was cut and bleeding. The blood didn't bother me, but I was afraid to touch him, in the same way I was afraid to look into his eyes. Give me a demon to kill, but not this. Give me a war, but not this.

Grant, Zee had called him. His name was Grant.

I forced myself to meet his gaze. A mistake. I felt naked when he looked at me, stripped down to bone, muscle, nothing but my sick, thundering heart shuddering behind my ribs. All he did was look, but that was enough to shatter a part of me that couldn't afford to be broken. Not now.

"You really don't remember me," he breathed, all kinds of pain wrapped up in that low, deep voice.

I shook my head. "Not even a little."

He sucked in his breath like I punched him. "You love me."

You're crazy, I almost said.

But I didn't. I kept my mouth shut.

Because all it took was the look in his eyes, and the way the boys had behaved around him, to know that he was telling the truth.

I had loved this man.

Just not anymore.

CHAPTER 3

I backed away from him, feeling cornered in that expansive room. My heel stepped in blood.

"Don't run from me," he said. "I'm the last person you should be afraid of."

"I'm not afraid."

He smiled, but it was tense and sad, and faintly bitter. "Liar."

I turned from him. Faced Jack's corpse. Took a moment, pretending to look at the body, when all I was doing was stitching my nerves back together. *Liar, liar, pants on fire.*

I didn't remember this man, no matter how tightly the boys hugged his legs. I didn't know him, no matter how he stared at me: like I was his. His, in that way that had to do with secrets and holding hands, breathing the same air. Naked skin.

Jesus, enough. You're a fighter.

So fight.

I sucked in my breath and focused on Jack. Worse than a roller coaster. My head was going to turn inside out, and my stomach punched upward into my throat like some ham-fisted drunk. I swallowed hard—pretended that I wasn't vomiting a little inside my mouth—and pushed past heartsickness and revulsion to look at his waxen face.

Throat cut. I had already seen that. I prowled the edges of his body, searching for anything else. Not much of a detective. I usually relied on the boys for small details, but that would have to wait until tonight.

Stupid. Should have had them check for scents.

Maybe they already had. Maybe there weren't any. Just ours. Maybe something had gone wrong. Wrong with *me*.

"You're being self-indulgent," said the man, behind me. "When you blame yourself. When you even *think* about it."

I froze, then turned my head, slowly. "What did you say?"

"You heard me." The man limped toward me, his expression so hard and cold I wondered what the hell I had been doing with him. "You always blame yourself first. You think the worst of who you are."

"I'm a killer," I found myself saying, even though I'd had no intention of speaking. "If you know me—"

"I know you," he rasped. "I know you, Maxine."

As he loomed over me, I held my ground and suffered a wash of heat from his body to mine. Smelled cinnamon, and other warm things. Made me think of sunlight, and fire.

He got close and stopped, studying me. I didn't know why it felt so unnerving. Other eyes from other men flashed through my memories—crazed, murderous, sly, cold—but none burned me like this man.

He was right: I was a liar. He scared me. I was an unbreakable woman, unless you started from the inside out.

"You going to talk, or look?" I asked, unable to speak above a whisper. "My grandfather is dead. You're standing in his blood."

"Jack's not dead. And you didn't murder his body. I'd bet my life on it." He searched my face. "How much *do* you remember? You know, don't you, that Jack isn't exactly . . ."

"Human. Yes."

"And you know where you are?"

"The Coop," I answered, more slowly, having a sense of where this was going and dreading it.

The man leaned back, frowning. "Why are you living here? *Who* are you living with?"

I swallowed hard and pointed at Jack's corpse. "Don't change the subject."

"Your memory *is* the subject."

"I would never love you," I said.

He leaned over his cane, not breathing. I bit my tongue, hating myself a little, and turned back to Jack. There was little to see that I hadn't already noted: cut throat, clothes in order. Men who fought for their lives usually tore something, or looked scuffed up. Not Jack. I crouched in his blood and picked up his hand. His skin was cooling. He was looking more like a shell to me, a wax figure. Unreal.

There was blood under his nails, but it all seemed to be his. Not that I had any way to know for certain. I picked up the knife, finally. The boys sucked the blood from the blade, leaving the metal gleaming in the lamplight.

"Was he lying like this when you found him?" asked the man, voice low, rough, a little too calm.

I hesitated. "He was on his side."

"No furniture has been knocked over. He doesn't look like he fought."

"Or had time to fight."

"Maybe you found him dead. Your memories could

have been . . . stolen . . . after that. It wouldn't be the first time."

I stood, avoiding the man's penetrating gaze. Wondering how much to say, when it seemed he already knew everything. I thought of the boys again, Raw and Aaz hugging the man's legs, burying their faces in his knees—and forced myself to look at him. Really look.

He had been wild-eyed when I first saw him, and that wildness was still there, but tempered now with a dull hurt that burned shadows into the angles of his face. Not a pretty man, but handsome. He looked capable. Nothing sly about him. Just . . . straightforward. Uncompromisingly so, if the relentlessness of his gaze was any indication.

"You're right," I said. "My mother stole my memories once, when I was eight. I got them back, later. I know Zee is capable of the same thing. He did it to my grandmother."

"Yes," replied the man, carefully. "You told me. You . . . traveled back in time to help her. Using that." He gestured toward the armor on my hand. "He stole the memory of you from her, afterward."

I exhaled, slowly. "If I hadn't seen the way the boys act around you—"

"You don't scare me," he interrupted. "If the boys hadn't remembered me—"

"You'd be missing that hand. Or worse." I walked toward the bedroom. My feet were sticky. I was tracking blood on the floor. I passed through the open doorway, switched on the light—stumbled, a little, at the sight of rumpled covers and clothes on the floor, mine, and a man's—and then kept walking toward the bathroom. There was a first-aid kit under the sink. I didn't question how I knew it was there. It just was, and I remembered that.

I set the knife aside. Washed my hands, even though I didn't need to. I saw a razor, a can of shaving cream; a black bra hanging from the door handle. I saw two sets of towels, and a man's dirty socks on the floor outside the hamper; two toothbrushes leaning together inside an ugly-ass mug shaped like the Statue of Liberty's head—*you flew to New York City on a plane, your first, to help an old woman, an old man*—*and you bought that at the airport because, why, why, someone said you should, because it was a joke and you laughed, but you didn't laugh alone, you weren't alone, and every time you look at that thing you remember laughing, and you smile again*—and I was smiling now, I realized, and scrubbed at my mouth with the back of my hand.

I was in another world, I thought. Twilight Zone. Losing my mind, my bearings. Other dimensions existed. Maybe I had slipped into one. I could blame interdimensional travel on all my problems, starting with my first ancestor, and the creatures that had made her and come to earth millennia ago.

My reflection offered no help. I looked like shit: black hair snarled, skin pasty, shadows under my eyes. I pulled back my hair and looked at the scar under my ear. Or tried to. It was hidden by one of the boys, a tattooed tail snaking out from beneath my hairline to hide a twist of lines engraved into my skin: a mark, lashed into me by a demon.

A distinctive mark, one that had frightened Jack, and others. An ancestor had carried this scar: a gift from the same demon who had given it to me.

Oturu. A being made of night, and knives, and nightmares. I dreamed of him, sometimes, but in those dreams I was always someone else—another woman—and there was blood, and death, and long hunts that seemed to span the distances between starlight.

Oturu had marked me because he said I reminded him of my ancestor: the woman in my dreams. Not exactly a compliment. According to my grandfather, the nicest thing anyone could say about her was that she had almost destroyed the world.

I clutched the first-aid kit to my chest and left the bathroom. The man leaned inside the bedroom door, waiting for me. Posture loose, at ease—except for those eyes. Like a wolf, I decided. Another kind of hunter.

"Your hand," I said.

"Jack," he replied.

"He can wait. Like you said, he's not dead." I almost couldn't say the words. I had to force them out until it sounded like I had a speech impediment. "Maybe he's looking for another body."

"Hopefully one outside the womb. I'd rather not wait for him to grow up and find us before we get some explanations."

I grunted, and gestured for him to back out of the room. But he gave me a look and limped to the bed. Sat down on the edge of it. And waited.

I wanted to kick his bad leg. The bed—and him sitting on it—reminded me of a bear trap. I had gotten caught in one of those in Alaska, during daylight hours. The teeth had broken off against my leg, but it had still been a bitch to open the jaws to free myself.

Hadn't smelled like sex, though.

I didn't sit beside him. I fumbled open the first-aid kit, laid it on the edge of the mattress, and found bandages, ointment. The man stared the entire time, which I hated. I didn't even know why I was doing this except I felt like I should.

"Give me your hand," I muttered.

"Take it," he replied, still holding his fist against his stomach. The front of his shirt was bloody.

"Don't play games with me."

He shook his head, his gaze never leaving mine. "This isn't a game."

"Touching you won't make my memories come back."

The corner of his mouth tilted up in that bitter smile. "Take my hand, Maxine. Or walk out of here."

Or punch you, I thought.

I grabbed his wrist. My tattooed fingers were slender and small compared to the rawboned muscle of his forearm, feminine, even, which wasn't a description I usually applied to myself. I was surprised, too, at the heat I felt from his skin. The boys normally left me desensitized during the day, unable to feel heat or cold unless it was on my face, or breathed in.

I didn't remember this man. I didn't remember ever *touching* a man, except in an exorcism. I didn't know how to be gentle.

But he winced, and I found myself trying. I loosened my grip, carefully drawing his hand away from his stomach. His fingers remained curled against his bleeding palm, and I slipped mine underneath—small, my hand small in comparison—carefully straightening them.

He could have done it on his own. He had offered to help me stand, earlier. But this was a test. He watched my face, wincing only one other time, when I said, "You're a manipulator."

"Maybe," he agreed, after a moment.

He said nothing more as I bandaged his cut hand. The blood made it seem worse than the actual damage, just surface lacerations that would hurt like hell. I didn't have much experience with fixing people, but I thought I did a passable job.

"I can't feel my fingers," he said. "I hope I still have them."

"Whiner," I muttered, watching him try to flex his hand.

He didn't have much luck. I had that gauze coiled around him tighter than a diamondback.

I shoved all the paper wrappers on the floor. Boys would eat them later—a thought that came so easily to me, I almost missed how strange it was to think it. Disturbing, even. It hit me again that this was home. Even the boys treated it like that. I could see their toys on the floor: half-eaten teddy bears, razor blades, *Playboy* magazines. A life-sized cardboard cutout of Bon Jovi stood in the corner, complete with big hair.

I pointed. "That's new."

"Zee used your credit card," replied the man. "Remember?"

"Yes," I said slowly, thinking about it. "Now I do. It arrived yesterday morning. I wasn't expecting it." I glanced at him, holding his gaze. "You thought I was lying about remembering?"

"No. I'm just puzzled why you remember *that* and not me."

"He has better hair," I said, walking from the bedroom. "Or maybe it's the leather."

He snorted, and called out, "What's my name, Maxine?"

I froze in midstep, then kept walking. "Zee called you Grant."

"Good," he replied, with bitter amusement. "Don't forget it."

CHAPTER 4

GROWING up, I had one friend, not including the boys.

My mother. The only person I could count on.

Larger than life, mean as hell in a fight, ruthless, cunning—and the best baker, ever. Her oatmeal cookies could raise the dead. Or make a little girl feel loved after a hard day of demons, and the endless road, and the knowledge that it would never end, that the days would only stretch out longer, and with sharper teeth.

And then she died. And for five years it was just the boys and me. Living in hotels and my car, traveling the country. Hunting demons.

Being alone was easier. No risk, just loneliness. No one ever died from that.

But something had changed inside me, I thought, approaching the kitchen of the homeless shelter. After years of living the straight and narrow—living alone—something had changed, and I couldn't remember what. I couldn't remember why I had settled down in this place, when everything about the way I had been raised screamed that I shouldn't.

Which made me think it had something—everything— to do with the man limping along behind me, grim-faced and silent.

Grant. I had told him not to come. I didn't want company. Especially his. Too much, too soon.

He wore clean clothes. So did I. Gloves, turtleneck. Covered from my neck down. I rarely showed my tattoos. Too many questions when they disappeared at night.

I glanced at him, then looked away, quick. Not before he noticed, though. He limped a little faster, and leaned in. "Don't look at me like that. I tried to warn you."

"I don't want to talk about it."

"We share an underwear drawer," he whispered tersely. "*Clean* underwear, thank you very much. It's not the end of the world."

"Did I say anything?"

"I think your eyes bled."

I shot him a look. "Later. We'll talk when we're not in public."

"Will you let me get that close?" Grant leaned in, his expression hard, unflinching. "Will you let me be alone with you again?"

Heat suffused my face. I was a tough woman. Covered in demons. Used to dealing with monsters. Sex with a stranger—and I assumed that we *were* sleeping together— was nothing. Really. Even if I did not remember being with *any* man, ever.

At all. Not even kissed.

"Fuck," I said, loudly. Heads turned, but when the volunteers saw it was me, their startled expressions faded, and they gave each other resigned looks that were a hairs-breadth from being disparaging. My middle finger twitched at them.

Grant never even blinked an eye, but his mouth soft-ened. "That's my girl."

I turned away. Something about his tone, the humor bur-ied in the hardness and anger—*that's my girl, that's my girl*—lodged inside the little cracks of my heart. Lodged like a ton of bricks. I wanted to vomit.

The kitchen was exactly as I remembered, which was some comfort. Journey blared, gruff voices rising and falling as crates of oranges were dropped on the floor, shoved side-ways around battered cardboard boxes filled with industrial-sized bags of pasta. Sausages sizzled as they were dumped inside metal serving bins, alongside pancakes and scrambled eggs—but those scents were nearly buried beneath the over-whelming sweetness of warm cinnamon buns being pulled fresh from the giant upright ovens. My stomach growled. I needed food—not just for me, but for the boys.

I didn't feel like eating, though.

Grant's cane stopped clicking. I told myself not to look, but I twisted around anyway and found him speaking to the men who had been unloading the oranges. Big guys with rough, dented faces, muscles that strained against their rain-spattered jackets, and gloves in their hands that they kept slapping against their thighs—impatient, wanting to get on with business. But they looked at Grant with respect. Listened to him with complete focus.

This was his place, I realized. His homeless shelter, his apartment.

Grant glanced at me. I felt another jolt when our gazes met, and broke eye contact, embarrassed and angry.

Focus, I told myself, grim. *Focus, or you're good for nothing.*

I scanned the kitchen for the person I had come down here to find. With Jack's body dead, there were other problems that could arise. Maybe. Perhaps. I wasn't sure. But it was nothing I wanted to take for granted. The old man was upstairs under a sheet. I didn't want anyone else to end up the same way.

Over in the corner I saw a girl stacking loaves of day-old wheat bread. A faded purple kerchief covered her braids, and she wore a patchwork apron that had definitely come from home. I didn't know her name. I told myself it was because I was an asshole and not some pothole amnesiac.

"Hey," I said, and the girl jumped, gasping. A tentative smile flitted across her mouth when she saw it was me, but there was a trace of nervousness, too. My sparkling reputation. I vaguely remembered seeing her yesterday, on the edge of a crowd that had watched me put a man down for harassing a woman. Broken his nose against the floor, in plain view of a dozen horrified people—which was stupid and smart. Stupid, because it drew attention to myself. Smart, because a little brutality made a good deterrent.

I was a woman of all trades around here, but mostly the muscle kind. If there was a problem with security, folks came to me. If there was a problem with anything else . . .

I couldn't remember. I couldn't even recall why these people knew me, just that they did. I had lived here for almost two years. Two mysterious years, for some mysterious reason.

I heard that cane clicking on the floor and smelled cinnamon. Told myself that was the oven and not the man who warmed my shoulder without touching me. He felt like a radiator.

The girl looked past me, and her smile widened into something genuine and sweet. I cleared my throat. "Byron is supposed to be here."

She tore her gaze from Grant, and frowned. "Oh. I haven't seen him." She turned, studying the kitchen, and her frown deepened. "That's strange, isn't it? He's never late."

I walked away without another word and headed for the doors. The moment I was in the hall, I started running. Grant called my name, but hearing him only made me run faster.

The homeless shelter had been built from a collection of linked warehouses, part of a former furniture factory just south of Seattle's downtown. There were beds for men, women, families, along with a small day care, and a job-training center. The Coop also had a second wing filled with short-term apartments, reserved for special cases.

Byron was a special case.

His room was at the end of the hall. I rapped on the door. Heard nothing on the other side and pulled a set of keys from my pocket. Listened to the muffled click of a cane on the stairs and felt ridiculous for trying to outrun a man with a bad leg—and for trying to escape him at all.

You live with him, I told myself, unlocking the door in front of me. *He knows your secrets. You wouldn't have made that decision lightly.*

And the boys wouldn't have tolerated it unless they liked him.

"Fuck," I said again, and opened the door.

It was dark inside. Some fresh air would have been nice. The room had been designed like a standard hotel space: bed, dresser, one window, a bathroom by the door. Movie posters covered the walls: *Hellboy*, *Blade Runner*, a few others that Byron and I had picked up over the last few months. Books had been stacked in islands along his desk, surrounding stacks of paper. No computer. He preferred longhand, and I didn't care if he mastered the Internet, or knew how to type. I just wanted him to learn. I had been homeschooled, and had somehow found myself doing the same for him. He was good with history and math. I dared any so-called college kid to match his brains and maturity.

The teen was still in bed. I didn't need to turn on the lights to see him. He was asleep, but restlessly so, half the covers kicked off, one sock hanging from his toes. He still wore his white T-shirt with its Shakespeare logo.

Grant appeared in the doorway. "Is he okay?"

I held up my hand and knelt by the bed. The boy's cheeks, usually bone-pale, were mottled red. I stripped off my glove and touched his brow. I felt heat through my tattoos. Too much heat.

I rubbed his shoulder, watching his eyelids twitch. "He has a fever."

A faucet turned on in the bathroom. Water ran. Grant reappeared, a wet rag dangling from his bandaged fingers. I placed it on the boy's brow, soothing back his dark hair, suffering a peculiarly breathless anxiety that, not for the first time, made me wonder if this was what it felt like to be a mother.

"How did you know?" Grant asked, quietly.

"I didn't. But he and Jack . . ." I stopped, still unable to get around the fact that this man, for all intents and purposes, was a stranger. I wasn't a kid anymore, but never talking to strangers still sounded like good advice. Safer. Fewer headaches. Required no effort.

Grant leveled a long look at me. "Jack experimented on the boy. Made him immortal, a chronic amnesiac. Neither of us have been able to determine why he did that—or when—but we know, based on what Zee has said, that it was before Pompeii went up in flames and ash." He pointed at the wall. "That enough for you? You can start banging your head now."

"Smart-ass."

"If our positions were reversed—"

"Stop—"

"—and I didn't know you—"

"I wouldn't care."

Grant leaned down, holding my gaze. "I would be cautious, too, Maxine. But not . . . willfully blind."

For some reason, that cut. "Don't lecture me."

"Don't push me away. Not yet."

I looked down at my hands, then the boy. I wanted to tell him that *not yet* was *now*, and that he could go to hell. But those words lodged in my throat, and all I could force out was, "I should have asked Jack more questions about what he did to Byron."

"Jack doesn't answer uncomfortable questions." Grant sat carefully on the bed's edge and laid his cane on the floor. He stared at Byron with that same unsettling intensity, long enough that I wondered if I should be concerned.

"You were right to worry," he said, suddenly. "It's not a virus that's causing his fever. Goes deeper than that, but I can't quite determine—"

Byron's eyes opened. Just a little, revealing narrow slits of dark feverish eyes. I held my breath when he looked at me, hit with memories, lightning flashes of images: seeing him for the first time inside a wet cardboard box; later, a zombie holding a gun to his head, his dark eyes wide with fear.

But the memories of him simply sitting with me, eating with me, reading with me, were the strongest—because Byron was like me, wary of people. Unused to having a friend.

He trusted me, though. God help him, but he trusted me.

"Kid," I said, gently.

Byron looked at me for a long moment, then his gaze ticked upward, sideways, toward Grant. "Why . . . are you both here?"

"Looks like you came down with something since last night." I flipped the washcloth to the cool side. "Tell me how you feel."

"Hot," he mumbled, and closed his eyes again. "Had a bad dream."

"Tell me."

"Woman. Or man. Don't know. Had a . . . collar. And her voice . . ." Byron touched his throat. "Didn't want to hear her . . . *him* . . . speak."

I frowned. Grant leaned in. "What did she look like?"

"Sharp," he whispered, and swallowed hard. "I'm thirsty."

"I'll get water," I said, and went to the bathroom, thinking about women who might be men, and collars, voices. Could be nothing, but the boy was sick, Jack was dead, and I didn't believe in coincidences.

Grant was speaking into his cell phone when I re-emerged. One hand rested on Byron's shoulder, but the boy was relaxed, not a trace of distrust or tension in his face. I felt as though I was observing Zee again—or Raw and Aaz, hugging the man's knees. Had to shake myself.

Grant hung up the phone. "Rex is going to find Mary, and have her sit with Byron."

I didn't ask how he knew that I wasn't going to stay with the boy. Or why he didn't volunteer. Not that I would trust him to. I wasn't certain I trusted him at all, but everyone else seemed to be falling down at his feet. I could take a hint. Not be . . . willfully blind . . . to the possibility that maybe, just maybe, there was a reason the boys—and this boy—trusted him.

The same reason my underwear was mixed with his.

God. That made me ill.

The boy sighed. "Mary's crazy."

"Just a little," I admitted, which was an understatement bordering on lies, lies, and more damn lies. Mary had been a soldier and bodyguard in another life, on another world, in another *dimension*. Now she was an old woman addicted to marijuana, knitting, and—

Nothing. I couldn't remember.

I couldn't remember *him*.

"She likes you," I told the boy, embarrassed I sounded so hoarse. "If she brings you weed—"

"I know," he replied, collapsing into the pillows. "I'm not . . . stupid."

I bit back a smile and ruffled his hair. "Don't go running any marathons before I get back. Do you want me to bring you anything?"

He shook his head, eyes too dark. "I don't feel right, Maxine." His fingers scratched at his throat, then his chest. "I don't feel right."

I'm scared, I imagined him saying. *I'm scared.*

I thought of Jack, dead on my floor. Waking up in his blood, seeing his throat cut. My grandfather. My grandfather murdered. I hadn't stopped it. Couldn't even remember how it happened.

I knelt and pressed my lips hard against Byron's brow, tasting his fever. The boy stopped breathing when I touched him, then his arms wrapped around my shoulders, and I stopped breathing, too.

"It's going to be all right," I whispered.

His fingers dug hard into my shoulders. "You always say that."

"Because you're mine." I almost couldn't hear my own voice. I didn't know why I spoke those words, except that I was afraid of losing the boy, too. First my grandfather, then Grant: a man I was supposed to love. Gone. My life, unraveling.

"You're mine," I said again, stubbornly. "Nothing's going to happen to you."

"Okay," whispered Byron, and patted me on the back. "I can't breathe."

I let him go and stood. "I'll be back soon."

I walked to the door. I didn't mean to look back, but I did, and felt terrible, filled with dread, when I saw the boy. Byron had already closed his eyes, but for a moment I imagined him dead, cold. Grant stepped between us, and pressed his mouth to my ear.

"You'll scare the boy if he sees you looking at him like that."

I ducked my head and backed away. I didn't stop until I was outside, in the hall. And then I kept walking. Grant caught up with me at the top of the stairs. He stayed silent. So did I.

We left the building. No one stopped us. I walked to my car, sucking down the cold wet air, savoring the rain on my face. The rain always felt real.

I had a little red Mustang. Classic design, like a sleek cherry jewel in the Seattle morning gloom. I got in. So did Grant. I gripped the wheel, and said, "You haven't asked where I'm going."

He wiped the rain off his hair. "I'm not letting you out of my sight."

"If I don't give you a choice?"

A smile flitted over his mouth, but it wasn't pleasant. "Just drive, Maxine."

So I did. I backed out fast, accelerated forward, and yanked hard on the wheel as we swerved from the parking lot into the road, narrowly missing a parked service van and the man getting out of it. He yelled; I slid down lower in the seat and jacked up the volume on the radio. "Eye of the Tiger" was playing. Grant gave me a sidelong look, the corner of his mouth twitching.

"What?" I muttered.

"Nothing," he said, and turned up the radio until I felt the bass in my chest. The boys began pulsing on my skin in time to the music.

Fifteen minutes later, we reached Thunderdome.

CHAPTER 5

THUNDERDOME was a bar, but the kind where yuppies and rich college kids could go to feel a little dangerous—without actually getting knifed on the way to the bathroom. Karaoke nights on Saturdays were popular, inviting drunken performances while standing on the surface of the bar, kicking drinks and empty glasses on other inebriated revelers. Something that happened not just on the weekends, but most nights when the owner herself took the opportunity to flash a lot of thigh and serve drinks with nothing but her cleavage. The place had been open for only a couple months, but every time I visited, it was packed.

But now it was Thursday morning, and the sidewalk out front smelled like vomit. So did the young man in jeans and a cashmere blazer—no shirt—sprawled in the doorway, snoring. I nudged him with the toe of my cowboy boot, but all he did was snort a little and rub at the dried remains of drinks and dinner—broccoli, maybe some hamburger—coating his face.

"After today, I'm never eating again," I said. "Ever."

"I think I may become an alcoholic," Grant replied, hitting the buzzer beside the door. "I'll develop an affinity for vodka and go down to the docks to learn Russian ditties from the sailors."

"My mother did that once." I stood back, staring at the curtained windows on the second floor. "Took me along. I was thirteen. I learned how to play poker from a one-eyed giant with no teeth and breath that smelled like a box of rotting armpits."

Grant stared. "I don't know that story."

"Well, good," I replied, as footsteps echoed on the other side of the scratched bar door. "I'm glad I still have some secrets."

The locks turned, and the door opened. A woman peered out. She was shorter than me, but all leg—a fact clearly visible given her denim cutoffs: so short I could see the lace of her pink underwear. She wore cherry red boots and a faded pink sweatshirt, slightly oversized and falling off one shoulder. She had short black hair, freckles on her nose; she was mostly Chinese, but with a little something else mixed in her blood.

"Who died?" she asked, eyeing me in particular.

"That's not funny," I replied.

"No, I was serious," she said. "Who the fuck died?"

"Killy," Grant rumbled, stepping awkwardly over the drunk man. "It was Jack."

She made a face, not a particularly grieved one, and backed away from the door. "Oh, man. His throat was cut."

It was not a question—nor was I surprised she knew. It was why I was here. I might be covered in demons, but

Killy had her own gift—an offshoot of ancient tampering with human DNA.

Gods and monsters, Jack had said, once. Heroes and myth, and strange beings from legend; walking in truth, made from the minds of beings who had too much power: creatures that had left earth, for the most part, after the war with the demons.

Jack had been one of those gods, once upon a time. I suppose he still was. Old Jack. Old Wolf.

It wasn't lost on me that Killy knew Grant.

I had known *her* for six months. We had met first in Shanghai during a particularly chilling encounter with one of Jack's kind—an Avatar who had been released from his prison on earth and begun genetic experiments on humans: making new monsters, with nothing but a thought.

But the moment I recalled Shanghai, I remembered, too, that I hadn't been in that city for her. Or that Avatar. I couldn't remember why—and the hole in my heart stretched wide and cold. I looked at Grant. Found him also watching me. Killy stared at us both.

"Wow," she said. "That sucks."

"Stop reading my mind," Grant told her, tearing his gaze from mine. But not before I saw something sad in his eyes, sad and small and grieving. He hid it well, with a sharp smile that he gave Killy—but it stayed with me. And it cut.

Inside, the air was dark and cool, and smelled like ashtrays and vanilla. Booths lined the walls, made of wood and steel bars, and the other tables that crammed the narrow space were round, square, long, and short, jammed together in a maze that offered barely enough space to walk. The bar top was three feet deep and almost as long as the room, dented and nicked like it had been used as a shield in war.

The three of us were alone. I heard water dripping. Above our heads, a thump—followed by chains clinking.

Grant said, "Is that really necessary?"

Killy grabbed a bottle of water off the counter. "He had a bad night."

"Define bad."

"He's still furry. And I think he ate a cat." She walked toward the revolving door that led to the kitchen. "Come on. He'll be happy to see you."

"We didn't come here to visit," I said. "I've got problems."

"You always have problems," Killy shot back. "You're a train wreck. You ruined my life."

"I bought you this bar."

"I loved my old one. In *China*." She scrubbed her face with her knuckles. "It's taken months to retrain my mind after what was done to me. Months, so that I can sleep at night without hearing every fucking thought on this block. And here you come, wanting help—when you know, damn well, that you're the *one* person whose mind I can't read."

I gritted my teeth. "You're the only psychic I know."

"Fuck that." Killy reached behind the bar and brought out a small metal flask. "I have my own problems, *not* including the *werewolf* upstairs who's having a crisis of conscience because he can't bring himself to quit the priesthood." She knocked back a long swallow of whatever was in the flask and choked, wiping her mouth with the back of her hand. "I really liked that cat."

Grant stared at his shoes a little too carefully. "My condolences."

Killy flipped him the middle finger. "You're no better than Maxine. Just another kind of nightmare. I shouldn't even let you talk to me." She turned, stabbing that same finger at my face. "You're here because Jack's dead, and you can't remember what happened. You're here because you can't remember Grant. Which is bizarre because you two are so mushy it makes me *sick*." She took another long drink, and between a rough bout of coughing, said, "I can't fix what was done to you. The only reason I know *something* happened is because I can pick things up from *him*." She pointed at Grant, giving him a hard look. "Speaking of which—"

But she snapped shut her mouth and didn't finish. Just turned on her heel and walked fast toward a swinging door framed with hundreds of nails that had been hammered into the wall, each one dead center in the forehead of a different cutout head, most from personal photographs—but a mix of public figures, too. Voodoo wall. Killy kept the hammer and nails behind the bar. Each one cost a dollar to use, and only if you were dead sober.

We passed the kitchen and marched up a narrow flight of stairs to the second floor, which was locked. The vanilla scent intensified on the other side, and I heard a low, murmuring voice that broke into a growl. Chains rattled. I thought of Jack, throat cut, and stopped walking.

"This is a waste of time," I said. "I'm sorry about Father Lawrence, but if you can't help me remember, then I'll need to find another way to get the information I need."

Killy gave me a piercing look. "Who will you go to, Maxine? Who else have you got?"

I said nothing. I felt heat against the small of my back. Grant's hand, hovering. Caution or reassurance, I wasn't sure which—but it bothered me.

Killy whispered, "You leave, you'll find nothing. You stay, you can make a hurting man feel better. So Jack's dead. Won't last. He's probably hovering over our heads right now. So fuck him."

No, please, I thought. *Fuck you.*

Grant cleared his throat. "Maybe I can do something for Frank."

"No one needs your kind of help." Killy pointed at a door near the end of the hall. "But I suppose the effort means more than the result."

His jaw tightened; with anger or mere irritation, I couldn't tell. I wondered what, exactly, she meant—what Grant could do that made Killy so protective of herself and Frank. Whatever it was, it obviously hadn't bothered me on a personal level. Not if I was getting . . . mushy . . . with him.

Mushy. Right.

I tried to remember. I thought of Mary, Rex, that bedroom with the rumpled covers. I fought to recall why I lived at the Coop. Why I had stopped running and finally settled down, here in rain-drenched Seattle.

But each time I felt like I was on the verge of knowing, I hit that hole in my head and heart, that yawning black hole. An emptiness, a scouring, like some rough hand had found the one thread that was this man, and yanked it free: haphazardly, without any regard to what was left behind. Bad enough I couldn't remember the circumstances of my own grandfather's murder. But that was a single event in time—as far as I knew.

With Grant, it was as though someone had tried to erase his very existence from my mind. All of it. But without any thought at all to the inconsistencies that would arise.

Grant limped ahead. I watched him, soaking in details: broad shoulders that strained against his fleece jacket, lean torso, nice ass. Unfamiliar, but nice.

"Staring won't help," Killy muttered. "Neither will having sex with him."

I blinked. "Excuse me?"

She gave me a hard look, but we were standing closer

now, and I could see that her eyes were bloodshot, the corner of her mouth sagging with exhaustion. She'd had her own long night.

"You're looking for a trigger. Or if you're not, you will be. Something that will shake up your memories. Staring won't be enough, and neither will sex. The first is too distant, the other too intimate."

"Then, what?" I folded my arms over my chest, feeling Zee shift between my breasts, stirring in his dreams. The armor on my right hand tingled. "What do I do?"

"Give it time," she said, as Grant stopped at the end of the hall and rapped his knuckles lightly against the door. "Don't think about it. Just . . . follow your instincts. Memories are *never* lost. Brain is too twisty for that. You can bury something, you can hide it, it can be knocked sideways—but it's always there."

"I don't remember him," I said simply, as Grant glanced back at us. His expression was inscrutable, but maybe that was because I hadn't been around him long enough to know his moods and what it meant when he looked at me, just so—a glint in his eye, his jaw set, that faint furrow in his brow.

I didn't look away until he did. Took a while. Not quite a contest, more like an appraisal. I felt studied by him, as though he was taking me apart with nothing but a look. I hated the sensation, but short of removing his eyes or knocking him unconscious—or just leaving—there was nothing I could do to stop him from seeing me.

And maybe that was the problem. I had never been seen before. Truly, deeply, seen.

Finally, he broke eye contact. Stared at nothing, thoughtful, gaze distant—and then opened the door and limped into the room, possessed of a peculiar calm strength that radiated more from his presence than anything physical.

"You don't remember him, but you feel *something*." Killy leaned against the wall, rubbing the back of her neck. "I can see it in your eyes. Trust that, and you'll get better results than knocking on my door at seven in the fucking morning."

"Right. Like you were asleep."

"I was thinking about it," she said, frowning, and glanced down the hall. "Damn. They're practically spooning each other."

I had not been up here in months, but I remembered a room of spare design, with little furniture and just as little light. Not much had changed, except the bed was gone and a table added—a rickety old thing with green paint peeling off, and its entire surface covered with lit white candles of varying sizes. Some were in jars, others leaked wax within small chipped bowls; and a dozen more burned inside a candelabrum that looked like it had been unearthed in the ruins of some Gothic love chamber. The light was soft and golden, and the intense vanilla scent finally made sense.

Across the room, a bed had been made on the floor. Soft pillows, a quilt, the Bible—and a pile of chains. Chains, binding a werewolf.

Brown fur covered a husky, stout body—rather round in the stomach, which hung over the waist of tight black sweatpants. I saw black claws, and long teeth, one eye that was crimson and gold, and another eye that was human brown. No wolf-head, no pointed ears, but there was a wildness in the man, in the werewolf, that was not human and never would be again.

Father Frank Lawrence. He might have been the only man in the world with his . . . particular condition . . . though given the proclivities of the creature that had made him, I had my doubts.

Over the last six months, I'd read newspaper reports

of strange sightings on the outskirts of Paris and Madrid: men and women covered in fur, attacking at random before running away from their victims—usually screaming for help. Media types blamed crazies in costumes. I blamed advanced genetic manipulation used as a weapon, a toy, by a creature who had thought himself a god.

Father Lawrence sat cross-legged, palms resting on his knees. Iron cuffs bound his wrists and ankles, but he didn't seem to notice them. He was focused entirely on Grant, who also sat on the bed, his cane resting upon his stretched-out legs. He was talking quietly, urgently, but stopped when we entered the room.

"Hey," I said, discomfited by the way both men looked at me: like I had walked into a locker room right after the jocks had stepped from the showers. Embarrassment flickered across their faces, then shut down into something far more secretive. It was an odd thing, feeling walls go up against me. Usually, it was the other way around.

"Maxine," greeted Father Lawrence, his voice little more than a growl. Against my legs, Raw and Aaz tugged toward him: dreaming my life, perhaps the lives of all the women who had come before. Ten thousand years, dreaming.

I eased into the room, face bathed in the heat of more than a dozen candles burning. "You're going to start a fire."

"Meditation," he rasped, giving me a smile that bared sharp white teeth. "I find my symptoms are eased with a little reflection."

"And the chains?"

His smile faded. "I need to reflect a little more."

Grant cleared his throat. "I was telling him . . . what happened."

I studied the candles. Thought about Jack and felt small and cold. "And?"

"I'd like to talk to you," Father Lawrence rasped, his words ending on a growl. "Alone."

Grant looked away, expression thoughtful but unsurprised. "Frank."

"Get out of here," he replied, not unkindly. "Ask Killy to eavesdrop for you."

Killy blew out her breath, looking down and scuffing one boot across the scratched hardwood. Grant jammed his cane into the floor and heaved himself onto his feet. His mouth tightened with pain as his leg straightened. I almost helped him. My first instinct.

But I stayed put and ignored the answering ache in my heart, the nagging sense that I was, indeed, cold and small—but in a different way entirely than I had felt earlier. I glanced at Frank, found him frowning at me. At least, I thought it was a frown. Hard to tell with all that fur.

I didn't look at Grant as he limped past—and he didn't look at me. But my gloved hand hung at my side as I stood next to that narrow doorway, and the edge of his hand, his little finger, brushed against mine. Not even close to a real touch—leather and demons between us—but Dek stirred against my palm, and I felt heat. I felt heat.

Grant turned his head, just a fraction. All I saw was the corner of his mouth, but even that carried the intensity I was beginning to associate with him, as though everything he did was charged.

Or maybe that's just you, and what you're seeing is what you feel.

I began to close the door behind him. Glimpsed Killy watching me from the hall. Nothing in her eyes but concern. Not for me, though.

I shut her out but didn't let go of the doorknob. "So."

"Sit down," he said quietly.

I almost refused, politely. But Father Lawrence was too

dignified and serious, even in fur and chains—and I had nothing to prove.

I kicked off my cowboy boots before stepping onto the quilt, then carefully, gingerly, slid down the wall beside him. Our elbows rubbed, and his fur made a scraping sound on my coat sleeve. All I could smell was vanilla, and the faintest hint of wet dog.

"Tell me what happened," he said.

"I don't want to," I replied bluntly. "I didn't come here for that."

Father Lawrence held up his furred hands, and the chains rattled. "Tough shit. None of us get what we want."

I stripped off my gloves and rubbed my eyes, which still felt bleary from my earlier tears. More tears than I had shed in years. "You don't really need those, do you?"

"Not all the time," he admitted. "Not when I'm in my human body. But when I shift . . . when I shift, I only need to be dangerous once. One time, to kill or ruin someone's life. These . . . precautions . . . are worth some discomfort. Besides," he added, with a grimace, "I think I ate a cat last night."

I patted his arm. "The boys ate a grizzly bear once. Manage that, and we can talk."

Father Lawrence grunted. "I'm sorry about Jack."

"He's not dead."

"Part of him is. The very physical part who knew your grandmother, and mother, and you. You only knew him as Jack Meddle, old man with crazy white hair and wrinkles. That body was precious. You can admit that, Maxine."

I stared at my tattooed hands, those red eyes glinting. The armor glimmered with candlelight, holding the light, so that when I turned my right hand, there was a delay in the movement of the reflected glow, as though part of it remained trapped, or lost in time within the armor.

"Seems ungrateful," I said quietly. "Too sentimental. The real Jack is nothing but energy. Energy with conscious intent. He told me that once. Called it the soul. And his soul . . ."

"Can do things. Occupy bodies. Alter bodies." Father Lawrence also stared at his hands. "You've never lost him before. Part of you isn't sure he'll be back."

"I can kill his kind." I closed my eyes, the candlelight making me dizzy. "Something inside me, Frank. Something about me. It scared Jack. *This* scared him." I tapped the scar on the edge of my jaw, beneath my ear. "Don't pretend it doesn't scare you. You've got it tattooed on your arm." I smiled, grim. "Any members of that cult still contact you?"

"Yes," he said, which surprised me just a little. "Not everyone was corrupted by Father Cribari and the Erl-King. There are those still dedicated to the mission that Jack created for our order, all those centuries ago."

"Watching my bloodline. Waiting for one of us women to destroy the world."

Father Lawrence nudged me. "Drama queen. Like you're something special."

I smiled, despite myself. He added, "Why aren't you talking to Grant about this?" And then, before I could say anything: "Pull up the edge of the blanket. I need something."

I did as he asked, biting back all kinds of nasty replies, and pulled out a clear bag filled with Oreo cookies. Some were smashed, the creamy filling smeared against the inside of the plastic.

I shook it. "What is this? Contraband?"

Father Lawrence patted his stomach. "I'm on a special diet. Open it up and tell me about Grant."

I shoved the bag into his furry hands. "Open it yourself. And forget about it. I'm not talking about that man."

"That man." Father Lawrence tried to open the bag, but his claws snared the plastic and everything ripped. Cookies fell out into his lap. He sighed, and gave me a reproachful look. "That man loves you. Actually, forget that. He *adores* you."

"I don't know him."

"You know him. You just don't remember."

"What does that even *mean*? Killy said the same thing, and I'm sick of hearing it. I don't remember him, I don't know him. He's a stranger. As far as I'm concerned, he can stay that way."

"Coward," Father Lawrence whispered. "You terrible coward."

I grabbed a cookie and shoved it into my mouth. "Maybe."

"Fine." The priest very delicately picked up a cookie between his claws and took a careful bite. His fangs shattered it into pieces that joined the other crumbs in his lap. "I won't presume to tell you anything then."

"Stop trying to be so polite," I muttered. "You have to put the whole thing in your mouth."

"But you loved him," he continued, sweeping crumbs into his palm and tipping them into his mouth. "By God, you loved him. And you need each other. More than you realize."

I closed my eyes, briefly—counted to ten—and then reached into the bag for a cookie. I held it against the priest's leathery lips. "Open up."

He gave me a sidelong look but did as I asked. I angled the entire cookie inside until his cheek bulged. "What I need, Frank, is to find out who murdered my grandfather."

"Mmm," he said. "Jack expected to be killed."

"Excuse me?"

"Jack warned me." Father Lawrence held up his arm, and I saw the outline of that twisted tattoo beneath his fur. "The Old Wolf is still my master, second only to God. And I am here to watch you, Hunter Kiss, and help when I can. Despite my . . . current indisposition." He lowered his arm, and the chains rattled.

"Jack," I said, trying to ignore everything else he had said. The idea that a small group of men and women had been following every move of my ancestors for the last several thousand years still didn't sit well with me.

Father Lawrence folded his furred, clawed hands over his round stomach. "Jack said, and I quote, 'The status quo would have to change.' That events had progressed to the point where he would have to take certain actions that might have . . . negative results."

"Yo," I said. "His throat was cut."

"That's . . . negative," he replied mildly. "But I think he was worried about something even bigger."

"I saw him last night, but he was fine, relaxed, all smiles. He didn't act like a man on the verge of anything terrible." I hesitated, staring at the candles. "But Grant . . . Grant said that Jack called in the middle of the night. That he needed to tell me something important."

"So he told you, or he didn't. But given the absence of your memories, my guess is that he *did* tell you something important."

"Something that someone else doesn't want me to remember." I leaned back, shaking my head. "The boys don't remember, either. And that . . . that should be impossible. They can't be tampered with."

"Except by those who made your bloodline. Or," he continued, holding up his dark furred hand, forestalling any comments from me, "some other force you aren't yet familiar with. How many surprises have you been given over the past year, Maxine? There's so much none of us understand. We're children, compared to the vastness that sleeps."

I was certain he didn't mean anything, but my hand touched my stomach, my ribs. "I know."

Father Lawrence struggled to feed himself another cookie. I let him do it on his own, and he managed to shove the whole thing in his mouth. He was a messy eater, but only because his mouth was awkwardly shaped. He mumbled, "Grant is another matter entirely."

"Oh, God," I said.

"There are things he needs to explain," he replied, with a great deal of seriousness. "And when he does, you need to ask yourself again why you don't remember him. *Why him?* What would be the benefit?"

"Why not make me forget everything? It seems as though that would be easier."

"Easier, yes. Assuming . . . assuming someone did steal your memories."

"Of course someone did." I frowned, searching his gaze, which was becoming distant, thoughtful. "What are you thinking?"

He hesitated, and the hush that fell down around us was thick, and the air hard to breathe.

"Both of us would do anything to protect the ones we love," Father Lawrence said. "I wear chains when I lose myself. I hide in this room with candles and prayer. But what would you do, Maxine, to protect Grant?"

"I don't know. I'm not that woman."

He gave me a sad, chilling smile. Against my skin, the boys stirred, tugging me toward the door. I didn't need to be asked twice. I stood and pulled on my boots, unable to look at Father Lawrence.

"I wondered if I killed him," I blurted out. "I still wonder. My knife was there. But I wouldn't have needed a weapon to finish it."

"I don't believe that," Father Lawrence said, gently. "You wouldn't hurt your own grandfather. And you're not a cold-blooded killer."

"But I do kill." Tears burned my eyes. I blinked them away. "I'll see you later, Frank. Stay out of trouble."

"And don't," I added as an afterthought, "keep stringing Killy along. You being here isn't easy for her. You know how she feels about you."

"Don't," he said.

"Don't," I echoed mockingly, and left the room.

CHAPTER 6

I knew something was wrong before I hit the stairs. The boys were too restless. Even the armor throbbed; but that felt odd, and separate from what Zee and the others were telling me. Which was worrisome enough.

I reached the bar. And found a shitload of zombies.

Almost two dozen, scattered like gnats on rotten fruit: ready to eat, ready to fly. Men, women, even a couple teenagers, all sporting black auras that flickered above their heads like storm clouds. They watched me with dead eyes and flat expressions. Sitting, standing in front of the door and windows. Business suits, street clothes, and a mother in sweats with a baby strapped to her chest and a pistol in her left hand.

Possessed humans. Ruled by parasites who fed on pain. Amongst them sat Killy and Grant. Killy was pale, tight-lipped, arms folded over her chest. The toe of her red boot tapped the floor with all the force of a machine gun.

Grant was far more still, but only in body. His palms pressed flat against the battered wooden tabletop, his jaw tight and that furrow deep between his eyes. But when I looked at him, only for a moment, the air seemed to shimmer around his body in waves of heat and light—not an aura, but something deeper, burning inside him.

He met my gaze. I saw no fear. None. Just grim confidence, rooted so deep, so unwavering, I might have also called it *faith*. Faith in what, I didn't know, didn't presume to guess. I wondered why I assumed he knew what surrounded him. Most humans couldn't tell a zombie from a peanut. Even being with me wouldn't have changed that. You had to see it. Feel it. Know it.

He does, I thought. *He damn well does.*

A woman sat with him and Killy, across the table. Aura thunderous, cut with flickers of red lightning that flowed from the crown of her head, down to her feet. She had red hair, and wore a red dress beneath a bone-colored trench coat. Red heels covered her feet, and her legs were long and bare, pale as snow and moisturized until they shone. She was nursing a cup of coffee, steaming hot, and smiled over the rim when she saw me.

"Hunter," Blood Mama whispered. "Dearest little Hunter."

❦

THERE were rules when it came to demons. Rules and hierarchies that I had only just begun to understand. My mother had never found it important to delineate between different kinds of demons—at least not to my face. If it wasn't human or animal, it was dead meat. If it was human or animal, and tried to hurt us, it was also dead meat. My mother did not fuck around.

The most dangerous of the demons, so the stories went, were the Reaper Kings.

World Eaters, some of my ancestors had called them. Living only for their bellies, and the hunt, and the kill.

I knew nothing else about the Reaper Kings, except that they were death—and the leaders of the demonic army. Imprisoned in the First Ward, the core of the veil, for the last ten thousand years. I had tried asking Jack about them, but of all the myriad things my grandfather had *not* wanted to discuss, *they* seemed to be at the top.

My mother had warned me, though. But not in so many words.

You won't be able to run from them, baby.

Stop them, you stop it all.

Right. Easy. Thanks for the advice.

The lowest of the low within the ranks of the imprisoned army were the parasites. Rats, cockroaches, fleas. Slipping between cracks in the outer ring of the prison veil to farm for pain. Some were young, others old. The old ones could exert complete control over hosts. The young ones simply rode along, choosing humans already predisposed to abuse, and merely . . . egging them on. I couldn't blame every random act of violence on a parasite turning some human into a zombie puppet, but if there was pain, and fear, and death—all three of those together—then a demonic parasite was probably close by, feeding on that dark energy.

And the zombie seated in front of me was their queen. Queen of the demonic parasites. Queen of the gutter rats.

I walked to the table, turned a chair around, and straddled it. My gloves were still off. I shrugged out of my jacket, and pushed up my sleeves. Tattoos rippled across my skin, scales shimmering and heaving, those red eyes on my palm glinting like fire. Grant and Killy watched me, but I didn't look at them. Just Blood Mama. Just that cold smile.

"Have something to drink," she said, as a stringy-haired zombie in jeans and Birkenstocks walked out from behind the bar and set down a tray filled with three cups of coffee, steaming. Killy gave the zombie a disgusted look.

I poured a little from each cup over my tattooed finger, allowing the boys a taste. Blood Mama said, "Poison, my dear, is for cave-dwelling types with no sophistication. I'm better than that."

"Bullets aren't better," I replied, and drank from the last cup tested; a slow sip that burned my lips and the inside of my mouth. I glanced at the others. "It's okay."

Grant's mouth twitched into a faint smile, which took me off guard. So did the fact that I almost smiled back. Just a little. Like this was some game. Which it was, but nothing that should have inspired kicks and giggles.

Don't know you. Better off not knowing you, I told him silently as he picked up a cup. Killy tapped her foot a little harder and gestured with her chin toward the zombie who had brought the coffee. "Don't. He just took a shit and didn't wash his hands. In fact, he *smelled* them afterward."

Grant hesitated. I put down my cup. The zombie edged away from the table and Blood Mama, who also stared at her coffee.

"Awkward," I said.

Blood Mama's hand shot out and grabbed the zombie's wrist. His aura sputtered like a flame, and sweat broke out on his pale forehead. He did not try to break free, though—frozen, frozen like a rabbit—and I sensed a shift in the other zombies, a hunger in their eyes that reminded me of a mob watching an execution. Horror and excitement, a strange arousal: the promise of a good feeding.

"Bad child," Blood Mama whispered. "I like this host. If I wanted it polluted with filth, I would find a sewer to roll in."

Her pale hand tightened. I heard a crack—bone, I thought—but that was the snap of the zombie's breath in his human lungs as his head snapped back, mouth open, eyes rolling in his head. His aura flared once, brilliantly dark, like a prairie storm cloud—and then sucked inward until it was the size of a fist. A scream vomited out of him, choking off into a strangled sob. Grant pushed back his chair.

"Stop this," he said, deadly quiet. "Give him to me if you don't want him, but stop this."

I stared. Blood Mama's lips peeled back over her teeth in a grotesque smile. "Another pet, Lightbringer? No. This one's *mine*."

She yanked hard on the zombie's arm, and he fell on his knees, mumbling and weeping. His aura writhed, cut with streaks of frantic light. Blood Mama leaned forward and slammed her mouth against his. Not a kiss. A feeding. Her aura surrounded the other zombie in a storm of red lightning, and I thought—I marveled—that any human could be so blind not to see this, or feel it, or fear it.

Grant reached for his cane, like he was going to stand. I grabbed his arm. He shot me a hard, haunted look—but it was too late for whatever the hell he thought he was going to do. I heard a popping sound. The human host collapsed on the floor at Blood Mama's feet, still pricked by her aura. She kicked at the body with one red heel—and dabbed delicately at her lips.

I knelt and touched his neck. Found a strong pulse. Just unconscious. He would wake with amnesia, and a host of sins on his shoulders—sins he'd have no memory committing. I felt completely sympathetic.

"Mmmm," she murmured. "I should do that more often."

"You ate your own child," Grant said.

"I'll make another." Blood Mama snapped her fingers, and a second zombie rushed forward to take away the coffee. "Now, what were we discussing?"

"Nothing," I said, returning to my chair—giving Grant a warning look. "Though it's no coincidence you're here."

"Why, did something happen?" Blood Mama smiled, still rubbing her lips. "Oh, yes. Jack."

"Jack," I echoed. "Word travels fast."

"Depends on the word." She glanced around the bar, her demeanor careless, relaxed. her fingers trailing up her leg, as though she couldn't stop touching her stolen human skin. "You mentioned coincidence, but that's merely a path finding its proper course. Call it destiny. And I am here, Hunter, because I felt something disturbing cross *my* path. All the way in the veil."

I leaned back in my chair, holding her gaze. "So you brought an army with you. Seems overdone. You and I both know we're not allowed to kill each other."

She tilted her head, mouth quirked with either puzzlement or amusement—and I wondered what I had said wrong. I glanced at those zombies standing around the bar, none of whom could meet my gaze. Auras shrank when I looked at them.

And when *they* looked at Grant.

I sat up straighter. "Last time I saw this many demons in a bar, I was eight years old. I'm sure you heard about that encounter."

Her red lips thinned. "Your mother should have killed you when she saw what you were capable of. She was young enough to have another child. A *safer* child."

"But you got me."

Blood Mama waved a dismissive hand—but the glint in her eyes was anything but. "Let's not waste time on the past. Your bloodline has always been an abomination. But a useful one. Even the war with those Avatar skins proved beneficial to me and mine. How else would we have thrived all these thousands of years while the rest of the old Lords were locked tight in their prisons?"

She leaned forward, her aura dancing with such quiet violence, I felt the table vibrate. "You and I both know the veil is cracking. Only a matter of time before the inner rings break, and the army goes free. And now those Avatars . . . those skins . . . will be returning, as well. Drawn by the murders of their own kind, here on earth. At both your hands." Blood Mama glanced at Grant. "Which is worse, I wonder? We, who want to eat you? Or those who wish to *play* with you?"

I couldn't speak. I wasn't even certain I could look at Grant, but I did, wondering who the hell he was—what he was. And maybe I wasn't careful, maybe I showed too much on my face, because I glanced back at Blood Mama and found her watching me with that same puzzled glint. And then, slowly, her gaze slid sideways to Grant.

"I'm sure you have an opinion," she remarked, softly. "Seeing as how you'll be the first person the Avatars enslave."

"I think you should be more worried about yourself," Grant rumbled. "Seeing as how I've made no bargains not to kill you."

"You talk so dirty. I don't suppose you're ready for me yet? I could do so much with your body."

"I could do so much with yours." Every word he spoke hummed through me, low and sonorous, making the boys shift against my skin, stretching themselves as though they were cats wrapped around a fireplace. Tingling warmth settled into my bones—and in my heart. A tug, like something clung there, pulling outward, toward *him*. I didn't know what it meant, but it felt real as a hand gripping my wrist, or the wind, or sunlight.

Blood Mama's eyes narrowed. "I did not come here for that. I will not let you control me."

"You won't have a choice," he said coldly. "I think it might do us all some good."

She bared her teeth, hissing. Grant barked out a single word—a word that sounded like a wild musical note—and the zombie's breath cracked in her throat, eyes flashing wide in rage, shock. Her aura shuddered.

"Fuck," I muttered, even as Killy scrambled to her feet. One of the zombies grabbed a barstool and ran toward Grant, swinging.

I swung off my chair and slammed into the possessed man. We tumbled hard into the bar, but I didn't feel a thing except for the soft yielding sensation of my nails piercing wool and flesh, fingers sinking straight through fat like a hot knife in butter. Blood spurted, instantly absorbed into my skin.

The zombie staggered away, holding his gut. It wasn't lethal what I'd done, but it would require stitches, a hospital. More damage than I usually did to a human host— those blameless hosts. I felt ill.

I got knocked off my feet, and hit the floor so hard I bounced. Wood cracked beneath the back of my skull. The boys howled in their sleep as zombies held me down: arms, legs, sitting on my stomach with hands around my throat. I smelled smoke: my clothes, burning. The boys, burning. Like sitting in water slowly boiling—the zombies didn't know what was happening until they fell away from me, hands on fire, choking on their screams.

I sat up, charred and smoking. Zombies stood between me and Blood Mama. I couldn't hear Grant. I couldn't see him. I couldn't—

—*feel him,* came the unbidden thought, and the fear that ripped through me was startling and fierce, tearing straight into the core of me, beneath my ribs, below my heart. Darkness, coiled. Blinking awake from deep slumber. Leaving me breathless, unsteady, sick with dread. It had been some time since I had felt . . . the creature . . . inside me. A spiritual force so strong it might as well have been physical—separate from me, but of me—with a mind of its own.

This was what Jack feared. This was what my mother had feared. Something inside me that no one could, or wanted, to explain. A force that slept, ever more lightly as time went on, and that seemed to be growing stronger with every terrible waking. It was connected to the falling of the prison veil—I knew that—just as I knew that if I let it, if I ever grew too weak to contain it, the thing would destroy all that I loved. Maybe even this world.

Like my ancestor had almost done.

I closed my eyes, ignoring everything around me. Focusing just on my heart, on quelling the ripening, throbbing sensation beating a drum in my gut: a body unwrapping like some worm made of endless night, stretching, unfolding like a butterfly beneath my spun skin.

My muscles and bones grew warm, liquid as mercury, and my veins filled with a fire that licked my heart into a pounding scream. *I* would have screamed, but all I could do was choke, and choke some more, on hunger.

No, I told the thing, fighting for control; afraid and sick, reminded again what it must feel like for those humans to be possessed. *Not now. Not here.*

The zombie with the baby stepped forward. The infant squirmed, making wet, sobbing sounds. No dark aura over its head. Kid had a devil for a mother, aiming a gun in my face. Blood Mama, hidden, barked out a sharp word. The zombie's right eye twitched, mouth twisting with displeasure—but she lowered the weapon and backed off, stepping around those possessed men and women who were clutching burned hands to their chests.

Most demons would have abandoned their hosts by now, but they were holding on. Because of their queen. The minute she left, those humans would be shed like yesterday's underwear, leaving them with headaches and palms that looked like hamburger.

Blood Mama glided around her zombie children, red heels clicking on the floor. Her smile was sly. But when she looked into my eyes, she froze—and that smile slipped like a cut ribbon.

"You're not yourself," she whispered, and the human skin she wore seemed to wither away under the force of her possession, flesh sucking into hollows, shadows, growing gaunt and tight against the bone.

"Maybe I don't want to be," I replied, barely able to speak, shivering uncontrollably as the thing inside me unwound a little more; and my hunger grew, a little more. A terrible hunger, not for food, not for anything I could name—except for the spark that made the living, burning at the root of a heartbeat, or a thought.

"Lady Whore," I breathed, two words that did not come from me. I had not thought them, did not know them, and the voice that spoke them hardly seemed born from me.

But Blood Mama flinched, fingers twitching, and something terrible entered her gaze: fear, maybe, or horror. She almost bowed her head—almost, I saw it—but her spine stiffened, and that aura flared, and she braced herself.

"Even you, dreamer, know the meaning of a promise," she said, each word forced out between clenched teeth, speaking at me, but not *to* me. "You will not use me again. Not now. Not *ever*."

Not ever, echoed a soft voice in my head, filled with distaste and disdain, and that endless reaching hunger.

I closed my eyes, fumbling for my right hand, pressing my fingers into the armor. I thought of good things, things I loved, my mother and Jack, and Zee, the boys. I thought of sunsets, and the open road, and the stars. And I felt a golden thread tug on my heart, outward, ever outward. I thought of Grant, even though I didn't want to.

And slowly, ever so slowly, the darkness settled.

I exhaled and opened my eyes.

The air of the bar felt too bright, tinged with blue—as if air could have a color—and even the shadows beneath the tables seemed to glow around the edges, pulsing like heartbeats.

Blood Mama stared at me, her face stone hard. I licked my cracked lips and tasted blood. "Grant. Killy."

"Here," growled a low voice, and some of the zombies shifted, revealing Father Lawrence. I had no clue when he had entered the fracas, or how he'd freed himself from his chains, but his claws were slick and dripping with blood, and the brown fur covering his body stood out on end, bristling over the contours of his arms and chest.

Behind him, Killy sat on the floor—leaning over Grant. My vision blurred again when I saw him, but not enough to block out the stain of blood on his collar, or his stillness. He was so still.

"Get out," I whispered to Blood Mama, fighting the chill that raced through me. It was always like this, afterward. Shock, adrenaline pouring out of me. I needed to sit down.

Blood Mama's aura trembled, but not the rest of her—human eyes flinty, jaw set. "Your mother was *such* a fool to let you live."

"Maybe." I walked toward her. "Lady Whore. What, I wonder, does that mean?"

Her mouth tightened. "I want to know what Jack told you."

I stopped in front of her. "What is this thing inside me? How do you know it?"

"Jack," she whispered, with a hint of desperation, aura straining against the bonds of her flesh. "Tell me what Jack said."

My eyes narrowed. "You came here for that. *Just* that. Jack."

"He told you something."

"Jack's a big talker. Why don't *you* tell me what you think he said if it's so important."

Blood Mama lifted her chin, ever so slightly. But instead of answering, she walked toward me, gliding gracefully, with a sway to her hips and her heels clicking sharp on the floor. She did not stop, or hesitate—simply held my gaze as she walked past me, our shoulders brushing. She showed nothing on her face as we touched, but her aura shuddered away from me.

"I was so certain," she murmured. "I felt the call. We all did."

I grabbed her arm. "Who killed Jack?"

"Jack's body, you mean." She looked into my eyes, her gaze flat, dead. "You must have been there. Don't *you* know?"

I leaned in close, tasting the heat of her breath, which smelled like coffee and roses. "Tell me."

I could count on one hand the number of times I had spoken with Blood Mama, and not once had she shown anything but cold cruel calm. But this time, again, her aura pulled away from me, and unease flickered in her gaze. It didn't give me any kind of thrill. Just dread.

"Hunter," she whispered. "The Old Wolf was, and always has been, a canny beast. If he let his body die, it was because it was time."

She pulled away from me. I let her go and stood aside as she walked on to the door. She stopped, though, with her hand on the knob, and looked back at me. "Take care, Hunter. There are knots unraveling, and you are . . . most certainly one of them."

"What am I, then?" I tapped my chest, and the armor tingled, as did the boys. "What is this . . . thing? No one will tell me."

A faint smile touched her mouth, but it was wry, and bitter, and even a little sad. All of which I found disturbing.

"You've been told, in so many different ways," said Blood Mama, opening the door. *"No one is more terrible than the leader of the Hunt. No one is more feared. Her desire is her outcome. Her wish, is the command."* She stepped outside, and closed her eyes against the breeze that ruffled her hair. "Jack's words, if I'm not mistaken. I think you know them."

"Just a riddle."

"Riddles are safer. Poor minds that puzzle merely give the riddle-maker a chance to run." Blood Mama's smile widened, just a fraction. "So take your time, Hunter."

She let the door close behind her, but it didn't stay that way. Zombies shuffled out, some calm, others pushing, a few who were injured dragging themselves, others carrying those who were unconscious.

I stepped in front of the zombie mother. Her baby still cried, but she wasn't doing a thing to comfort it. The gun had disappeared into her purse. She reached for it, but it was too little, too late. I slammed my tattooed hand against her brow, murmuring words my mother had taught me in a language that might have been thousands of years dead.

The parasite inside her screamed. *She* screamed. Her aura struggled to free itself from its bonds of flesh, but I kept chanting through gritted teeth, and the boys, my hungry boys, tugged in that fucker like a fish on a line.

Until the parasite was gone. Eaten. And the woman was free.

I caught her before she fell. Father Lawrence helped, and we settled her into a chair. She was unconscious, but her baby wasn't, and continued to scream. Father Lawrence made a shushing sound, and swept his furred hand over the baby's head. The kid stopped crying and stared up at him with huge eyes.

I turned around. All the zombies were gone. I smelled sweat and fear, and burned flesh. A little bit of wet dog. Killy was staring at the exorcised woman, muttering to herself.

Grant still wasn't sitting up. But his eyes were open, watching me.

I walked to him, and knelt. Glass crunched beneath my knees. Sometime, during the fight, those coffee cups had gotten smashed on the floor. Coffee soaked through my jeans, but the boys sucked it up, and within moments, my denim was dry again.

"Someday," he said, like that word was an old joke, just between us. And for a moment, I wanted it to be. I was desperate for something good, and warm.

"You don't want me to remember you," I said, as close to begging as I'd ever been in my life. "Not when it means this. This violence."

He did not smile, but somehow I felt it rise out of him. I felt the heat in his eyes and in the brief touch of his fingers against the back of my hand, and I began to believe how it was possible I might have fallen for this man. Maybe, just a little.

Grant struggled to sit up. This time I helped him. I didn't think about it until it was too late, and his arm was looped over my shoulder. His rough cheek rubbed against mine. I closed my eyes.

"You always say things like that," he whispered. "But I'm still here, Maxine. So don't remember me. Don't remember. Just remember me from now on."

"I will," I said.

CHAPTER 7

KILLY didn't want our help cleaning up her bar. I didn't blame her. I seemed to have a bad habit of bringing violence into her establishments.

Grant and I drove back to the Coop. The rain beat down hard against the windshield, drowning out the radio until all I heard were drums and snatches of melody. Grant stared out the window, humming to himself. I could not place the song, but I could hear him more clearly than the rain and radio, and his voice rolled through me, over me. The boys stretched and shivered.

"Stop," I said.

Grant looked at me but didn't play dumb. "There are things I need to tell you."

Father Lawrence had warned me about this. I hadn't believed him.

Why did you forget this man? I asked myself. *Why him?*

"Your voice," I said, frowning uneasily. "What you did to Blood Mama, the things she said to you. She called you something."

"Lightbringer." Grant fiddled with his cane. "It's a name I'm uncomfortable with. But it *is* a name that's mine. In the same way that the demons call you Hunter."

Lightbringer. I had heard that name before, from Jack. The context was fuzzy, but I felt it resonate inside my heart.

I pulled into a gas station and parked. Listened to the rain on the roof, the windshield wipers, the radio busting a move with "Bohemian Rhapsody." I listened to the lyrics and could imagine the boys singing along, inside my head.

No escape from reality. Open your eyes.
Open your eyes.

I left the engine running and got out of the car. Grant, this time, did not follow. Inside the station, the aisles were clean and the air bright with artificial light. A girl in a dirty brown sweatshirt watched me from behind the counter. I ignored her and went straight to the hot food. I hardly looked at what was there. Just grabbed hamburgers wrapped in foil, juggling them in one arm while I walked quickly to the freezers for ice-cream bars. I picked up sodas, too. Some of the hamburgers fell on my way to the counter, but I didn't try to pick them up. I kicked them across the floor like soft hockey pucks. The girl watched me like she wanted to hit her security alarm. I wondered if there was blood on my face from the fight. Or maybe I smelled like burned flesh. My clothes were a little charred.

I paid for the food, and she threw it in a plastic bag. When I slid back into the car, "Bohemian Rhapsody" was still playing. Grant watched me, silent.

I grabbed a hamburger and shoved the rest of the sack

toward him. He peered inside and, after a moment, removed an ice-cream bar. It was hard for him to unwrap it with one hand bandaged, but he managed.

"You know," he said, "the first night we met, we went to a McDonald's for ice cream and hamburgers."

I choked a little.

Grant watched me finish off the hamburger in three bites and reach for another. "I thought you were never going to eat again."

"I thought you were going to become a drunk."

"Mmm," he said; and then: "Ask."

"I don't know how." I finished the second burger. Cheap, but good. I hadn't eaten one of these in a long time. I had gotten used to real food, not road fare. I unwrapped the foil from a third hamburger. "What you did, what you seemed to be doing, shouldn't have been possible."

"What did you think I was going to do?"

I stopped eating and put down the hamburger. "Possess her. Kill her."

"Possession," he echoed thoughtfully. "We've never called it that. But yes, more or less *that's* true. I would have . . . changed her."

"She brought all that extra muscle for you. Not me. In case you tried."

Grant touched his bandaged hand against the lump swelling just at his hairline. "If there hadn't been . . . inter- ference . . . I might have managed something permanent. Maybe. I've never tried before, with her."

He said it so easily. Possessing a demon, no big deal. Controlling the queen of them, an interesting experiment. *Managing something permanent*, as though he'd have her trading red high heels for bunny slippers, or eating chili peppers instead of souls. I couldn't imagine it.

"I don't have horns," he said, and I blinked, coming back

to myself, staring at him. He wasn't smiling, but he wasn't frowning, either. His eyes were just . . . warm.

"Not yet," he added.

"I didn't say anything," I replied.

"We've had this conversation before. History isn't exactly repeating itself, but close. You're not as grim as you used to be."

"Grim."

"You had good reasons."

I looked away, out the window. Watched a man pump gas into his truck. Ordinary, everyday. He wasn't a zombie. A woman walked past him into the station, head down against the rain, tugging fretfully at her tight pink sweater. He never looked at her. Both of them in their own little worlds, alone.

"When did we meet?" I asked.

"When do you remember coming to Seattle? Where did you stay? Where did you go?"

His questions irritated me. "Almost two years ago. I stayed at the Hyatt. I was going to leave that night, but I went to Pike Place Market for a walk . . . even though I knew it was trouble. The prison veil is weak there." I looked at him, frowning. "My next memory is . . . later. Moving into the Coop."

"But you don't know why."

"Stop," I said wearily. He did, and ate his ice cream. I watched the girl in the pink sweater come out of the station, still tugging on her sweater and carrying a gallon of milk. She looked miserable, lonely, like someone had stomped on her dreams this morning and told her to go sit in a ditch and die.

I glanced at Grant and found him watching the girl, too. He looked sad.

"She's thinking about killing herself," he said, twisting

in his seat, watching as she climbed into a beat-up rusted sedan. "She won't, but the germ is in her."

I believed him. I couldn't help it. I almost wanted to run after the girl, shake her up, and didn't know why. Not my problem. I had enough on my plate. "Are you like Killy?"

"No," he said. "I'm something else."

The girl drove away. I felt cold when she did, a little empty, like I had done someone wrong.

I dumped the rest of the hamburgers from the plastic bag but left the ice cream inside. I wrapped it up until it resembled a brick, then pressed it, lightly, against Grant's swelling head. He held still. I did not meet his gaze. "Let's say you're telling the truth."

"Generous of you."

"Yes," I said. "Blood Mama should have killed you by now. Or tried to take over your body."

"She made that attempt, a little over a year ago." Grant placed his bandaged hand over mine. "That's how we met. You saved my life. At Pike Place Market."

I withdrew my hand, letting him hold the softening cold pack against his head. "And I never left."

"I think you decided you liked me. Just a little."

More than a little, if we were sharing a bed. I was beginning to feel too curious for my own good about how all that had come about. "What *are* you?"

"Human," he said, and his tone was serious, dark, that one word hanging heavy in the air, like it meant more than what I knew. Or maybe I did know, in a different way than I could remember. I was human, and not. Human and demon, and other parts thrown together, in ways I could not comprehend.

Human. I was human. And a little bit not.

"When I was a kid, I was diagnosed with synesthesia," Grant said. "You know what that is, right? A neurological

condition where the different senses—auditory, visual—
get mixed up. For some people it's letters or numbers
that evoke smells, even personalities. For me, when I hear
sounds . . . I see color."

I knew about the condition. I liked music. Years ago I'd
read about Duke Ellington, Jean Sibelius, seeing colors in
notes, melodies. "So when I crumple this foil—"

"I see flashes of bright orange. The sound of the rain
looks like dark silver pearls. When the car engine runs, I
see a deep gravel gray that resembles teeth, and when I
hear 'Bohemian Rhapsody,' I'm surrounded by a rainbow
of purples and reds that . . . spike . . . then melt together
like hot wax."

"And when I talk?"

"I see light," he said, and it surprised me to see his
eyes grow a little too bright, red-rimmed, hot. "I see light,
Maxine."

I forced myself to breathe. "And?"

"I don't just see sound. I see energy. Auras. Around people." Grant looked away from me, and stared at the half-
eaten ice-cream bar in his other hand. "I can change those
auras. I can . . . manipulate them."

The hamburgers felt heavy in my stomach. "What does
that mean?"

Grant stopped holding the plastic bag to his head and
tossed the remains of his ice cream inside. "I can change
people. Alter who they are, down to the soul. Not just
people."

"Demons."

"Anything that lives."

"Me?"

"You're immune. God knows, I think you might be
the only one who is. And even if you weren't . . ." Grant
stopped, and the silence was long and deep, and I was

grateful for the boys, then, on my skin, with their heart-beats pulsing in time to mine.

"I wouldn't hurt you," he whispered, "but there are lines, Maxine, that I could cross. And sometimes I think I have."

I picked up the trash around me. Grant handed over the plastic bag. I got out, threw everything away. Breathed long and deep, though the air tasted like exhaust. I heard sirens in the distance. Zee tugged, once—

—and the armor twisted on my skin. A very physical jerk, as though it were trying to pull away from me. I clutched my hand to my stomach, breathing through clenched teeth.

It happened again. I ripped off my glove. The armor's surface was moving, shimmering, those engraved knots and roses oozing across the organic metal like petals and threads cast on water. I stopped breathing. And didn't start again until, abruptly, the armor stilled.

I slid back into the car. Grant's frown deepened. "What's wrong?"

"Mind reader, too?"

"I know you."

"Guess you do," I said quietly, and gripped the wheel with trembling hands. "Buckle up. We've got trouble."

GRANT and I drove back to the Coop. We heard the sirens before we saw them. I told myself it had nothing to do with the corpse in the apartment, but I was already thinking about new aliases for Grant and Byron. Mary, too. We'd go to Texas, I thought. Back to the old farm where my mother was buried. Or maybe drive to Chicago or New York. I had inherited homes there, filled with cash, weapons, papers. Everything a girl needed to start over.

I didn't question why I included Grant. I told myself it was because I wasn't done yet with his mystery, our mystery—the who and what and why of him. I guess that was true.

It was raining hard, skies dark, which was why we didn't see the smoke sooner.

Not that we needed to. An ambulance sped through the intersection ahead of us, followed by two fire trucks. Grant leaned forward until his nose bumped the dashboard, staring intently through the windshield. Zee wrestled even more violently against my skin, and the armor felt hot, then ice-cold; and then it pulsed like a heartbeat, making my right hand twitch uncontrollably. It felt like an electrical current was jamming up my muscles. I peeled my fingers off the wheel and stuck my hand beneath me, holding it still as best I could. Grant watched but said nothing.

I turned the corner and saw the Coop. Fire trucks and ambulances surrounded the homeless shelter, which took up an entire city block in the warehouse district. The place was immense.

And it was on fire. Just the second wing. The floor with the apartments. Where Byron was.

I slammed on the brakes. Grant jerked against his seat belt, bracing himself against the dashboard. Maybe I put the car in park. Didn't know, didn't care. I was out on the road, running.

A crowd had gathered on the sidewalk and in the garden, volunteers and homeless trying to calm each other. Firemen were cordoning off the area. I slammed through them all, ignoring shouts, screams. I glanced up just before I entered the building, and looked at the smoke billowing black through the windows—one of which had already exploded outward. Looked like someone had set off a bomb.

Then I was inside. The downstairs hall was smoky, but

mostly clear. I passed firemen wearing masks. Several tried
to grab me, but I wrenched free and punched one man who
was too persistent. I cracked his mask, and he slammed
hard against the wall. I didn't stop. I flew up the stairs,
and it was like entering another world, hot and thick with
smoke and ash. My eyes and lungs burned.

Not for long. The boys slipped over my face and mouth,
and then my nostrils. Strange sensation. Felt like I was
drowning. I tripped on the stairs, panicked, and touched
my mouth. I found only smooth skin. Touched my nostrils
and found them gone. When I blinked, my eyes felt thicker,
heavier; and the world darkened, veiled in silver and pearl.

When I breathed, air filled my lungs. It tasted warm,
like sulfur. The boys, breathing for me. They had saved me
from drowning before, just like this. They had probably
saved my grandmother like this, as well. She had been in
Hiroshima when the bomb was dropped. Lost, in the inferno, watching bodies blast into ash.

I did not feel the heat. I reached the second floor in
moments and saw flames climbing the walls and ceiling,
sweeping across the carpet in waves of light. I ran through
the fire, and my clothing burned. My hair burned. I felt it
sizzle away as I passed through solid walls of flame.

I watched for breaks in the floor as I raced toward Byron's room. The smoke was thick, blinding, but the boys
were wild and tugged me forward with their own unerring
instincts. Below my heart, the darkness stirred—the creature, reaching upward—but I slammed it down, ruthless.
I listened for screams, cries for help from the adjoining
rooms, and heard none.

I found a dead body in front of Byron's room.

The man was one of the few things not entirely on fire;
in fact, it looked as though he had simply dropped dead
from smoke inhalation. I didn't recognize his face. He was

pale, well built, and the remains of his clothing looked like linen, the kind those Seattle Earth Father types liked to wear when they were pretending to be yogis. Parts of it were burning, but slowly, as though something in the material retarded the flames.

He looked peaceful, and that frightened me.

Byron's door stood ajar. I stepped over the body, pushed it all the way open. All I saw was fire and smoke. If he was here, if he had not been spirited out—

But his bed was empty. On fire and empty. I turned a quick circle, making certain he was gone.

And found someone else entirely.

A woman. She came out of the bathroom, moving through the smoke like a pale ghost, unbothered by the fire. I thought she was naked, but her clothes were merely the same color as her skin and clung to her in wispy waves, like silk. Flames touched her, but nothing burned. She had a very long neck, and around her throat sat an iron collar. Her hair was short and red.

Trouble. I knew that. This was big damn trouble.

I stood my ground, waiting. She did the same. The building was burning down around us, and we had all the time in the world.

Until she moved. And, abruptly, she was no longer a woman, but a man. The transformation was complete, startling, and when I looked closer she—he—was still the same person. Just caught at a different angle.

"You are a Guardian," she said, tilting her head, just so, becoming a woman again, the firelight hot on her sharp cheekbones. "Warden. Made woman."

I could not speak. I had no mouth. I stepped closer, and that woman's gaze dropped, studying my burning clothes, which were falling away to reveal my naked tattooed skin. She looked at my breasts, my stomach, lower and lower, her gaze lingering on the armor covering my right hand. Her eyes fluttered closed. She tilted back her head as though in pleasure, or pain.

"I feel him," she whispered, swaying.

And she vanished. Gone, into thin air. Gone as though she had never existed. Like magic.

Except it wasn't magic. I had seen it done before. By Jack, by others. Even I could slide through space using the armor on my hand. But there was a price to that travel, for me. There was always a price.

I heard shouts, distant and tinny. I tore my gaze from where the woman had been standing, thinking of Byron, Jack—*I feel him, I feel him*—and ran to the doorway. I looked down the hall and saw a hulking figure beyond the wall of flames.

One of the firemen. Coming to look for the stupid woman who had run into the building and punched one of their own. The fires raged around him, thick and hot, snaking up the walls and licking the ceiling above his head. I stared, torn. I wasn't certain he had seen me. I couldn't let him see me.

But my feet vibrated, then my legs, and a groan rolled through my ears into my muscles and bones. This floor was going down.

I ran toward the fireman. He was already backing away toward the stairs, but he was too slow, too late. He noticed me coming at the last moment, and I don't know what he saw, but his eyes widened behind his mask and his scream was louder than the crack of the beams above our heads. I slammed into him just as the ceiling collapsed.

I had been hit by a bus once before, and this felt the same. I didn't feel pain, but the weight dragged me down on top of the man, and for a moment I saw my face reflected in his mask.

Except I had no face. No mouth. No nose. Even my eyes were lost in black scales and mercury knots, every inch of my skin covered in demonic bodies. Scariest thing I had ever seen. And I was bald.

I looked past my reflection into the fireman's eyes. He was still staring, screaming, and his fear had nothing to do with the ceiling crushing us, or the fire. I rolled my right hand into a fist, and the armor tingled.

A moment later, we slipped into darkness.

Lasted only a heartbeat, a heartbeat a thousand years long, but in that place *between* I felt smashed with the old horror; lost, forever, in darkness: no body, no heart, no ground beneath my feet; feeling nothing but the boys on my skin, the boys who were the shell around my emptiness, and my mind, screaming.

We were spat out into another part of the Coop, a hall near the lobby, where children had painted the walls with rainbows and castles. We slid across the floor, and I rolled off the man. Naked, except for the remains of my cowboy boots. The leather was still on fire. His yellow suit smoked. He scrabbled backward, staring at me with such horror.

I couldn't even tell him it would be okay.

I slammed my armored fist into the ground, thinking of Byron, Jack—Grant.

And I was gone.

CHAPTER 8

THERE was no such thing as magic.
Miracles, maybe. But not magic.

Arthur C. Clarke said it best, that any sufficiently advanced technology was indistinguishable from magic. Matches, mirrors, even the force of a magnet might be voodoo to a caveman, capable of being used, but without any understanding of what the object was or how it had come to be. Just a gift, maybe, from the gods—an invention of spirits and lightning, and the ghosts of bloodied ancestors.

I might as well have been a caveman, a Neanderthal, even a slug still crawling from the sea. The armor was that far ahead of me, a piece of another world where reality was shaped by possibilities, and dreams, and the force of free will. A key that not even time could bind.

But it was mine. Mine until I died.

God help us all.

❧

WHEN I entered the world again, I found myself in the apartment. Books, brick walls, and my grandfather on the floor, covered in a blood-soaked sheet.

I was not alone.

I saw Mary first. She stood by the couch, clad in a house-dress embroidered with sunflowers and butterflies, cinched tight at the waist with an old leather belt. Her legs and feet were bare, spidery with dark veins. Old track marks covered her sinewy arms. Thick gray hair stood out from her head, bristling, wild.

She clenched a butcher knife in each hand. Standing very still, watching the woman from the fire.

I watched, too. The woman knelt beside Jack's covered body, her head bowed so low her brow nearly touched the blood-sticky floor. Her palms lay flat and still, her spine curved in a perfect arc of obeisance. If she was breathing, I couldn't tell. If she was alive, then she'd had a lifetime of practice prostrating on floors.

I looked around but didn't see Byron.

Mary's gaze slid sideways when I joined her, silently assessing my face. No glimmer of surprise or shock, just a faint tightening of the wrinkles around her eyes. I touched my mouth and felt only skin. No lips. No nostrils. I could feel my tongue, though, locked inside my closed mouth, and it tasted like sulfur and blood.

Mary extended one of her knives to me. I shook my head.

Maybe our movements drew her attention—or maybe not at all—but the woman stirred and sat up slowly. She did not look at us, her gaze instead drifting upward toward the ceiling, eyelids fluttering, her mouth moving in some silent prayer.

Not human, I thought, able to see her better. Not human, in so many little ways: the length of her neck, the small size of her eyes, the stark angle of her cheekbones. I called her a woman, but it was difficult to determine her gender with any certainty—when the light shifted, I could have just as easily identified her as a man.

She was not from this world, though. I knew it, just like I knew what water was, or fire. She had not been born on earth.

Those fluttering eyelids stilled, closed—and then blinked open slowly, like an owl's.

She looked at me. I steadied myself, glad for the boys resting so heavily on my skin. I had dealt with crazies all my life, crazy and dangerous, but there was something in this woman's eyes that made me feel small on the inside. Small and cold. I didn't want her near anyone I cared about, not even the dead.

"Warden," she said. "The skin of our Maker lies defiled, and yet you live. Explain this."

I wished I could—though I had to wonder why she didn't ask Mary, as she was the one standing around with the knives.

I walked toward the woman, silent except for the scuff of my smoking bootheels on the floor. The boys shifted across my face, just enough to give me back my mouth and nose. Cool air flooded my lungs. I wet my lips, and they tasted like iron. The woman watched me, small eyes narrowing, thin mouth tensing into a hard line.

"Answer me," she snapped. I stopped, but only out of surprise. Her voice sounded so different, like she had plugged her vocal cords into a stereo and electric guitar, and hit the ON switch. Those two words spilled over me with all the force of a shock wave, pulsing with power.

Reminded me of Grant.

Mary muttered, "Slave. Baby born, cut and bred."

I wanted Mary to stay silent, but the woman didn't look at her. Just me, her gaze growing darker, even smaller.

"You *will* speak," she said again, with that same voice: more tone than words, more melody than tone, rising and falling as though part of a lullaby to a baby hurricane. The boys lapped it up, rolling over my skin. Tickled.

I smiled. "Who are you? Why are you here?"

The woman blinked, staring. And then, slowly, rose to her feet. By the time she was fully standing, she resembled a man again in both body and face. She'd had no breasts to begin with, but her cheeks, and the line of her jaw, moved effortlessly from feminine to masculine, and back again.

I wasn't sure she would answer me, but she whispered, "Praise be their will," and placed her hand over the iron collar. "I am the Messenger. I have been sent for our Maker, our Aetar Master, praise be his light in the Divine Organic."

Praise be his light. Our Maker. Our Aetar Master. All of those, words to describe my grandfather. Jack Meddle. Old man. Immortal. Avatar.

She said it like she meant it. I touched my own throat, purposely mirroring her posture. "Why were you sent?"

"You must know." The woman glided away from Jack's body, her gaze never leaving mine, though I sensed she was taking in the apartment—the space of it, the books, the windows—perfectly and kinesthetically aware of herself in relation to everything around her. "Our Makers felt two of their own murdered on this world. *Impossible* murders. None have ever been so taken, not since the war with the Reaper Kings. But the veil"—she closed her eyes, tilting her head—"the veil still holds. And so something else has murdered our gods and Makers."

The woman pointed at Jack's remains. "One remains. I am to bring him to the others for questioning."

"That will be difficult. He's gone from his skin."

"He will find another. I think, perhaps, he already has." She tilted her head, still studying me. "Why did you allow his skin to be defiled?"

"Murdered, you mean." I moved closer, holding her gaze. "I allowed nothing to happen. I found him. I'm looking for his killer."

"Look all you wish. You have failed already by allowing the desecration of your Maker. If you have honor"—she slid her finger across her throat—"you will kill yourself once his defiler is found. I will help you."

Spoken simply, matter-of-factly and without malice. Her version of benevolence, maybe. My smile never slipped. "Too kind. And if our . . . Maker . . . doesn't wish to leave with you?"

"I am the Messenger. I am the voice of our Aetar Masters. Their word is the will, and I am their hand through the Labyrinth. He *must* come." The woman said it as though the idea of resistance was inconceivable, as though her words should mean something to me. Make me quake in my boots, maybe. Jump to, with a salute.

I wasn't that smart. But I had a pretty good idea of where this was headed.

Until she looked at Mary.

I had assumed she'd already noticed the old woman, but there was a particular stillness that fell over the Messenger when she fixed her gaze on her. An ever-so-subtle widening of the eyes, a twitch in her mouth. A small but vital reaction. I didn't like it.

"You are different," said the woman to Mary. "You feel . . . old."

I didn't think she was referring to wrinkles and gray

hair. She said *old* in the same way that myths were old, or mountains, or the pyramids. A deeper old, the kind that stories were made of.

Mary very deliberately ran her tongue over the flat side of the butcher knife. She did the same to the other blade. Her gaze, locked steady on the Messenger. It would have been a ridiculous gesture with anyone else, but not Mary.

"Old as sin," she said, lips parting in a terrible smile. "Sins of your Makers. Skinners. Sluts."

"Stop," I said.

The Messenger drew back, ignoring me. "You will not say such things."

Mary's smile turned darker, fiercer. "No chains around *my* heart."

And she attacked.

I was expecting it, knowing Mary as I did—though when she moved, I was surprised at her speed. I couldn't have stopped her even had I wanted to. The old woman was made of muscle and adrenaline, and flew past me with those knives flashing. Dead silent.

The other woman leapt backward. Mary stayed close. Neither made a sound, both moving faster and faster, knives and fists entwined in a terrible dance of block and attack. Inhuman, between the two of them; nothing anyone of this world could have matched. But the woman, the Messenger, had the advantage.

She was young.

And she had claws.

I saw them in flashes. She hadn't possessed claws earlier, but sometime during the fight, her fingernails had pushed outward, riding the backs of elongated fingertips that were sharp as needle points. I saw them most clearly when she finally managed to land a blow against Mary.

Mary jerked backward at the last moment, and the

Messenger—instead of taking out her throat—raked her fingers down the old woman's chest, snaring her dress and ripping it open. Long wrinkled breasts sagged like pears—and between them, embedded in her sternum, glittered a golden circle of coiled knotted lines—twisting, into a maze. A labyrinth.

I had seen the disc before, and the design. Seeing it again made me feel dizzy, lost, heart aching around that deep black hole of amnesia—which was beginning to take on the shape of one peculiar man.

Grant. For a moment, I thought I remembered him from before this morning—born in flashes: me, running toward him as a zombie pointed a gun in his face; his face buried in my hair as we stood on the ocean's edge; his voice, singing.

Then, nothing.

Those memories slipped away, as if imagined.

The Messenger froze, staring at Mary and the golden disc embedded in her sternum. Blood dripped from the tips of her fingers.

"No," she whispered.

Mary bared her teeth and jutted out her bleeding chest. I half expected her to thump it with her fists, which still clenched the butcher knives.

"We live yet," she said, and lunged again. The woman did not jump back. She grabbed both knives in her hands, blades sinking into her flesh—and held on with little more than a grunt of pain.

"Impossible," she gritted out, teeth clenched. "That bloodline was *culled*."

Power, in that last word—a terrible sinking power that pushed through me. I was not affected by it; but Mary let out a rattling hiss and threw back her head as though in pain.

"How did you escape?" asked the woman. "Are there others?"

Others. I didn't need my memories to know that there was one other.

Grant.

Mary cried out. I grabbed the Messenger around the neck, wrenching backward and twisting with all my strength. Breaking necks was never as easy as it looked on television; but I heard the crack, and the woman went down.

So did Mary, her knives clattering across the floor. Her skin was ashen, hollow, as though the life had been drained right out of her. I checked her pulse. Found it rapid, weak.

I glanced over at the Messenger, expecting a corpse.

But she wasn't dead. Just paralyzed. Her eyes blinked, mouth gaping, but that was all that moved. I knelt, breathing hard.

"Enough," I said. "You're not taking anyone from this world."

She stared at me. I didn't think I would ever forget the accusation in her eyes, the betrayal, as though I had violated some sacred promise between the two of us.

One "made" woman to another, I realized. Like comrades in arms. She had expected me to be on her side. Assumed it.

"Defiler," she breathed, and tears rolled from the corners of her eyes, across the bridge of her nose and cheek.

"No," I said, hating myself. "There are things in this place you don't understand."

She closed her eyes. "I am the Messenger. I am the voice of our Aetar Masters. Their word is the will, and I am their hand through the Labyrinth. That is *all* I need to understand."

"You're wrong," I told her, but refrained from saying

more. I heard a clicking sound outside the apartment. A cane.

I didn't remember Grant before this morning, but I recalled other things, strange things around the *periphery* of him—memories swelling in hits and waves. Enough, so that I had a growing sense of the larger picture. A crazy, profoundly disturbing, picture.

There was no way, *no way*, this woman should be allowed to see him. Not until I understood exactly what was going on. Not even after that.

I ran toward the door. But I was too late.

Grant limped inside—and stopped, staring. Déjà vu filled me, as though life had rewound itself to that predawn moment, seeing him for the first time. His expression was the same, concerned and weary, more than a little wild. Soot covered his cheek and clothing. His hair was slick with rain. He looked at me, then past me, at the woman on the ground.

"What—" he began, but she made an ugly choking sound, staring at him like a normal human would stare at Bigfoot, or little gray men from outer space, or even the Easter Bunny wielding a chain saw—with horror and shock, and disbelief. It made her look young to me. My hands felt dirty for hurting her.

"Lightbringer," she breathed. "Abomination."

I pushed Grant back toward the door. "Get out."

He staggered, staring over my head. "Maxine. She's—"

"*Go.*"

"—like me," he finished.

The woman screamed at him. Not in fear or pain—but rage. Her voice sounded like the siren wail of an electric guitar, inhuman and unearthly, cut from something wild. The boys rippled across my skin when they heard that cry.

Mary's body twitched, then broke into a full seizure.

Grant shoved me aside, so violently he almost lost his cane. He staggered, caught himself, and shouted.

Just one word, but a word that became a soaring note that rose out of his throat like thunder. I felt an answering tug inside my heart, as though my body was connected to the power in his voice.

I remembered, too, what he had told me—energy, auras, *I can change people*—and whipped around, staring at the woman, who was still screaming at him, screaming like she didn't need to breathe.

I had broken her neck. Heard the crack, seen the paralysis. But she was moving again, hands twitching, legs trembling. Mary was still unconscious, breath rattling in her throat. Her seizure had stopped, but she was withering away like there was a tube jammed in her heart, sucking out blood, sparks.

Her life, stolen away to heal another.

Grant snarled. I crossed the room in two steps and drove myself down onto the Messenger, slamming my knee into her chest. Bone cracked. I wrapped my hands around her throat. Her voice choked off. A small part of me screamed and screamed as I strangled her, screamed like I was a little girl watching a horror movie, but I gritted my teeth and didn't stop.

She looked up at me. No fear in her eyes. Just a promise. I had a feeling she was good at keeping those.

I wasn't surprised when she disappeared—leaving my hands empty, my ears ringing with silence. What surprised me was how disappointed I felt for not killing her sooner.

A mistake I could rectify. My left hand closed over my right, holding the armor tight. I closed my eyes, focusing on the woman with all my strength. I had to follow. I had to finish this, for all our sakes.

Ice spiked from the metal into my bones—ice becoming fire, striking straight into the marrow of my fingers and wrist. I braced myself.

But nothing happened. I didn't slide into the darkness.

I opened my eyes, staring at the armor. I'd never known what I was doing when I used it. Just instinct. Drive. Hunger. It had always given me what I needed most, but what I needed and what I wanted weren't always the same things.

I needed to kill that woman. I needed to kill her before she hurt anyone else. I couldn't let that wait.

"Don't do this," I said to the armor. "Not now."

The armor pulsed twice: two heartbeats. Like it was saying, *Fuck you.*

I tried again, focusing on my need, even shaking my right fist like that would be the magic bullet. Got nothing in return. I had been told the armor had a mind of its own. Fine. It could go fuck itself. I might just cut off my own arm out of spite.

I looked over my shoulder. Grant was on the floor, hauling Mary into his lap. His jaw was tight, eyes hard, but I knew that look for what it was now—anger and grief, and determination.

"She's alive," he said, not looking at me. "Barely."

I stood, swaying—and then sat down again, hard. My head hurt. It was hard to breathe. Nothing had been done to me, I wasn't injured—but I felt like parts of my body had been turned inside out. Including my mind.

I kept seeing things when I looked at Mary and the apartment—memories overlaying reality, sparks of light, snatches of music—piano, a flute—the feeling of warm arms around me while my fingers banged out a rough version of "Chopsticks"—the scent of popcorn, the crunch of chewed nails—the boys giggling while watching old Disney movies starring Dean Jones—

And that scent of cinnamon all around me, in my hair, on my clothes, buried in my skin.

I remembered those things. I hadn't forgotten them. But having them so near the surface of my mind made me feel distant, removed, out-of-body. As though I was living another woman's life.

I looked at the armor again and clenched my hand into a fist. The woman could be anywhere. I couldn't hunt without help, and it was still daylight. I was stuck. A sitting duck. And that woman was out there, probably using her voice on another unlucky soul. I wondered how many lives it took to heal a broken neck.

I scooted closer. "Will Mary be okay?"

"Yes," Grant said firmly, but in a tone of voice that really meant *No, but I'll make it happen if I have to rip a hole in hell.*

"Who was that woman?" Grant asked, then shook his head. "Wait. Get me my flute first."

"Where is it?"

"Over there, beneath the window."

I managed to stand again and staggered in the direction he pointed. I saw the table, and several flutes—most of them made of wood—but there was one that gleamed golden, a lovely instrument. I had a feeling that was the one he wanted. I picked it up, turned—and stopped.

My mother's chest was on the floor beside the table. Old-fashioned, solid wood. Nothing fancy except for what it held. Journals, photographs, weapons, all the little pieces that were left of my mother's life and my childhood. It was hard to look away. I could remember carrying it up the stairs into this apartment, I could recall placing it in different spots, trying to find just the right place to store it.

I could see, in my mind, removing pictures and spreading them on a table, pointing out my mother's face, and saying, *You're right, we do look alike. But all of us always do.*

I walked back to Grant. He was humming. Sounded like something from *Swan Lake*. I gave him the flute, but he grabbed my hand before I pulled away.

"Are you hurt?" he asked, and it hit me that I was naked. No one—no one I remembered—had ever seen me like this. I had never imagined anyone would. Too much, too insane. Demons covered my skin. Maybe they resembled tattoos, but I knew the truth.

But Grant didn't look at my body. Just my eyes.

"Maxine," he said, squeezing my hand. "Maxine, answer me."

I tried to pull free. "I can't be hurt. If you know anything about me—"

He stopped me by kissing my hand. Just one kiss, but it was gentle and desperate, and my voice choked into silence. I shouldn't have felt that kiss, but I did—the boys let me—and the heat of it sank through my muscles and bones.

My first kiss.

Grant pressed his cheek against my hand, and let me go. "Better get dressed," he said hoarsely. "Someone's going to come looking for us soon. Might come up here."

I nodded, unable to find my voice. I went and locked the front door, then walked past him and Mary to the bedroom. I spared a glance for Jack's body, still covered by the sheet. My grandfather. Praise be his light.

He was starting to smell.

Grant began playing the flute. A mournful melody filled the air, achingly beautiful, cutting through my chest like a blade made of exquisite light: first light, dawnlight; that soft morning glow, the kind that filled windows and warmed skin and sheets.

I felt that light inside me when I heard his music. I felt five hearts beating against my skin, in steady time to that rise and fall of perfect notes. Five hearts, my heart, all of us together, as one.

And a sixth, I realized. A sixth heartbeat, pulsing softly below my heart.

There and gone. I touched the spot, breathless. Waiting to feel it again.

I was still waiting, even after I started looking for clothes.

CHAPTER 9

I wanted to stay away from the bathroom mirror. Just one glimpse was enough. I was bald. Tattoos covered my entire head. I looked like a circus freak from circus hell, the kind where clowns ruled. My worst nightmare. I hated clowns.

"Hey," I said, rubbing my cheeks, rubbing and rubbing until Dek and Mal got the message and receded from my face. Pale skin appeared from beneath black scales and silver claws, and my lips went from gray to pink. I think the boys would have stopped at my former hairline, but I had no wig, no hat or scarf. Until I could find something to cover my head, the boys would just have to sit out the day below my jawline.

I rubbed the scar beneath my ear. I looked like shit.

My cowboy boots were ruined. I peeled them off. Slid on new jeans, a turtleneck and slim vest. Found running shoes and socks. I looked almost normal when I was done.

Except for the shadows in my eyes. And the fact that I had no hair.

Fortunately, I still had some eyebrows. Not very good ones, but at that point, I was happy for anything.

I tugged on gloves last of all. Held up my right hand and turned it around, studying the armor. It had grown, as I'd known it would when I transported myself from that hall downstairs. Not much, just a fraction of an inch up my wrist—but that was a fraction of an inch I'd never recover.

"Fuck you back," I said to it. "I hope you had a good reason."

Grant had stopped playing his flute. I hesitated before leaving the bedroom, but when I opened the door, he was still seated on the floor. Mary's eyes were open. She was smiling at him, so sweetly it almost hurt to see. She gave me the same smile though it slipped a little.

It was enough, though. The old woman didn't smile for just anyone.

"Alive," she said, patting Grant's hand. "Good song."

She looked healthy. Pink skin, bright eyes. I imagined her hair appeared a little less gray; and some of her wrinkles had smoothed away.

"What did you do?" I asked Grant.

"Gave her back what was taken. Plus a little extra." He rubbed his face. "It was close."

Close. He looked tired. I sat back, thinking hard about what I had seen, what I had been told, what I remembered. Piecing it all together.

I had questions, but all of them but one could wait.

"Mary," I said. "Where's Byron?"

❧

POLICE were everywhere. I had a feeling they would be looking for Grant—based on the same feeling I had that he owned the place—but he stayed with me as we made our way to the basement. Mary came with us, after changing into some of my clothes. Pants looked strange on her. So did long sleeves. I made her leave the butcher knives in the kitchen.

No one saw us. A quick glance outside the windows showed that the police were still keeping everyone outside the building; but I heard voices echoing down the smoky halls, using words like *arson* and *structural integrity*.

The basement didn't smell like smoke, and the air was cool and damp. Years ago, the warehouses that made up the Coop had been part of a furniture manufacturer, and some of the old equipment was still stored in the dark underbelly— massive iron structures whose purpose I couldn't guess though the boys liked to come down sometimes and climb all over them. Good diversion while hunting rats. During their last adventure, they had worn safari hats and carried machetes. Eaten both, along with the rodents.

There were few lights in the basement, and none was turned on. I left it that way. I could see light from Mary's room, shining from beneath the closed door. It made a path across the concrete floor, and our footsteps, along with Grant's cane, echoed loudly. I heard no one else but us. Mary started humming "Oh, What a Beautiful Morning," and twirled on her toes like a dancer.

I hadn't been down to Mary's room for weeks. Not much had changed. Racks lined the walls, filled with wooden flatbed containers brimming over with young marijuana plants and blazing sunlamps. On my last visit I'd had the boys eat her plants—and equipment. These couldn't be the same ones. But here we were—and here those plants were. I just hoped the police didn't come into the basement looking for anyone.

Byron lay on a cot in the corner, covered by a thin blanket and about fifty balls of brightly colored yarn. A zombie sat with him, holding a gun.

Rex. For a split second I didn't recognize him, but then the memories returned. I hung back at the door while the others went in and studied that thunderous aura. Old parasite. Oldest one I had seen in quite some time, including this morning's run-in at Killy's bar. The dark cloud of his aura hovered over a grizzled brown face creased with wrinkles and other signs of age and stress. Rex's host had lived a hard life before being possessed.

But that didn't explain why I was tolerating the presence of a demonic parasite. Or why it felt natural, as though it was the right thing to do.

Conversion. The word filled my head. *Conversion.*

I gave Grant a sharp look. *Demons. Grant can change demons. Alter what they are.*

I closed my eyes, glad for the doorway I was leaning on. I sought out memories of Rex, and other zombies who inhabited the Coop. Possessed men and women who came and went, but often stayed. Always uneasy around me but willing to take the risk. Because they were . . . they were . . .

Converts. Breaking themselves to become something new. Feeding, not on pain, but . . .

I opened my eyes. Rex was staring at me. So was Grant, but there was only compassion in his eyes. I couldn't remember the last time someone had looked at me with such acceptance, as though it was okay, I was okay: who I was, what I did, was *okay.*

Should have bothered me, just out of sheer contrariness. Should have scared me, because he was a strange man and I was a strange woman, and there was a very strange history between us I didn't remember or understand.

But I was past that. I had bigger problems.

And I liked the way he looked at me.

I inclined my head toward the gun in Rex's hand. "Expecting trouble?"

"Just you," he said, aura flaring. "I don't like the look in your eyes. Makes me feel like I should start running."

"Maybe you should. Get away from the boy." I pushed myself off the doorway and walked to the bed. Rex stood and got out of my way. I ignored him. Byron's eyes were closed, his breathing steady. I touched his brow. He was warm, but his color was better.

I wanted to wake him up and forced myself to back up a step. "What is all this?"

"Rainbows," Mary said, tweaking a strand of purple yarn.

Rex rolled his eyes and slid the gun into the waist of his jeans. "She said there was trouble coming and made me bring the boy down here. Told me to stand guard while she went to go cut a motherfucker."

Grant studied the boy, and frowned. He said, absently, "There was a fire. The entire second wing burned down."

Rex stared. Mary tore a marijuana leaf off the stem and jammed it in her mouth. "Forced gate," she muttered, chewing hard. "Labyrinth burns when torn."

The Labyrinth.

It always came down to that place. That *road*.

Demons were not of earth. Demons weren't even really demons—not in the biblical sense. Just a name that suited creatures that hunted and fed on humans—in the same way that the zombies I hunted weren't movie zombies but simply human puppets, possessed. Names were conveniences only.

Demons, like the Avatars—and humans—had traveled to earth via a network of interdimensional highways. A crossroads between here and there—a place beyond space, or time, or anything that I could possibly comprehend. Only that it was the Labyrinth, the quantum rose, a maze of knotted roads between countless worlds.

Earth, being one of them.

I thought of the dead man in front of Byron's door. "You're saying she exited the Labyrinth inside the Coop itself?"

"She comes with a need, and needs make gates." Mary tapped her chest and pointed to the boy. "She hunts the Old Wolf. And his skins."

"Byron's not a skin," I said firmly.

"Everyone's a skin," Rex replied. "What's going on?"

"Stop." Grant held up his hand, tearing his gaze from Byron. "Who was that woman? Why would she want Jack?"

Faces and names flashed through my mind. Ahsen. Mr. King. Avatars, both of them insane. Too dangerous to live.

I could hear their screams. I remembered killing them. The first with my bare hands. The second . . . with someone else.

Who was just a hole in my memories.

I looked at Grant. "She's come because of those two Avatars who died. Jack's kind felt their murders and sent her to bring him back."

"Back."

"Two of your own get murdered, you don't come yourself. You send someone else to investigate."

"Someone who can control an Avatar." Grant glanced at Mary. "That woman and I share the same gift. How is that possible? I thought there were no others."

"No *free* others." Mary reached out and tenderly brushed his hair from his face. "Babies stolen into chains, raised in chains, modified and cut and slaved in chains. An army in chains."

I gave up trying to stay away from Byron. I sat down on the bed, balls of yarn falling to the floor around my feet. The boy never stirred. He breathed, but his sleep was so deep. I touched his wrist, feeling his pulse. Strong, steady.

"I remember," I said. "I remember Jack talking about this. But the details are so unclear."

"Probably because it has to do with me." Grant sighed, rubbing his face. "I'm not from this world, Maxine. My mother brought me here when I was a baby. We came through the Labyrinth."

"You were escaping the Avatars."

"Yes." He gave me a cautious look. "What else do you remember?"

I remembered only what I had been told by Jack. But that was enough. I could still hear his relentless, urgent voice.

The Lightbringers and the people they watched over were the first humans. Found on one world. One distant, now-dead, world. All humans, my dear—every human—is descended from them.

We stole their bodies. We bred them, molded their flesh. And when a particular breed of human was conceived, a world was found through the Labyrinth and seeded with that strain of flesh. Allowed to evolve, and become. Time moves differently in the Labyrinth. What took millions, billions, of years, we could have instantly, merely by opening and closing a door.

Worlds, seeded with life by the Avatars. Worlds, used as playgrounds and castles in the sky. Worlds upon fantastic worlds, linked together through the Labyrinth, that maze of infinite possibilities.

Humans had been brought to Earth as proteins and molecules. *Part of the lab, the farm,* my grandfather had said. *The grand experiment. A reservoir for bodies.*

Bodies descended from the Lightbringers. The first humans.

I finally remembered hearing that name, in its proper context. Jack, speaking of Lightbringers in desperate tones, calling them guardians, judges, truth-sayers, warriors. Hunted and murdered because of their ability to manipulate energy. And, by extension, the Avatars.

Blood Mama was right. I didn't know if the demons could be any worse.

And if Grant *was* a Lightbringer, then that meant . . . that meant . . .

I closed my eyes, trying to focus. "What matters is that . . . woman . . . saw you. She recognized what you are. We can't let her leave and tell anyone she's found a Lightbringer here."

"She might have already left this world," Grant said.

Mary plucked at the yarn and shook her head. "Not without Wolf. Slaves obey."

"She wants Jack, which means we have to find him first. We have to protect him. We have to stop *her*."

Grant made a frustrated sound. "I hate this."

I stood. "What can we do to protect the boy? She was drawn to him before. Probably because of Jack's connection with him."

Mary pushed aside the blanket. A golden pendant lay heavy on Byron's chest, a compact disc that was nothing more than a tangled coil with no end, no beginning, just layers of roped metal that knotted together in a design that tricked the eye. When I looked at the pendant, its center seemed impossibly deep and far away, as though I could touch it and find my hand swallowed. Looking at it made me dizzy.

But the design was familiar. I had just seen something similar embedded in Mary's sternum.

"That's my mother's," Grant said.

"Masks his mark," Mary replied, with a sly smile. But that was all she said. I heard a clanging sound outside the room and the echo of voices.

"Police," Rex muttered. "Shit."

Grant tightened his grip on the cane. "I'll take care of this. Watch the boy."

He limped out of Mary's room. After a moment, I followed.

Men were coming down the stairs with flashlights. I hurried ahead of Grant, moving silently in my soft-soled shoes, and flipped the switch on the wall. Lights came on. I heard grunts of surprise, and peered up at three men in uniform—one police officer and two guys from the fire department. The police officer had a familiar face, but I couldn't remember his name. I was bad with names.

"Sorry," I said. "We're so used to this place, we don't really need the lights."

I'm not sure the men believed—or heard—me. They seemed to be too busy staring at my bald head. I had forgotten my missing hair. Didn't know how. My scalp felt light, cold. I almost touched it, self-conscious.

Grant limped close, drawing their gazes. "Ralph. Were you looking for me?"

The police officer, a lean man in his early forties, flashed him an apologetic smile. "Sorry, Father Cooperon. One of the ladies said you come down here sometimes to, um, take care of one of residents."

"Yes," Grant said, with surprising composure and authority. "I planned on finding you after I was done calming her. Has something else happened?"

Ralph's expression of regret deepened. "I know this has been a tough morning, Father, but I need you to look at a . . . a body . . . we pulled from the fire. Just one," he added hastily. "A white male, maybe in his twenties. No ID. We're hoping you'll recognize his face."

I barely heard him. My brain was finally catching up to something he'd said at the beginning. *Father Cooperon. Father Cooperon.*

As though Grant was a priest.

Ralph glanced down at me. "Ma'am. You cut your hair."

"Burned it all off in the fire," I said weakly, which got me a laugh. I glanced at the other men. "How are your guys who went into the building?"

They hesitated, glancing at each other. "Fine."

"Bullshit," muttered Ralph, climbing up the stairs. "McKenzie is having a nervous breakdown. Says he saw a monster. Pansy."

One of the guys gave me a lopsided grin. "No face, he told us. Covered in scales. Snake lady."

I pretended to shiver. And then shivered for real when the other man gave me a long look, and said, "Except for the hair, you look just like the woman McKenzie went in after. We still haven't found any trace of her."

Ralph, now at the top of the stairs, turned around. "Leave her alone. You hear a cough, you smell smoke on her? Jeee-sus. Anyone who went into that hell is gonna need a morgue for being too stupid to live."

Grant coughed. I gave him a dirty look. A faint smile tugged the corner of his mouth, and he tweaked my hip as he limped past. I flinched. He ducked his head, brushed his mouth against my ear, and whispered, "You look beautiful, snake lady."

He was insane. I kept telling myself that as we climbed the stairs.

It had stopped raining. Most of the people still hanging around outside the Coop were volunteers. Some of the homeless regulars had disappeared, but I blamed the presence of the police for that. I didn't feel comfortable being near them, either. I had broken too many laws over the years.

Grant had no trouble with them. I hung back, watching for stress fractures, tension, but every person in uniform looked at him with deference and respect. Just a man, leaning on a cane, dressed in faded jeans and a thick flannel shirt. Just a straightforward, unruffled, man.

Big, sexy man, I thought, unable to help myself. A man who looked like a wolf compared to everyone around him, something a little *other*, a little sharp around the edges.

Not born on earth. Able to manipulate people with his voice. Able to change a demon, down to the core of its being.

Capable of killing an Avatar.

I didn't remember that, but I knew it was true. Who knew what else he could do.

You had a taste, with Blood Mama.

Blood Mama. A demon queen. And, even though I couldn't remember Grant, not before this morning, I recalled those Avatars, Ahsen and Mr. King, who had been afraid of something, someone, around me. Afraid, and hungry.

Of him.

And of something inside me. The darkness, that slept so lightly.

"Lightbringer," I breathed to myself, tasting the word. It didn't stir memories, but for some reason, I felt compelled to touch my chest. Listening for that sixth heartbeat.

I stopped, after a moment. I didn't want to think about that. Scared me. Even Grant scared me. He was dangerous. My mother might have killed him for nothing more than the *possibility* he could go bad. There wasn't anyone alive who should have that kind of power.

Including me.

I joined Grant as he was led to a body bag. One of the cops, a woman, gave me a quick once-over, followed by a tight smile. "Donate your hair to charity?"

"Yes," I lied, and saw behind her the fireman whom I had rescued. He sat on the end of an ambulance, staring into space, a blanket over his shoulders and an oxygen mask on his face. I turned slightly, so my back was to him.

Ralph donned latex gloves and unzipped the body bag. I wasn't surprised to see the man I'd found outside Byron's door. Burned yes, but not as much as I would have expected. Even the fragment of clothing I saw appeared minimally charred.

What bothered me, though, was that his features were disturbingly bland, even for a dead man. As though someone had taken an eraser and rubbed out everything but a mouth, nose, and eyes. He looked . . . unreal. Like a doll.

"Never seen him before," Grant said grimly. "I can't imagine why he was up there. Was he the only one?"

"Thankfully." Ralph hesitated. "Know anyone who'd want to burn you out?"

"No." Grant looked him dead in the eyes. "I hope this was an accident."

Ralph seemed to have trouble tearing his gaze away. "The investigators will figure that out."

He asked some more questions, promised to be in touch, then freed us up to the volunteers, who had begun pressing near the police tape, watching Grant with anxious eyes. Me, I got a few looks. But it was clear who folks responded to.

It didn't take long to reassure everyone. Grant told the volunteers to go home, that the shelter would be closed for a few days. He asked several of the women to make some calls and find beds for all the regulars. Told her to pay for hotel rooms if she needed to, and gave her his credit card. No one argued, no one whined. I watched the crowd and listened to his voice.

"You didn't use your . . . gift," I said, as we walked back inside the building.

"I didn't need to." Grant glanced down at me. "People can be reasonable, you know. Decent, too."

"Pollyanna."

"Pessimist."

"Can you *see* . . . decency?" I fluttered my fingers like I was tracing the outline of a person. "When you look at someone?"

"I see a lot of things. More than I want to, sometimes. More than I can . . . resist, occasionally." He shrugged, grim-faced. "People come here with problems. Addictions, mental disorders, rage. I . . . tweak . . . them."

"You change them."

"I help them."

"Are they the same people when you're done?"

"Yes." He glanced at me. "Mostly."

"Giving yourself some wiggle room, there."

"A wife-beater won't be the same person when I'm done with him," he admitted. "But he won't be a robot, either. I don't possess people, Maxine."

"But you play God. Just a little."

Grant hesitated. "You do, too."

I said nothing. A little stung. A little hungry for more. I hadn't had a conversation like this in . . . well, longer than I could remember. Which didn't mean much, apparently.

But I was hungry for words. Hungrier than I should have been.

I had never gone to school. Kids my own age were seen from afar, and even up close they might as well have been a million miles away. I said hello to some boys when I was growing up, but it was just in passing: in the aisles of a library, or in a grocery store when my mom and I would roll into some town to stock up on food. We never stayed anywhere long enough for more than hello. Even if we had, my mom wouldn't have allowed it. We had too many secrets. And she had too many demons who needed killing.

I read a lot, though. I learned about the world through books and television, and my own eyes. I figured there were kids who had it worse, by a lot. I always knew I was loved. I was always protected.

But being with Grant, here and now, made me realize again how much I had missed out on—and how much I still wanted some semblance of a normal life. A good, simple life.

Right. Now *I* was the crazy one.

Grant limped past the basement door. I stared at his back. "Where are you going?"

He glanced over his shoulder, but didn't answer. I listened to the boys on my skin, flexed my hands, but they were silent. No danger around us. Not for the moment.

Grant led me to an office. Not much furniture, just a table, a couple chairs. No phone. A framed picture, about the size of my hand. I was in it. So was Grant. We were sitting together on driftwood, at the beach. Both of us smiling. Not forced smiles, but the kind that begin and end on a laugh.

"I look happy," I whispered.

"Remember that." Grant pulled the picture out of the frame. He pushed it into my hands. "You're not alone, Maxine. You're not . . . unloved."

I exhaled, sharply. "Just means I have more to lose."

"More to fight for."

"More pains in the ass I've got to deal with."

Grant smiled. "But I have a nice ass."

I laughed. Bubbled out of me before I could stop it. Not

a big sound, not a giggle, but just a good laugh that made me feel warm, and more like myself than I had felt since waking up this morning in a pool of blood.

Grant sat on the edge of the table, watching me. "What do you think is going on, Maxine? Is that woman part of the reason you've lost your memory?"

I shook my head, still looking at the photo. "I think Jack knew she was coming. I think that's why he wanted to talk to me. What happened last night . . ." I stopped, and leaned against the wall. "You should have seen the look on her face, the way she . . . prostrated . . . herself in front of Jack's body. She worships his kind. She thinks they're gods. She accused me of not protecting him, as though the fact that I was alive and his human body was dead was a mark against me. I think . . . I think she believes I killed him. She called me his defiler."

"Sounds like a zealot."

"A zealot who uses her voice to drain the life out of an old woman?"

"That man up there, in the body bag. He was drained."

"How can you tell?"

"He was . . . emptier . . . than a regular dead person. A new corpse still retains some residual energy. That man had *nothing*. Mary would have died the same way if you hadn't stopped that woman."

"You might have stopped her."

"I was too busy pouring energy into Mary." Grant smiled grimly. "I should have done something different. Attacked."

"You followed your instincts. You saved her. There's nothing wrong with that."

"Except the woman is gone. Out there now. Probably hurting others." Grant looked down at his hands. "She knows what she's doing. She's had training. Not like me,

Maxine. I still don't understand everything I can do. I've spent my life playing this thing by ear."

"Your mother?"

"Never told me. She died when I was in my teens." He gestured at the picture in my hands. "I've learned more about myself in the past two years than I ever imagined. More than I *wanted* to imagine. Without you . . . it would have been difficult."

"I can't imagine I made it easier. I'm no bargain."

Grant shook his head, mouth tilting into a wry smile. "You're my only friend, Maxine. Before you, I had no one. No one I could talk to about who I am. No one I could be honest with. I think you understand what that means. Better than anyone."

I stared. No one could look at me like that and be lying. No liar could live around me this long without being murdered by the boys. And no one but this man could see me bald and tattooed, strangling a woman with my bare hands, exorcising demons, talking about the end of the world—and not even bat an eye.

What had I lost?

"I just scared you," Grant said quietly.

"Yes. You scare me a lot."

"Scared of being happy?"

I held up the photo. "This is overwhelming. I should have spent my entire life alone."

"But you made a home."

"I made a home," I agreed. "I wish I remembered you."

Grant pushed himself off the table, leaning hard on the cane. "Come on. Mary and Rex are probably rolling joints by now."

I slid the photo into my vest pocket. "That cop called you something. *Father Cooperon.* Anything else you want to tell me?"

Grant smiled and held open the office door. "What do you think it means?"

"You don't want to know what I think."

He leaned down close to my ear. I didn't move, didn't breathe, didn't blink. But instead of speaking, he moved a fraction, and kissed my cheek. Softly, gently, his mouth lingering against my skin. Heat washed over me. My heart pounded. I wanted very much to turn my head and see what his lips tasted like. Cinnamon, maybe. Or sunlight.

But I didn't. And he pulled away before I could take the leap.

My second kiss, I thought.

We didn't talk as we walked back to the basement. I wanted to. I had more questions. No time to waste on silence. But I felt off-balance. I couldn't count on my voice to work.

At the bottom of the stairs, Zee began to twitch. Not exactly a warning, but nothing I wanted to take for granted. I left Grant behind and jogged to Mary's room.

I opened the door. First thing I saw was Byron, sitting up. Rex and Mary stood on the other side of the crammed space, staring at him. Neither had pleasant looks on their faces.

"Hey," I said to the boy, walking quickly to the bed. "Are you—"

Byron looked at me, and I stopped. He was not my blood, not my child, but I knew him. I knew that kid as well as anyone could.

But I didn't know the boy in front of me.

"Maxine," said Byron. "Oh, my sweet girl."

I clutched the rack beside me, needing something to hold on to. The metal rail crumpled beneath my grip. The boy flinched. For a moment, just one, I imagined fear in his eyes.

"Forgive me," said the boy, but his voice was deeper, his accent refined, and his eyes—the way he looked at me—

Byron was gone. Jack had found his new skin.

CHAPTER 10

JACK Meddle. Meddling Man, Zee called him. Full of riddles. But I suppose when your grandfather was older than a star, you made allowances for eccentricities and secrets.

Except the ones that cost lives.

"HOW could you?" I asked, feeling lucky I could speak at all. We'd been so happy last night.

Even Byron. Byron, who had done the dishes and washed away the entire aftermath of Jack's pie-making carnage—because it was my birthday, and he knew I would have cleaned up for the old man.

I remembered the boy, in the apron. I remembered his small, satisfied smile.

A full-bodied shudder wracked Jack, and the look he

gave me was nothing I had ever seen on Byron's face, or even the old man's: fear, uncertainty, self-loathing. He raised a trembling hand, as though warding me off. "Don't say it. I can't bear to hear it again. I know my apologies are worthless, but please, we *never* meant to hurt you, or any of the women in your bloodline. We were *desperate*. It was the *only* way."

I had thought I understood him until then. "What?"

He stilled. Grant said, "This has nothing to do with last night, old man."

Jack's face turned waxen, pale. I tried to move, and couldn't. I felt so heavy, my legs weak. When I breathed, no air reached my lungs.

"Old Wolf," I managed, finally. "Get out of that boy."

"The boy." He spoke slowly, as though the words were foreign, as though he'd forgotten where he was, who he was inhabiting. "He's not being harmed."

I grabbed his wrist—that stolen, knobby wrist—and leaned down into his face. Killed me to see those eyes, those eyes that were not Byron's eyes. Not Byron's soul. Not the spark that was the boy, and the boy alone.

"How dare you," I said. "How dare you do this to him."

My grandfather tugged his wrist free and swung his legs over the bed's edge—moving unsteadily, wincing as though in pain.

"This *is* temporary," he replied, but all I could hear was Byron's voice, stolen from him; and all I could think of was the boy, somewhere inside, maybe watching, maybe aware— locked out of his own body. Possessed against his will.

I blocked Jack from standing. "It's one thing to take an embryo in the womb, or even a coma patient . . . but this is something else. Byron is *not* yours."

Jack took hold of my arm and squeezed. Desperation, in his eyes. Fear. Grief.

"I wouldn't have done this if there were another way. Do you understand? *There's no time, Maxine.* Why else do you think I came to you last night?"

"I don't remember last night, Jack. I woke up in your blood. Beside your corpse." A cold hard knot settled in my gut—same knot that had been in me all day, only larger, like a tumor. "What happened? Who cut your throat?"

Rex made a small sound of surprise. Grant gave him a warning look, while Mary settled against the racks, stroking the leaves of her plants while giving Jack a long, thoughtful look.

My grandfather didn't answer my question. Just sat back, staring like he'd never seen me before. "How could you possibly forget?"

"You tell me." I looked so hard into his eyes I thought my head would pop. "Someone's come for you. Now you've made Byron a target. If she hurts his body, if she takes him to God knows where because of you . . ."

Jack rocked forward. "Who has come?"

"Another hound," Mary spoke up, tapping her chest with a long bony finger. "Has your scent, Wolf."

"Shit," Rex muttered, his aura twisting down his shoulders like snakes. "This world is getting too crowded."

"She calls herself the Messenger," I said, ignoring him. "Sent by her Aetar Masters. *Praise be their light.*"

Pure revulsion roped down my spine when I said those words. My mouth felt dirty. "I saw the look in her eyes. She's going to keep coming until she's dead, or you're back in the Labyrinth. And if she doesn't return home, your kind will just send another. Or am I wrong?"

Jack's expression was so grim. He looked down, saw the amulet hanging around his neck, and shuddered. He stuffed it beneath his shirt. "Let me up."

Grant edged me aside. Gentle, when he touched me—

but there was nothing mild about his expression. "Give me one good reason to leave you inside that boy."

"I can't," Jack said, looking like he wanted nothing more than to melt back into the covers and pull them over his head. "But we have no time for anything else. Not the womb, not some coma victim whose brain I must repair. I would *never* have done this if there were another way."

"This is sick," I said. "All of this is sick."

"It's life," Jack replied, hoarse. "Survival."

"I'm not going to let Byron's throat get cut."

"Put aside your concerns for the boy, just for a moment. What we need to discuss has nothing to do with my . . . death."

"What, then?"

He shifted uneasily, rubbing his hands in a washing gesture, scrubbing at them until his skin looked red. Out, damned spot. "You don't remember. You should remember."

I grabbed his wrist, stilling him. "You'll break his skin if you keep that up."

"It wouldn't matter." Jack closed his eyes. "Do you know how many times this boy has died over the last three thousand years—through murder and beatings, and simple starvation?"

I froze, cold to the pit of my stomach. Zee twisted against my skin. I touched my breastbone, steadying him, and me.

Jack whispered, "You love Byron so much."

"I love him." I could barely speak. "He's not my child, but I love him."

His face crumpled, raw misery and heartache filling his eyes—fleeting, before he rubbed them hard and sighed. Amazing, how much of the old man I could see in Bryon: the way he set his jaw, the tilt of his head, how he studied Grant, then me. Like a rough caricature, superimposed upon the teen. I had to look away.

Jack said, "It shouldn't have been like this. I realized, last night after the party, that someone was coming for me. I could feel a ripple from the Labyrinth—and there were things you needed to know in case the encounter went badly. Now I have to tell you again."

Something in his voice made me afraid. I couldn't even swallow. Grant said, "What is it, Jack?"

"The truth about who Maxine really is." My grandfather looked from him to me. "Because I love you, my dear. I should not have loved your grandmother, but I did. I should not have loved the daughter I made with her, but I did, with all my heart. Just as I love you. Please, remember that."

Zee was struggling harder now. All the boys were. Even the armor tingled. I clenched my hand into a fist and pushed it against my stomach, hard. The boys pushed back.

Jack said, "The others should tie you down. Rope won't be strong enough. Neither will chains, but they may have to do."

Grant made a small sound. I stared.

My grandfather gave us a dark, hollow look. "It's a kindness."

"You think I'll hurt Byron. To get to *you*," I said, stunned with the realization; and then, "Oh, my God."

Grant's hand tensed. I pushed him away, backing up until I hit the racks. "I *did* kill you. I cut your throat."

"No," Jack said gently. "But you didn't stop Zee when *he* did."

Grant stepped between us. "Enough."

"No," Jack said, again. I could not see him around Grant. His voice sounded distant, far away. I wanted to melt into the floor, or explode through my skin. I wanted to run like hell and never come back.

"No," Jack said, a third time, even more softly, as though the word was a chant, or prayer.

I stepped out from behind Grant and faced my grandfather. "Zee killed you because of something you told us."

"It was an emotional reaction. Happened so quickly I'm not certain you could have stopped him, even had you wanted to."

"Maxine would never condone hurting you," Grant said tightly.

"Lightbringer," Jack said. "Maybe you don't see as much as you think."

I glanced around the room but saw no rope, no chains, nothing at all to tie me down with. I didn't feel particularly in need of restraints, all things considered. Just answers. Something to cut the pressure building in my skull.

"Tell me," I said. "The boys are asleep. I'm unarmed. I won't hurt Byron. I won't hurt *you*, no matter what you have to say."

Jack was quiet for such a long time, I wasn't certain whether to feel insulted or frightened. He hardly seemed to breathe. Grant was also still, tension and power crackling in his silence. I wished I could see through his eyes. I wanted to know what the world looked like as energy and light. I wanted to know what he saw inside me, what he saw that did not scare him.

Jack edged close, and extended his hand. Byron's hand. I took it, and Dek trembled against my skin. Grant grabbed my other hand and squeezed. Heat traveled through my palm, up my arm, into my heart.

"I have a story to tell you," Jack said.

"Make it simple. Tell me the truth."

"You're not who you think you are," he replied, with all the pain of a man confessing murder. "Your bloodline isn't what you think. My kind didn't create the Wardens to guard the prison veil, and though your ancestors might have lived amongst them, and believed they were one of them, those mothers and daughters were never Wardens to begin with."

He paused, pale and sweating. Rex made a low, dismayed sound—as though something had just clicked into place for him. I didn't look in his direction, but I felt him on the periphery, shrinking back against the racks. Staring at both of us with unmistakable horror.

I whispered, "Jack."

"I need a drink," he said.

"Jack," I said again, just as the boys began trembling on my skin, quivering with a simmering rage that felt like shallow earthquakes, or sandpaper scraping.

Outside the room, I heard a shuffling sound. Jack's head snapped up. Mary glided toward the door, muscles tight with the promise of violence. Rex reached for his gun.

The door opened.

The Messenger stood on the other side.

Time slowed. I watched her. She watched me. Her small eyes glinted golden in the basement light. Alien, in the details—her neck too long, her eyes too small, her cheeks a little too sharp and delicate. She could pass for human, but with a double take. Mothers might hide their children. I would. Not because of her bone structure. She radiated an *otherness* that was not simply eerie, but cold, aloof, menacing in the way a predator menaced—with stillness, and patience, and promise.

So much promise.

She was not alone. I saw two men and a woman behind her, deep in the shadows: not zombies, just human, wearing jeans, a business suit, a jogging outfit. Nothing in their eyes. Mouths slack.

"There is no place you can hide from me," she said

softly, her voice lilting with power. "For I am the hand, and the light, and I am justice, swift, in the name of our Aetar Masters. Praise be their light."

Grant stepped in front of me. I began to cut him off, but Jack was even faster, darting around the both of us. Slender, young in body, old as a star.

The Messenger had been focused on Grant and me—but when she saw Jack, a shudder ripped through her. She hadn't expected to find him here—that much was clear. The amulet had worked.

The shudder faded into a quiver—a tremor that made her eyelid tick—and then down, down she went, her knees hitting the floor so hard I heard a crack. That tremor faded into perfect stillness.

"Maker," she said. "Praise be your light."

"No, don't," Jack said. *"Don't."*

For a split second I thought he was telling her not to worship him. And maybe for a split second that was the case. But the Messenger's head lashed up, staring at Grant, then past him at me.

"You will not defile him again," she said, and grabbed Jack's arm. I had already started moving, but two seconds was an eternity. Two seconds couldn't compete with the speed of a thought.

Jack's eyes widened. I reached out—

They disappeared. So did the three humans. I staggered into Jack's last position, hit on all sides by the air in the room, rushing to take up the space that five people had just been occupying.

I fell on my knees. Slammed my armored fist into the floor. Concrete cracked, and went flying. Grant grabbed my shoulder. I didn't try to push him away. Instead, I stared at the armor.

Please, I thought. *This needs to happen.*

The armor pulsed, once. I imagined a voice reply: *Yes, it does.*

Then, nothing. My vision slipped sideways, fading to black. Hearts thundered on my skin. I felt the cold of the void in my soul—and just when I thought I'd been lost too long, too long for that soul—I hit rock.

Daylight. Sky silver, leaking mist and a fine rain. I could see my breath, and smelled sap. Above the thick tree cover, shrouded in clouds, loomed the craggy stone fingers of a mountain buried in snow.

Heavy breathing. A low grunt of pain. I found Grant on his knees, clutching his cane in a white-knuckled grip. His bottom lip bled. Bitten, maybe. He was very pale, deathly so—but if he was afraid, I didn't see it in his eyes.

"Behind me," he said. "Listen."

I didn't need to listen. That woman's voice was everywhere, flowing through the trees in a strange, minor key that sounded like a distant cousin to nails on a chalkboard. Made the boys ripple on my skin. Even Grant, now, had spoken with power in his tones, each one rolling over me like a hard ocean wave. Except I was the reef, the mountain, with my roots in stone.

"Stay here," I told Grant, but he grabbed my wrist and used me to haul himself to his feet. His strength surprised me. And once he was standing, I didn't waste time trying to convince him to sit back down. All he had to do was look at me. Intense, thoughtful, grim. And then the corner of his mouth twitched, and his gaze filled with warmth and resolve. Like this, what we were about to do—whatever that might be—was nothing.

I gave up. Any man who could scare Blood Mama—any man who could kill an Avatar with nothing but his voice—was no fool, and no one who needed to be protected.

Even though I would. With my last breath.

I turned, ran. Grant jammed his cane into the ground and kept up, only a few steps behind. He moved fast for a man with a bad leg.

I saw Jack first. Standing with his eyes closed, face uplifted to the sky. Quivering. Shaking. Cold, or under terrible strain. I thought it might be the latter. The Messenger stood beside him, her face also uplifted, mouth open so wide she could have swallowed a large man's fist. Her jaw had come unhinged. The vein in her long neck vibrated like a hummingbird's wings. Grotesque. So was her voice.

I'd heard strains of a melody in the beginning, but it was as though something had been keyed in, locked, and all she needed now was power. The three humans lay on the ground in a crumpled heap. They looked dead. As though they had been out in the desert for a week, drying under the sun.

I didn't stop running. I picked up speed and slammed into the Messenger with all my strength. We flew into the nearest tree. I heard a massive cracking sound. Bone. Wood. Didn't feel a thing, but the Messenger coughed blood, and her jaw sagged like old underwear.

Her voice, though, still rose from her chest, rising and rising. Even her coughs were melodic. Every sound, laced with power. Every sound, energy.

She stared at me. I gritted my teeth and slammed her head into the tree. I wasn't going to let her get away. Not again. She continued to look at me. Her gaze never wavered. Uncanny, golden. I didn't blink. Least I could do was not flinch when I killed her.

"No," Jack said, behind me. Grant fell down on his knees, close, and slammed his hand against the woman's brow. She gasped, trying to free herself from him, but I climbed on top of her body and held her still.

"Open your eyes," Grant said, each word shimmering

in the air and clinging to his voice, his voice that sank into my heart. My heart, that was stronger than my brain, because I saw things in that moment, flashes of heat and memory filled with Grant: standing on the beach with him, laughing as the wind lashed us so hard we spread our arms, pretending to fly; or nights in candlelight, in little restaurants where the booths were deep and private, and our toes wrestled beneath the table; or his hands sliding down my bare shoulders, against my back, holding me to him, tight, tighter, always—

I gasped, touching my head. Drowning, overwhelmed. I tried to remember more, but there was too much, all at once. My head hurt. I had to lean hard on the tree.

"No, don't," Jack said once more, still out of sight. "You can't."

"Open your eyes," Grant said again to the woman, ignoring my grandfather. I knew what he was trying to do. I knew, because I knew *him*. I remembered.

She screamed. Jack cried out. Grant winced but dug in harder, his face almost unrecognizable. He was humming, but so low it was barely audible. I felt it, though. The ground vibrated with his voice. Fallen evergreen needles trembled. So did rocks, shaking loose from the hard dirt. The boys raged against my skin, flowing upward over my face and head.

Her scream didn't end. Just rose and rose, her jaw flopping sideways as she tried twisting away from Grant. His eyes glowed. So did hers. I didn't tell him to stop. I was afraid to. I heard more cracking sounds, but they were beneath us, in the ground, in the trees. The armor rippled and shimmered. So did the silver veins running across my hands, and the red eyes burning hot in my skin. Everything was burning. Every breath, hot. I smelled sulfur.

Jack collapsed beside me. Blood trickled from his

nostrils. His eyes, wild. He tried to grab me, but his hand bounced off the air around my body, and he clutched it to his chest. My grandfather. Byron. Looking at me with such horror.

"It's tearing," he breathed. "Maxine."

I was still distracted by Grant, my memories. I didn't understand what he was telling me. Not until I vomited.

There was nothing in my stomach, but the act was violent and shocking. I never got sick. Never.

Except for one time, only. For one reason, only.

Pain spiked inside my head. Zee pulled so hard on my skin I felt certain he would break free. He was trying. All of them were, with all their strength. I looked around, heart hammering in my throat—

—and the world bled light. A storm of light. A wild, aching light that was white-hot, and caressed with undertones of rich reds and purples, kisses of turquoise that broke apart like hissing sparks. I was blind, for light.

Until I looked up and saw darkness.

I blinked, and the light disappeared, the forest slamming back into my vision like a slap. I still felt blind, though— only because the world appeared so dull: gray, bled out, drained.

But the darkness was there. In the sky, above our heads. A crack in the sky, a seam shaped like a lightning bolt, red and bleeding through the clouds. I smelled blood. I heard screams on the other side.

"Maxine," Jack whispered.

I see it, I wanted to tell him, but my voice wouldn't work.

The prison veil was open. And something bigger than a parasite was about to come through.

CHAPTER 11

I felt like a kid in one of those nightmares where the halls never ended and the doors were all locked, and even though you couldn't turn to see what was behind you, you heard the hard breathing and felt the heat on your neck, and knew that if you stopped, even for a moment, something worse than death would happen.

Right now, the halls were going on forever. Doors locked. Except there was no running. I'd see the monster coming.

The screams intensified, and the wind shuddered through the forest with one wild heave, tearing at my clothes and making the trees sway and groan. I smelled blood—thick, cloying—and beneath those harrowing cries I imagined the sound of crashing waves, full of storm.

Grant was finally silent, watching the sky with grim horror. Even the Messenger stared past his shoulder, her small eyes opened wide. I looked at Jack, but he was staring at the woman.

"You fool," he said to her. "You thought you were opening the Labyrinth? *There is more than one kind of door.*"

The Messenger flinched. I grabbed Jack's arm. "Can it be closed?"

"Not by me." He looked at the others. "Not alone."

"Tell me how," Grant said.

"Lad," Jack replied slowly. "I told you. It took almost all of my kind to build the veil, and the effort still killed some of us. You can't."

Grant stilled. "We don't have a choice but to try."

I rose on unsteady feet and stared up at the sky. I felt the weight of something coming, but some of that weight was inside: a part of me, reaching for that hole with aching hunger, a yearning that bordered on homesickness. As though whatever was up there, I needed to find. I needed to touch, and breathe, and see.

Yours, all of it, a sinuous voice said in my mind. *Yours to lead, to hold.*

I tore my gaze from the hole to look down at Jack. It was a struggle. I didn't see him at first, even though I stared into his face. My head was still in the sky, and my mouth was dry. "Go. If you can cut space, then go. Take Grant, take *her*, and get the hell out."

"No," Grant said, trying to stand. Jack shook his head, looking only at me. His eyes frightened me. I was afraid of what he could see in my eyes.

I grabbed the Messenger by the throat. Her dazed gaze cleared, focusing hard on me.

"There are things happening you don't understand," I said, desperation making my voice break. "Maybe you can't. Maybe you're not wired that way. *But you keep them safe.* You protect them. That, I think you understand."

She shook her head, face screwed up as though in agony. "I understand you are one of them. And that *he* . . . the

Lightbringer . . . did something to me." Her trembling fingers brushed her brow, and her already pained gaze turned haunted. "I owe you no honor."

The Messenger tried to grab Jack's wrist. My grandfather wrenched backward, out of her grip, giving her a horrified look. "No, we will not run. We will *not*. She is my blood. She is the blood of my skin and soul—"

I cut him off, ruthless. "You remember what they did to Ahsen because she was an Avatar." I looked at the Messenger. "I don't care what happens to me. You protect them."

The Messenger looked from Jack to me, her gaze sharper, but in a different way. Thoughtful, almost.

"If you are certain," she said.

"No," Jack snapped.

I forced myself to smile. "I love you, Old Wolf. Take care of Byron." I looked at Grant. "Go."

"Not a chance." His hand shot out to grab the Messenger's shoulder. "Remember what I told you."

"My eyes were always open," she said, her voice cracking on the last word.

Grant stayed silent. Jack reached for me, and I backed away. The armor rippled over my hand, pulsing in cold waves. That awful weight bearing down on my shoulders grew a little heavier, and inside me, below my heart, a stirring—the darkness, shedding its shallow sleep.

We were never asleep, whispered that voice, again. *Simply waiting.*

I breathed through my teeth and met Jack's haunted gaze. "Remember what *I* said."

His face crumpled. "No—"

But it was too late. The Messenger lunged forward to wrap her arms around him—

—and they disappeared. I wished very much I could follow.

Grant's hand slid around my waist. Memories crashed. His touch, both familiar and strange.

"You should have left," I told him, trembling. "I wish you had."

Grant kissed the knuckles of his other hand and made the sign of the cross. Then he kissed the top of my head and pulled me near. "Life's too short to waste on running. I won't leave you alone."

I swallowed hard, swaying. "I'm not the one who can die."

"Then why is it you always tell me that I'll outlive you?" Grant brushed his thumb over my mouth. "You and me, Maxine."

I grabbed the front of his shirt, stood on my toes, and kissed him hard on the mouth. He tasted hot and sweet—familiar and new—and the darkness stirred a little more, rising, uncoiling to fill my skin. I could see it in my mind, encircling the second golden pulse that surrounded my heart, a pulse that belonged to Grant.

Our link, I remembered—a connection that bound us, into the soul. I could feel our bond, and him, burning through me, as though the sun lived inside my heart. I wondered how I could have forgotten anything about this man.

The Messenger had created bonds with humans to steal their energy. Grant also needed a source of power when he used his gift—but he didn't have to steal it. Not from me.

Two hearts live, I thought, holding him even more tightly, digging my fingers into his shoulders.

Grant shivered, and against my mouth murmured, "I think we may be fine."

I sensed movement overhead, and we pulled apart. Zee raged upward, against my skin. All the boys, screaming in their sleep. The darkness stirred again, but I did not push it away.

A single eye open inside my mind—*its* eye—and I thought, *Yes, this time I need you.*

They need you, said that sinuous voice, just a hiss in my mind, like a thought captured between dreams and waking. *You are tangled in all those bleeding bones, and war-hearts. Your knots run deep as death, and the endless night.*

"No," I said, out loud. Grant glanced at me, but only a moment. Bodies dropped from the cut in the sky. My heart charged up my throat like I was going to turn inside out, and keep turning, and turning.

I counted dozens, maybe a hundred, falling through the sky—a cloud of silver bodies that cut through the mist like pale ghosts. I felt removed from myself as I cataloged all the alien details—long, naked limbs, flying hair, humanoid masculine bodies—until, closer yet, I saw the holes of their eyes; and closer, the sharp angles of their faces; until they slammed into the earth in front of us, so hard the world shook. Some landed in the conifers, breaking branches, but none of the demons fell—simply leapt, light as air, onto the ground to join their brothers.

Grant slid around me to stand at my back, watching the ones who landed behind us. My spine and chest began vibrating, like a tuning fork was pressed between my shoulder blades. His voice, rumbling so low I could only feel it. I flexed my hand, and the armor shimmered, white-hot, blinding—

—until I held a sword in my hand.

It was a familiar weapon. An extension of the armor itself. A chain ran from the pommel to my wrist; delicate as the blade, which was long and slender, engraved with runes. The metal gleamed with inner light—moonlight, starlight, icelight—and when I scraped the edge with my thumb, sparks flew. I felt good holding the blade. Better. Grounded.

I forced myself to breathe, slow and deep, and thought of my mother. My fearless mother.

She'd eat these bastards for breakfast. You can have them for lunch.

There were so many. Pale and gray as the dead, with silver hair that spiked high in bristled tendrils before falling into long, knotted braids. Wiry, gaunt, dressed in leather belts and little else. Their fingers resembled the tines of pitchforks and their faces were almost as sharp. Silver eyes and silver lips, and chains of chiming silver hooks, hanging from ears to narrow nostrils. Most of them lacked at least one arm, or chunks of flesh from thighs; and their fists were full of smoky parasites, Blood Mama's children, who screamed and screamed.

They ate those parasites. Ripped heads off with their teeth, then tossed aside the smoky remains. I felt no disgust or pity while I watched them consume those lesser demons. Zee and the boys did the same when they could.

Except I wanted a taste, too. The desire hit me hard, in the chest, where the darkness rolled.

The demons watched us—perfectly, eerily still. Eyes glinting, faces hollow with hunger. Saliva trickled from their lips. I found them disturbingly human, or so close that I wondered at their origins. I wondered, too, what Grant saw when he looked at them.

I wanted to know why they hadn't tried to kill us yet.

"They're waiting," Grant said, as though he read my mind. "Something's coming."

Something, from above.

A solitary figure dropped through the crack in the sky. I could tell, even some distance away, that he was larger than the other demons, who stirred and looked up, and jostled each other aside to make room. Cracking sounds filled the air, deep amongst the crowded bodies. I heard chewing, and remembered the humans that the Messenger had drained to death. I tried to feel pity for them, or even disgust, but the sounds of eating intensified, and the demons began fighting to reach that spot where I'd last seen the bodies. I watched, and all I felt was a strange pride, or pleasure: like a lioness watching her cubs feed.

I bit the inside of my cheek, then my tongue. Ruthless. Desperate. I tasted blood, and the sharp spike of pain was enough to shake me loose and bring me back to myself.

But I felt that pride, that pleasure, waiting like an iron cape ready to settle on my shoulders, in my heart. I felt it, so strong, just on the other side of me.

Not me, I thought desperately. *None of that is me.*

But it is under your skin, said the voice. *So close. So close. We are so close.*

The newcomer landed softly, despite his size: a giant, the ropes of his braided hair tied around his body like some strange armor. Silver glinted at his waist. He had all his limbs and was not missing chunks of flesh. Of all the demons present, he had meat on his bones.

He studied me. Just me. His eyes were green, a startling color against the dull gray of his skin. His long, deadly fingers tapped gently against his powerful thigh. He was thoughtful.

"Bring them to me," he said to the others.

The words had hardly left his mouth before the demons swarmed—striking like vipers, with hisses and howls. The sword flashed in my hand, swung like a baseball bat arcing lightning against the demons that tried to slam me. Blood spilled. So did limbs. I did not look at Grant, but I heard him, his voice moving through me as it rose like a crashing wail of thunder, primal and inhuman. I concentrated on his voice. As long as he sang, he was alive.

And so was I. The boys raged against me, burning hot—

and inside the darkness rose, filling my skin with its spirit flesh, shedding sleep as it blinked a lazy eye inside my mind.

I got knocked down. Twisted, as I fell, and saw Grant also on the ground, kneeling with his eyes closed, his hands clenched in fists. Sharp fingers hovered perilously close to his face, but the demons stood frozen, staring at him, mouths slack and their eyes rolling back in their heads.

Others, behind them, tried clawing over their bodies to reach Grant. Some turned at the last moment and attacked their own brothers, protecting him. Those who did were torn down without mercy. More took their place. I could not imagine what it was costing Grant to control so many minds.

Fingers stabbed me and broke. Hair lashed like whips, harmless against my face. I kicked out, hard, swinging the sword—and the blood I spilled was crimson and beautiful; and so were the screams, and the fear I saw, and the unease that arose in faces that were hollow with ten thousand years of hunger. Zee raged, between my breasts. All the boys, churning with such heat and violence I felt as though the surface of my skin were made of lava.

Grant still sang. When I thought of him, the golden light of our bond flared hot inside my chest, surrounding the darkness. The thing did not flee, or flinch—but purred—and fed the bond part of its own spirit flesh.

Grant's voice faltered.

All around him jaws snapped shut, and a collective twitch raced through those demons held by his rumbling song. I spun, burning on instinct, sword swinging—and hacked off the sharp hands and fingers that jerked down toward his vulnerable face.

I didn't stop moving. I grabbed his arm and hauled him to his feet, tight against me. His breathing was harsh, his skin warm as fire. He pressed his lips against the back of my head, and his mouth stayed there.

And I started to laugh.

It was not my laughter. But it spilled out of me, triumphant and confident, and the sound had a physical shape inside my mouth, like a long tongue tasting the air; finding it delicious with blood, and death.

Hunger filled me. Aching, wild, hunger. Old, deep, and endless.

Grant stilled against me. The demons attacking us hesitated. I didn't. I lunged forward and grabbed a one-armed, scarred demon whose black eyes were too human with confusion—and, for a moment, despair. The boys howled in my hand when I touched him, and my laughter deepened.

The demon gazed upon me with horror and screamed.

He was still screaming when he turned to ash. His arm dissolved first, blowing away like silver snow, then his shoulder crumbled and his feet, his legs, his torso falling, shattering on impact like soft glass, and his face was last— his jaw, his skull, his eyes staring at me as they faded, and formed lumps that scattered.

I tasted the echo of his screams, inside me, like wine: rolling each note on my tongue, tasting the layers of his terror, and finding them pure and good, and sweet. My fist was full of his ashes, and I lifted them and dribbled his remains into my mouth.

Part of me screamed, too—but the darkness rolled with pleasure, and when I mixed those ashes with my saliva and swallowed, it was not just my body anymore. I was a passenger. My mouth tasted like poison.

Every demon stood frozen, staring. I felt Grant behind me, but not his touch.

I looked for the giant, and found him standing a head

above the other demons. His green eyes glittered, and his gaze did not leave my face as he walked toward us. The demons parted for him, and those who moved too slowly were knocked aside. On the periphery of my vision, I saw the dead being surreptitiously pulled into the horde. I heard more bones crack and the soft whisper of flesh tearing.

The giant stopped in front of us. He didn't talk. He got down on one knee, pressed his long, sharp hand to his chest, and bowed his head. The other demons dropped to the ground without hesitation, following his example. Kneeling to me. Heads lowered. Eyes closed.

I stared at them, stricken, but the darkness rose in my throat with a smile that tasted like death.

"Forgive me," rumbled the demon. "Forgive us all. We did not recognize you."

The sword glowed, runes rippling over its surface, down into the armor around my hand. I thought it spoke to me, but all I felt was a heartbeat in the metal, then five more on my skin. Hearts, burning, inside my chest. Burning like my bond with Grant, which seemed so far away—as though, beneath my skin, my soul stood on a dark plain, watching his light with miles between us, miles and miles.

The darkness clawed into my mouth and breathed words on my tongue.

"Ha'an," it whispered through me. *"How stand the other Lords?"*

"I do not know," he said, chancing a look at my face. "We were in the second ring, and the break only reached as far as us. I know nothing of Draean, K'ra'an, or the others—but the Lady Whore still stands, and her children will feed our bellies until we may hunt." He hesitated. "You freed us. We thought . . . perhaps, you were gone forever."

"We are forever," said the darkness. *"But this is the dreaming time."*

The demon's expression was surprisingly human. He frowned, like any man would who was confused.

"The veil is open, my Kings. These are but a fraction of the Mahati who are ready to serve you, should you but ask. All we beg for is food. A good hunt." He looked past me at Grant. "The humans still abide, it seems. They will suffice."

"No," I said, and this time it was all me. The darkness rested in my throat, but it seemed content to let me speak that word.

"No," echoed the demon, and anger flickered in his green eyes. "We have suffered, and you deny us?"

"This is not your world."

"And it is *yours*?" His words were challenging, full of bite, and the other demons stirred uneasily.

I straightened, flushed with an anger that might have been me, or the darkness, but that felt righteous, strong. I stared that demon dead in the eyes, and knew—knew, in my gut—that I could kill him. With just a touch. A kiss.

The power of that knowledge felt too good.

His mouth snapped shut, and he looked away. "Forgive me."

I walked toward him, stopping only when I would have touched him. I circled his body, staring from him to the rest of the demons. I glimpsed Grant, but looking at him made something in me burn, and the darkness flinched away—as did I. It was enough, though, to see his eyes: dark, fathomless, watching me like I was a stranger.

"This world is mine," I said, and the darkness consumed my tongue, and added, *"You are mine. All of you."*

"Forgive me," he said again, shoulders rigid. "Of course, we are yours. The Mahati have always been loyal. But if the others go free, they will say what is already in my heart. We must hunt, or die."

"Then you will die," I said.

The demon—Ha'an—looked at me. And then Grant. Uncertainty filled his gaze, followed by hard defiance, and a determination so cold, so visceral, I felt it in my spine, in the pit of my stomach where all my fear huddled in a tiny, weeping lump.

"This is not right," he said softly. "This is not what was. You are different, my Kings. And not *just* in your choice of vessel."

He rose, towering. "Kill me if that serves your pleasure, but *I* am the Mahati Lord, and we are the last survivors. I will not sacrifice our lives—our lives, that have already been sacrificed in dignity and flesh—when I do not know if you can still be trusted."

I waited for the darkness to speak, but it said nothing. And so neither did I. All I did was stare into the eyes of Ha'an—and smile.

The demon lord didn't quite flinch, but whatever he saw in my eyes was enough to make him sway backward.

"Lead us," he said, almost begging. "Please. If you do not, if you give us up, the other Lords will not rest until they take power. And we are not as strong as them."

I said nothing. Ha'an backed away, shaking his head. "Only you can bind us. You, our Reaper Kings."

I froze at the sound of that name. Zee twisted on my skin, a lurch that felt like a sob.

Thankfully, Ha'an had already turned away. He looked at the demons surrounding him, and the darkness watched them, too—filled with a different kind of hunger, a sensation like the rise of a car on a roller coaster, inching toward the crest of that first wild fall. The darkness wanted to fall. It wanted to hunt.

Ha'an glanced over his shoulder at me. "Three days is all I can give you, my Kings. Three days . . . or however long time is judged on this world. Then you will kill us, or lead us."

Ha'an leapt upward, straight into the sky toward the crack in the veil. I did not expect him to fly, but he did so as easily as walking.

The other demons followed, carrying the dead. None looked back. I watched, unable to move or breathe, growing ever more light-headed as those silver-bullet bodies disappeared into the red haze of the open prison veil.

The darkness wanted to follow—or maybe I did—my heart wound so tight around that entity, I couldn't tell what was me anymore. All I knew was that I wanted to follow the Mahati. I wanted to enter the veil and see the army amassed, and breathe the air, and touch those bodies that were mine, mine, *mine to lead*—

Hands touched me. I flinched.

Grant's chest moved against my back. Breathing. He was breathing—and then, so was I. Deep breaths. I had been suffocating that entire time, I realized. Afraid to act like I needed air in front of a demon.

Afraid of myself.

"Maxine," Grant said. He was shaking, I realized. Trembling.

"Don't talk yet," I breathed, and lifted the sword to my lips. I kissed the blade, and it shimmered like a mirage, and faded into the armor. I kissed the armor, then, too.

"Jack," I said.

And we fell.

CHAPTER 12

THE women in my family kept journals. Not for self-reflection, but to teach from the grave.

My ancestor—an Englishwoman named Rebecca—wrote once about the Reaper Kings. No specific date, just a year—1857. She'd been in London, and was planning a move to Paris, followed by a journey to Africa. Ready to explore all those remote jungles where no white man could go.

She mentioned the Reaper Kings at the end, and only in passing.

We are, by necessity, lonely women, adrift, as it were, in shadows and violence. So it is no surprise, I suppose, that I wish to explore the dark continent that so many speak of with both superiority and fear. I do not fear, for I am protected; I do not feel superior, for I know the cut of being judged. We are all human, in all the ways that matter—but one would not know that for all the ways we become blind to each other, for the smallest trivialities.

I think of the daemons, when I think of humans. There are many daemons in the veil—the army, so goes the lore, is vast. Not all daemons will be the same as their brothers, I know this. Nor do I believe—after my years of hunting the weaker breeds who escape the veil—that all daemons share one heart, one eye with which to view the world. It cannot be. The weaker daemons fear their Lords, for they have told me so before death—and they have said, too, that their Lords are full of cunning and spite, against each other.

Like humans. So much like humans.

And that is worse, I think. Because no army of conflicting individuals has ever been ruled with a light hand.

The Reaper Kings must be frightful, indeed . . .

IF I had known where the armor would take us, I would have been more specific. I would have said that Jack could wait. That my questions could wait. That the demons in the veil could wait and rot in their hell—while I did the same in mine. I would have said all those things if I had known.

Grant and I stepped from the void into a kitchen.

It was an old kitchen, with cream-colored cabinets, dusty green polka-dot curtains, and a checkered linoleum floor that, after almost seven years, carried a bloodstain not even the boys had been able to scrub out.

Home. In the room where my mother was murdered.

Sunlight poured through the windows. The air tasted hot, and smelled musty and tired. I didn't have any strength. My brain and heart were somewhere else.

But when I saw the stain—when it sank in—the rest of me caught up.

My knees buckled. I sat down hard on the floor, swaying backward. I would have stretched out all the way if my shoulders hadn't connected with the old Frigidaire. I leaned against it, overwhelmed, lost in cracked-eggshell walls and peeling-linoleum countertop. The kitchen table was still there, the heavy wooden chairs, just as I'd left them; and the board I had nailed over the north window, where the bullet had blasted through the glass and ripped apart my mother's head.

I could still smell the cake. Chocolate.

"Maxine," Grant said, falling down on the floor at my side. I held up my hand, wishing he would stay silent. Everything, too much. Demons. My mother. Me.

Us, said the voice of the darkness, as it curled beneath my heart. *It is not complicated.*

I was losing my mind. This was it. This was what Jack had been afraid of, what my ancestor had faced. Losing her mind to the thing resting so heavily inside—part of me, but not. Overwhelmed by voices, crawling with hunger, consuming demons . . .

I tasted that ash in my mouth, and leaned sideways, gagging.

Grant pulled me into his arms. I tried to push him away, but he was strong, and I wanted to be held. I needed an anchor. I balled his shirt up in my fist.

"I'm a monster," I said.

He shook his head. "Never."

"You saw, you heard—"

"Maxine," he interrupted roughly, but said nothing else. I remembered that glimpse of his eyes, looking at me as though I were a stranger—and the shame, and grief, that roared after that memory were almost more than I could bear. Zee twisted, and the others did the same, rough—then gentle—tugging on my skin until I wanted to hit myself, hit them, and scream. I didn't own my body. Not inside, not out.

I stared at the bloodstain on the floor. My mother.

No one owns you, she would have said. *No one but you.*

"I'm sorry," Grant whispered. "For everything."

"I asked for it," I said. "That night. Cake."

He stilled, then said, very softly, "Maxine."

"We could have gone out," I told him, unable to stop. "Would have been a public place. But I wanted cake. Her cake."

He was silent, again, for a long moment. "You didn't know what would happen. It wouldn't have stopped anything."

"A day. One day more. Maybe two, three, a week. Anything would have been better. More time."

Grant slid his hand around mine, his thumb stroking my wrist. Warm. Strong. Solid.

Familiar. I remembered him holding my hand that way, but other memories were distant, hanging by fingertips on the edges of my mind. I was afraid to touch them, that they would scatter.

"Are you hurt?" I asked him. "Did any of them—"

"No," he interrupted. "You?"

I closed my eyes. "I don't understand what just happened."

"You stopped an army."

"I almost lost myself."

You found yourself, said the voice.

I pulled away from Grant, intent on standing, running— but had to stop, nauseous. I leaned on my hands, trying not to vomit. My elbows shook. Grant placed his hand on my back.

"They can't be the Reapers," I whispered. "Not my boys. Not the thing inside me."

"Would it matter?"

I gave him a wild look. "You can ask that?"

"I know the boys. I know you."

"You saw inside me. Out there. I saw the way you looked at me, Grant, like I was a—"

"—stranger," he finished gravely.

The word cut deep. Made me feel small. I looked away from him. "Good. That's . . . good. You're not safe around me anyway."

"I'm safer than you are," he replied, unmoving. "What I said wasn't a mark against your character, Maxine. Not a rejection, either."

I still couldn't look at him. "I wanted to go with them. I wanted to . . . do things."

"It wasn't you."

"Some of it felt like me."

He shook his head. "I see you, Maxine. I see inside you, all the time, every day, when I watch you sleep, when you talk to me, when you just sit and read, or stare into space, and think no one sees you. But I see you. I see what sleeps inside you. I saw it more clearly, just now."

I finally met his gaze. "What *did* you see?"

"Same thing I've always seen. You. Power." Grant reached out and brushed his thumb over my mouth, tenderly. "Just . . . power. You told me once that the boys are only as good as the woman who leads them. Only as good as what's in there." He pointed at my heart. "What makes you think this is different?"

"It's alive, hungry. Has a mind of its own. Took over my body during the fight. It could overwhelm me permanently."

"But not the both of us." Grant leaned close, peering into my eyes. "I'm not much, but I'm something. You're not alone, Maxine, no matter what happens."

I wanted to tell him he was wrong, but my heartbeat carried a second pulse that rode out of the light binding us together: that light, his light, as deep inside me as the darkness bathing in its glow.

Never alone, said that dark spirit. *We are one. All of us, one.*

I sucked in a deep breath. "I can hear it in my head."

"So talk to it," Grant said, like it was nothing. "Maybe what you think you know is wrong."

"Wrong," I echoed, incredulous. "Grant, if we assume for a moment that the demon was correct, and the boys, the thing inside me, are all somehow part of the Reaper Kings . . ." I stopped, shuddering, feeling like my guts were going to crawl up my throat.

"Maxine," he said. "If they are, if you are—"

I held up my hand, stopping him—and then had to cover my mouth to keep from being sick. "You don't understand. The Reaper Kings, if they get loose, are supposed to destroy *everything*. You heard that demon. He wanted me to lead his people to hunt *humans*. For food."

"I heard him. I also heard you say no. Rather emphatically." Grant grabbed my hand. "Some call me a Lightbringer. And an abomination. But I don't feel like any of those things. I know who I am. I know who I was raised to be. So do you, Maxine."

I wrenched my hand away. "You're going to tell me you weren't afraid."

"I was terrified. If I were a weaker man, I'd need to change my pants right now."

"That's not funny. This thing inside me—"

"Saved us." He rubbed his chest. "I think it . . . touched me."

I was going to be sick again. I bowed my head, closing my eyes, focusing on the dark spirit curled so tightly in the nooks of my soul. I could feel it, separate from me, like a cancer made of iron, heavy and dull, with a metallic taste like blood.

Or maybe that was my bitten tongue. It hurt. I bit it again.

Stay away from him, I told the darkness inside me. *Stay the fuck away from him.*

I felt the thing smile, and turned my head away from Grant, afraid my mouth would mirror its pleasure.

We are you, you are him, he is you. All of us are one, together, whispered that supple voice. *You cannot break that bond, now that we have tasted it.*

I won't let you hurt him.

We would not hurt ourselves.

I believed that. But there were other ways to hurt someone, and this thing inside was operating on a different standard of right and wrong. I could still taste that ash in my mouth, and the ache of a nameless hunger that I did not think would ever be satisfied.

Hunt, and you will be satisfied, said the voice. *Sip death, and your thirst will abate.*

Fuck you, I thought, and opened my eyes—finding that old bloodstain directly in front of me. I stared at it, then reached out and pressed my hand against the dull patch of linoleum. I didn't feel anything; but Dek tugged, and Zee rolled in his sleep, all the boys restless.

"It touched you through our link," I said. "If it does that again . . ."

I couldn't finish. Grant gave me a sharp look. "How do you know about the link?"

I tilted my shoulder in a weary shrug. "Maybe there are some things I remember."

Love. Friendship. Acceptance. Everything I couldn't bear to lose. All reasons I needed to save him from me.

A floorboard creaked in the other room. We stiffened, staring out the door. I heard it again.

Old farmhouse. Almost every hinge and stair and board had a song—familiar to me, even after seven years. I could still hear my mother on those floors, or me, or the boys; and it was hard to breathe.

I stood, gesturing for Grant to stay down. I hopped over the noisy spots in the kitchen floor and peered into the living room.

The Messenger stood in the shadows.

She was alone, facing the kitchen. Seeing her in my mother's home felt wrong. No one should have been here. Not even me.

I walked into plain view. The Messenger did not move, or acknowledge me. All she did was stare: blankly, as though her mind was very far away.

Grant's cane clicked across the floor. It wasn't until he appeared in her line of sight that she moved. Just a little. A blink, a tightening of her mouth. A tremble.

"You survived," she whispered.

"You thought we wouldn't?" I asked sharply. Grant touched the small of my back. Cautioning me. His touch sparked déjà vu, a riot of memories that I felt more than saw, and which instantly faded into the back of my head. I tried not to sway.

"I did not know what to think," she said simply. "You ran?"

"We fought," Grant told her. "Pushed them back."

Her entire body twitched. I said, "Where's Jack?"

"What is this place?" asked the Messenger, instead of answering me. Her voice sounded hollow, faint. "I feel things in the walls. Echoes. Someone strong lived here." She fixed me with a hard look. "She was like you."

I said nothing. I walked through the living room toward

the front door. The boys, dreaming on my skin, tugged backward, ever so slightly, toward the kitchen. Remembering. I touched my chest, then studied my tattooed hands. Dek and Mal stared back, red eyes glinting. Against my legs, Raw and Aaz clung heavy and warm.

My boys.

I stood on the covered porch. It was late afternoon outside. Blue blinding skies, and a golden meadow that stretched as far as the eye could see. The gravel driveway was overgrown with weeds, and the paint was peeling— but nothing much had changed in seven years. Time had frozen on the night of my mother's death, and only I was different.

Everything, inside me, was different.

I soaked in the fresh scent of wild grass and clean, hot winds. Early spring in Texas was comfortable, pleasing on the eye. I had forgotten what unremitting sunlight looked like.

Precious world, I thought, shivering—and then, to the darkness inside me: *This is a precious, beautiful world. I won't let you hurt it. I won't let you use me to hurt it.*

I received no response.

My hand still felt the weight of the sword. I heard screams inside my head. Blood, war, death. I gripped the rail, leaning hard, and glimpsed movement near the old oaks—some distance away, on a small hill near the creek. I stared for a long time, watching the figure sitting hunched in the grass, filled with dread and hunger. My own clean hunger, nothing born from darkness, which coiled now, as though asleep.

Pretender, I told it.

I walked off the porch, across the driveway, into the grass. I kept the oaks in sight, and the teen who sat there.

Jack had his back to me, but I wasn't quiet in my approach. He knew I was coming. He sat with his chin resting on his knees, his hands digging into the ground beside him, gripping clumps of grass as he stared at my mother's grave.

It was unmarked, except for a giant slab of limestone the boys had placed on top. Zee had carved her name into the rock with his claws. We'd done it all the same night she died. The boys dug the grave. I sat with her body. We buried her, and I did not leave the spot until the next night, when the sun set.

Seven years. Everything was the same, except the grass had grown.

"You're safe," Jack said, not looking at me.

"You knew I would be," I replied. "Safe in body, anyway."

"An important distinction." Jack stared at his hands. "Grant?"

"Alive." I sat beside him and touched my mother's headstone. "They called themselves the Mahati."

He shivered. "Scouts."

"They wanted me to lead them."

Jack finally met my gaze. "What did you say?"

"I'm sitting here. What do you think?"

"I think," he said slowly, and stopped. "I don't know what to think, my dear."

My mother's name looked raw on the stone, and had been cut so deep, my finger fit into the grooves.

Jolene Kiss. Daughter of Jean.

I pressed my forehead against the stone. "I wanted to say yes. I wanted to, Jack. I wanted to . . . feel that power."

"The power over life and death," he said. "Once tasted, you can never really let go."

"Speaking from experience?"

He looked away, staring at my mother's grave. I did the

same, trying not to think of her burial. Trying to remember her face, her wry smile, that glint in her eyes.

I fixed her image in my mind, then lay down in the grass, listening to the wind and watching the blue sky. No rifts, anywhere to be seen. No hint of trouble. Just another day, another night, for six billion human beings.

"I don't come here often enough," he said. "It pains me."

"Been seven years for me." I closed my eyes, finding it difficult to breathe past the lump in my throat. "Jack. What am I? Tell me the truth. That's all I want. No riddles."

"No riddles," he echoed, and I heard a shuffling sound in the grass. Pried open one eye, just enough to see Grant join us. He looked solemn, but a strong steady strength burned at the back of his eyes. I could have called it compassion, or faith, but it was something deeper than that, and I had no name to give it except that it felt like the sun was being compressed into my heart—a wild light bigger than my life, but so much a part of me, I thought I might just keep burning, even if I died.

He stayed with you. He fought at your back. He did not flinch.

My man, I thought.

I held out my hand. He tickled my palm with his fingers as he sat heavily in the grass beside me, then took my hand fully, warm, in his. Jack watched us, regret in his eyes, something painfully wistful.

"I don't know where Jeannie is buried," he murmured.

"Neither do I," I said. "Mom never told me."

Jack bowed his head, running his hands—Byron's hands—over his face. I couldn't breathe, watching him. I couldn't think, or move. Even Grant was still.

"We were losing the war," Jack said.

I waited, but he didn't speak again, not right away.

Grant pulled me a little closer. I didn't fight him, didn't think about all the reasons that I should. I guess I'd been over that, again and again, for the last two years. We were still together. Some things in life were just stubborn, that way.

"Old Wolf," I said.

"Maxine," he replied, hoarse. "The armies of the demon lords could not be possessed by my kind, and they hunted humans—our humans—for food and slaves. We could have suffered that—there were so many worlds we inhabited—except for the existence of the Reaper Kings."

Zee tugged against my skin, agitated. "They could kill your kind."

"We couldn't hide from them. It was as though they tasted us in the air. Five demons, sharing one mind. Possessing . . . unimaginable power. I cannot tell you, Maxine, the things I saw them do."

"Don't try," I said. "Really, don't."

I wasn't certain Jack heard me; his gaze was so distant. "No one thought it would work, but we were desperate. We needed something that would break them down, separate them from the bulk of their powers. So we found a human woman, modifying her just enough. And then we . . . we bound the Reapers to her. We bound them to mortal flesh, on a . . . a quantum . . . level."

Grant's hands tightened. "How is that even possible? I know you did it, because Maxine is the evidence, but *how*?"

Jack shook his head. "I can't explain it. You have to *be* us to understand. What we did that day . . . it wouldn't be possible to repeat. It was . . . luck and power. More power than any of us imagined we'd have to use. Many died making that prison. Even I almost lost my life. And even so, we always . . . we always knew it wouldn't last."

"Jack," I breathed.

"There were two prisons," he went on, blinking tears from his eyes. "The first is the prison you saw today. A place beyond this world that holds an army. But that wasn't the prison the Wardens were guarding, all those millennia ago. Not the prison that will destroy the world when it falls." He shuddered, looking down at his hands, those black-painted fingernails bitten to the quick. "*You* are the second prison, Maxine. Your body, your soul. Your bloodline. And you are the *only* prison that matters. Because the demons you're holding . . ."

"The Reaper Kings," I whispered, and the boys stirred. I rested my hand over the spot where Zee slept. I felt sick, dizzy, very small. A cat could have picked me up in its mouth, I felt so small.

I wanted my mother, but she was in the grave.

"My boys," I said hoarsely. "My boys aren't like that, Jack."

"They've changed," he admitted. "But I don't know if that's because they've been separated from the power that made them . . . or whether it's possible they've truly . . . become something different. Ten thousand years is not a long time, my dear."

"It is if you're mortal," Grant rumbled, wrapping himself around me so tightly I could barely breathe. It still wasn't tight enough. I laced my fingers through his, and his rough, bristled jaw rested against my ear.

Again, I suffered déjà vu, a surge of *knowing* that was accompanied by flashes of memory, one in particular: us sitting like this, in bed, his large hand splayed over my stomach; and his whisper, *One of these days I want to be a father.*

I sucked in a sharp breath. Grant's arms tightened, and in a cold voice, he said, "Jack. Maxine isn't going to destroy anything."

"Destruction and rebirth go hand in hand," murmured my grandfather, looking back at my mother's grave. "The two are the same. Everything breaks. When broken, born again."

"I'm not evil," I said.

Jack gave me a sharp look. "I know. You're a good person. That's the reason I came to you last night. I wanted you to know. I wanted to do things differently, this time. Your ancestor lost her mind, and in her madness . . . her rage . . . she nearly destroyed the world. The veil was strong then, not like it is now, but even so, she seemed able to . . . access . . . the controlled energy of the Reaper Kings. Sometimes I think that if I had just told her, helped her understand . . ." He stopped, rubbing his face. "I was too tied up in secrets. And I was afraid of her. Shamefully afraid."

She feared herself, said the darkness, its voice drifting through me. *But she still hunted.*

I held my breath. Grant said, "You immortals. Afraid of so much. I've known children with more guts."

"So have I," Jack said, touching my mother's headstone with heartbreaking reverence. "I've learned a great deal from them."

Too much. All of it, too much. I struggled out of Grant's arms. "What do I do?"

"Nothing. Except be *you.*"

"Me," I echoed. "I wasn't *me* just now when I fought those demons. I let that thing inside me take over, Jack. And it felt . . . too good."

"Maxine," Grant said roughly, touching my hand. I looked at him, and was surprised—not just by the warning in his eyes, but that I understood what he was trying to tell me. It had been a long time since I'd known anyone that well.

And then, suddenly, it didn't feel like such a long time.

I remembered him. I remembered the sensation of meeting his gaze in a crowd, and knowing everything about him based on the tick of his smile, the glint of his eye. That small, precious kernel of a memory settled warm in my chest.

Later, he said now with his eyes. *We'll talk later.*

When we were alone. Away from Jack.

I glanced at my grandfather, and found him watching us with a great deal of uncertainty. Except for his eyes, it could have been Byron sitting there, and I wanted to press my head into the grass, be a little girl again, and cry. Just cry my heart out, for everything.

But that wasn't going to keep anyone safe.

I stood on unsteady legs and gazed down the hill at the farmhouse. The Messenger stood on the porch, watching us.

"What about her?" I asked.

Grant followed my gaze and was silent a long time.

"I opened her eyes," he said quietly.

"What does that mean?"

"He broke her conditioning." Jack openly studied Grant. "No one has ever done that."

"No one tried."

"Some tried, long ago, with other Messengers, other descendents of those stolen Lightbringers." He smiled bitterly. "But I don't think that's a story you want to hear right now."

Grant frowned, as though he disagreed. "I know when you're lying, old man. I can see right through you. How come she doesn't?"

"She can't read my kind. We're blank slates to her and those bred like her. That was the first thing we modified. Truth is poison, lad."

I looked at my grandfather, sitting so small and alone by his daughter's grave. I could see the old man in his eyes, those stolen eyes, in that stolen skin, and it hurt. I walked to him, and laid my hand on his shoulder, and kissed the top of his head. Jack stilled, holding his breath.

"That's not the reaction I had last night, is it?" I said grimly.

"I don't want to remember your reaction," Jack murmured. "In hindsight, it's probably best that you don't, either."

I could live with that. I glanced at Grant. "Is she a threat?"

"Not to me," he said quietly. "I'll watch her."

I nodded, and kissed him, too, on the mouth.

"I love you," I whispered, for his ears only.

I walked away and didn't look back.

CHAPTER 13

M Y mother had owned many homes, and a great deal of land—across the world, inherited from our ancestors. I had never set foot in most of them. Never lived longer than a year in those I had. All of it, mine now. I had never thought much about it.

But I walked until sunset and didn't see a fence, or another human being.

I was in the old pine forest when the sun went down, seated on a soft patch of ground. I felt the tingle, the weight of night bearing down on my skin. I knew the exact moment when the horizon swallowed the sun.

The boys woke up.

Happened fast. I fell backward, suffering the sensation of hot razor blades skinning me alive: between my legs, under my fingernails, against my breasts and arms. Everywhere the boys slept, every part of me they peeled away from.

Razed with pain. I gritted my teeth and bore it, watching as smoke flowed from beneath my clothing, smoke that trembled with red lightning. No different from any other waking that I had watched since childhood—first on my mother, then on me.

But it felt different. I saw it with different eyes.

Two long bodies settled around my neck, hot tongues caressing the backs of my ears and naked scalp. I closed my eyes and listened to sweet high voices hum, "I Just Called to Say I Love You."

I love you, I love you, I thought back, heart breaking. I had never considered myself particularly innocent, but I felt as though a knife had jabbed into a part of me still wholesome and young—and killed it.

Small clawed hands wrapped tightly around mine. So familiar and warm.

"You heard," I said. "You heard it all."

"Heard," Zee rasped, so softly, his voice thick with grief.

I rolled over, shivering. Raw and Aaz burrowed against my back, their bodies warm as fire. Dek and Mal wrapped more tightly around my neck. Zee's shoulders were hunched, knuckles dragging. His spikes drooped.

"You knew," I said.

"Like a bad dream," he said softly. "Faraway dream, strong as clouds breaking."

I stared, helpless and horrified. "But none of you are . . ."

I didn't know how to finish. What was I going to say? That none of them were evil? That Reaper Kings didn't clutch teddy bears or read *Playboy*? That the very worst and most dangerous of the demons didn't . . . love? Or need love?

Because I knew they did. My boys loved. I had always

known it. Alongside my mother they had practically raised me: changed my diapers, held my bottle, put me to sleep. Sung me nursery rhymes and helped teach me to read. I had even been granted a vision of them in the past, raising an orphaned Hunter—a newborn infant. I could still see them singing the funeral dirge of that baby's mother—and then taking the child, protecting her, holding her with such care. And not just because their survival depended on it . . . but because they loved her.

That couldn't be faked. Not with my boys.

"Maxine," whispered Zee. "We fear."

I feared, too. Raw wrapped his arms around me, pressing his face against my back. Aaz shuffled a couple steps sideways, and returned moments later to push a paper cup into my hands. Starbucks. I smelled hot chocolate.

Yes. We were definitely agents of the apocalypse.

I sat up, Raw still clinging to me, and sipped the drink. It made me feel better. Rooted me closer to earth. I held Zee's gaze, and thought of all the strange things I'd heard over the years—from Ahsen, the Erl-King, even Blood Mama. I thought about my mother, and Jack. Snatches of memories, things that had never made sense. Pieces, falling into place.

But it was still too much. I was going to drown. I grabbed Zee's arm, but all he did was rock on his heels and shudder. He looked so small.

"Why are you afraid? If you've always known, what could you possibly fear? You, Reaper Kings." I wanted to cringe when I said that name. It sounded ridiculous to even think about Zee that way.

But he closed his eyes, as though the weight of hearing it spoken out loud was almost too much to bear.

"Hush the name," he said.

"But it's what you are, right?"

The little demon snarled—all the boys did—but not at me. It was as though the name—that awful name, the very *thought*—caused them pain.

Zee pulled free. "Not us. Old days gone. Not us, Maxine."

I sat back, staring at him. Raw's arms tightened around my waist, while Dek and Mal were a solid, comfortable weight. Aaz picked his nose—ate the black steaming slime on the tip of his claw—and gave me a weak, toothy smile.

I could not smile back. Zee wasn't looking at me. Just down, down, like he was afraid to see my eyes. Afraid of me.

There were many things I could take, but not that. Not in this lifetime. It didn't matter what the truth was. Truth was shit. Truth wasn't always real.

Real was what you felt. Real was what you knew, in your heart.

"Hey," I said softly. "Look at me."

Zee did, reluctantly. I grabbed his arm again, but this time it was to pull him close. "Who are those bozo Reaper Kings, anyway? Fuck them. They've got nothing to do with my boys. My brave, dangerous boys."

Zee bowed his head. "Maxine."

"Are we, or are we not, family?" I ran my hand up his sharp face, burying it in his spiked hair—and tugged back his head until he looked me in the eyes.

"Are we family?" I asked him again.

"In our blood, beyond death," he rasped.

"Then don't be afraid," I told him, grim. "And I won't be, either."

Zee stared at me—all the boys, so still—and I saw something in his eyes that made me glad to be alive, to be here, to be who I was with all my burdens, and all the danger. I couldn't name it, I didn't want to, but I felt it strong as life. And I knew the boys felt it, too.

"Hard road," Zee whispered.

"Always," I replied. "But we've got hard heads."

Zee squeezed shut his eyes—exhaled sharply—and then bared his teeth in a toothy, breathless grin.

"Yeah," I said. "That's what I mean."

I let him go. Zee sidled backward, but not far. He kept one clawed hand on my knee. Dek and Mal were purring so loudly my eardrums rattled. Raw and Aaz tumbled into my lap. Somewhere from the shadows they had pulled out baseball hats—Yankees tonight—and jammed them on their heads. I tugged the brims low.

"Mom knew," I said. "Didn't she?"

"Truth given." Zee hunched down until he resembled a mushroom in the shadows. "All kinds of truths."

"Jack told her."

"No." The little demon traced a claw through fallen pine needles, making a circle of tangled lines that formed a knot. A maze.

"The Labyrinth." I touched the circle's edge. "She was in the Labyrinth. Before she had me."

"Slipped sideways. Accident." Zee hesitated. "Followed strange paths."

"Strange enough that she found out about you there? Strange enough that she found someone in the Labyrinth who knew the truth?"

Zee shifted uncomfortably. All the boys did. I wanted to ask more, but I knew that look: no answers tonight, not about that.

I lay down, and all the boys drew close, pushing against me, wrapping their arms around my body. I hugged them. We stared up through the swaying pines at the first stars of evening.

"What," I asked quietly, "do you remember? Before . . . this?"

"Hunger," Zee said. "Darkness and hunger."

I touched my chest. "That's what's inside me. This thing . . . it's part of you."

Zee stayed silent. Raw and Aaz shivered, while Dek and Mal hummed "Ask the Lonely" from Journey. I closed my eyes. "You should have told me years ago. I would have preferred hearing it from you. Not from those demons. Not Jack."

"Truth cuts," Zee muttered. "Truth cuts *us*. Scarred you, hurt you, burned your heart to knots. Ruined your life, with truth. Old mother felt the same. Laid you clues, riddles. To ease you. To save you."

"To save me," I echoed roughly. "From this?"

Zee laid his clawed hand on top of my chest, above my heart. "Worst part of us."

Tears burned my throat and eyes, followed by a feeling of helplessness so vast, so terrible, I thought it would rip me apart. "How? How did she plan to save me?"

"Your heart," he rasped. "Sweet heart. Sweet Maxine."

My mother had been a good woman, but not sweet. Hard as nails. Never easy to laugh or smile. She had raised me to be good, too, and strong, but there had been no lessons in sweetness. Just the right thing. Always, the right thing, no matter what.

I covered Zee's hand with mine. "What will happen when the veil falls?"

Zee laid his head upon my stomach. "Mystery. We become what we were, or you become . . . something other."

"And if I die first?"

All the boys stiffened. Zee said, "No."

"It'd be worth the sacrifice."

"No," he said again. "Better chance with you alive."

"What chance?"

"Always chance. Always possibilities." Zee closed his eyes. "Dwell there."

I rubbed his head. "Why do you care? I'm your prison. *All of us* have been your prison."

"No secret. Knew us captured."

"But you're not *just* demons. What you are—"

"Five hearts," Zee rasped, tapping my chest five times. "Five hearts. Now six. Now seven. Will be eight, in time. All one. All strong."

I wrapped my hand around his. "Mine is the sixth."

"Lightbringer is seven. Baby, when she future blooms—"

"Eight." I drew in a deep breath. "Why do you care, Zee?"

Raw and Aaz whispered to each other. Dek and Mal stopped humming. Zee murmured, "We raged. Over many lives we raged."

I waited for more, but he said nothing else. I did not push. I wanted to, but I was afraid—as though I stood on the edge of a terrible precipice, a descent into a darkness that would never end, and if I breathed wrong, if I moved even a little in a bad direction—I would fall. Lost, forever.

The boys were the Reaper Kings. My boys. My dangerous little boys. I could not comprehend it.

I could not comprehend what that made *me*.

Zee patted my head, gently. "Rest, Maxine. We guard your dreams."

"Guard Grant and Jack," I told him, closing my eyes. "The Messenger is still with them. If she tries anything—"

"We kill her."

I did not disagree, but the idea of more death made me sad, and sick. I had no right to take her life. Less right now than I'd had before. It wasn't that I had something to prove.

Just that, if everyone was correct, my capacity to do harm had become unthinkable. The way I felt, I might have to put down the sword and pull a Gandhi on someone's ass.

"I don't know what I'm going to do," I said.

Zee didn't answer me. I only meant to close my eyes for a moment. A little peace, with the boys. Maybe we were monsters, but not to each other.

Dek and Mal sang me to sleep.

⊰⊱

I dreamed, and no one saved me.

I had been lost, before, in darkness. Lost, in the Wasteland—a place inside the Labyrinth beyond the road of worlds, where lives and dreams were thrown away to be forgotten. An oubliette for the soul.

I had escaped, when no one ever had. I lived there, when I shouldn't have lived at all—but the boys had shared their strength with me, and finally their breath, and kept me alive.

If I died, they would die. That was how the story went. But I no longer knew if that was true.

Nothing was true.

Except your heart, I heard my mother whisper.

She wasn't in my dream. I was back in the Wasteland; only the maze I traveled was made of flesh instead of stone; and I was not in the Labyrinth, but instead the belly of a vast wyrm.

There were stars within the wyrm, glittering in the darkness of its stomach, and beyond the stars I saw the spinning tops of galaxies, churning lazily.

We are vast, whispered a deep, soft voice. *We are the other side of light. Born from the first spark, of the first moment, of the first breath of the mouth that opened and never*

closed. And the mouth still opens and never closes, and
from it springs worlds and dreams, and the fire of count-
less stars. We are vaster than the stars, for we are older
than them, and we have sung at the cradles of new life, and
tasted of that life.

We always taste. For we are always hungry.

The stars blinked out.

But there are things we have never known.

The galaxies disappeared.

And so we abide.

The belly of the wyrm faded.

Listening, listening, to the other side of light.

I had already begun to fall before that voice finished
speaking, and the words chased me as I plummeted through
darkness. I could not tell up from down—I spun, blind, listening to my heart pound.

Until, abruptly, I was elsewhere. And I was not alone.

I stood at the head of an army, vast as the night—a
throbbing pulsing army shuddering with cries and hunger.
At my side, wolves. Wolves, who resembled my boys. My
laughing, ready boys.

Upon my head, a crown of thorns. And the stars above,
bleeding light.

I wore no clothes. My skin, clad only in blood. And
when I screamed, and raised the sword I held within my
fist, my army screamed with me—

—and followed, as I charged.

❈

I saw stars when I awoke. It was still night. Not even close
to dawn, or else I would have felt the sun rising on my
skin.

I smelled pizza. Heard a stuffed animal squeak. I looked

for the boys and found them less than an arm's length away, sitting in the leaves amongst some of their favorite things. Dek and Mal purred in my ears. I rubbed their backs, wondering how, in any reality, it was possible that these two could lead an army.

"Are we setting up camp?" I asked. My voice sounded rusty.

Raw flinched, and stopped dribbling melted cheese on a chain-saw blade. Zee said, "Waiting."

Dek and Mal hiccuped. Raw gave Zee a strained look, and shoved the chain-saw blade down his throat. The chewing sounds he made were like fingernails on a chalkboard. I didn't see Aaz.

"Waiting for what?" I asked.

Raw made a mewling sound and hugged his stomach. I opened my arms to him and he crawled into my lap. I dragged over a teddy bear and put it in his claws. He began chewing the ear. The acid in his saliva made the fur smoke. I rubbed his tummy, and felt it rumble. Cheese and chain saws. Never a good combination.

"Zee," I said again. "Answer me."

But he didn't need to. Moments later, the scar tingled, beneath my ear. Pins and needles.

I knew that sensation. I understood what it meant, and forgot to breathe.

"Maxine," Zee rasped.

I hardly heard him. Sweat broke. Dek and Mal coiled tighter around my neck, their hums fading into silence. Raw rolled out of my lap, and Aaz loped from the shadows, dragging a hubcap behind him. He skidded to a stop and clutched the disc so tightly to his chest it tore in two, delicate as lace.

All of them stared at the sky.

I craned my neck. Glimpsed movement across the stars,

darker than night—blocking out the stars like a comet, eating light. A dagger in the sky.

"For you," said Zee. "We called him."

Cold air blasted over my body, and the dagger slammed into the ground in front of us.

Earth cracked, the split of stone sharper than a gunshot. Raw grabbed my shoulders to steady me, as did Zee. I hardly felt them. I should have remembered, but I had forgotten. I had forgotten everything about the immense figure who stood before me, towering like a pillar of black flames: the barest semblance of a man.

I had never seen his eyes. A wide-brimmed hat swept low over a pale face, revealing only a sharp jaw and thin mouth. No arms. No wind, either, but long black hair moved wildly in all directions, the very tips writhing like snakes. His feet resembled steak knives: fistfuls of glittering blades as long as my forearm, digging point first into the earth as if performing a lethal pirouette.

I could not move. I could not blink. Cold raced through my blood—cold, then heat, a flush of fear and a small dangerous thrill—because here, here, was a dance: the only creature in the world whom the boys would allow to kill me. Without so much as a fight.

"Oturu," I breathed.

"Our Lady Hunter," whispered the demon. "We have missed your face."

CHAPTER 14

DESPITE everything, I'd lived a small life. A full life, but small. I'd been raised to believe one thing, and for the first twenty-five years of my life, I hadn't questioned that. I'd questioned other parts of my life, but *not* that.

Demons were bad. Except for the boys.

The boys didn't count. Even my mother had been clear on that. The boys were family. The boys were only as good as the heart that led them, but that capacity for goodness went deeper than just orders and expectations. The boys knew right from wrong. The boys had compassion—when they chose to wield it.

But the rest . . . the rest had to be killed.

Then I'd come to Seattle. Met Grant. Started looking at demons differently. They still had to die. But I killed them now, knowing they were capable of choosing to change their natures.

That was a hard knowledge. It was easy to kill something when you thought it was a menace, like stamping out a flea, or a tick. Parasites had to die. But if Grant could modify the instincts of demons—if demons could even *desire* to be modified—then that choice, that ability to contemplate and accept such deep fundamental change away from the nature of one's birth, created disturbing possibilities.

Which, if followed to their natural, logical conclusions, meant I had been wrong. That my *mother* had been wrong. All the women in my bloodline, mistaken.

Or maybe, just maybe, I was finally learning something they had known all along and chosen to ignore: that, like people, demons were not so easy to judge.

Like Oturu.

Like me.

Like the boys.

I watched the dagger tips of Oturu's feet float upon the leaves. Starlight did not touch him; or perhaps the abyss of his cloak was too vast, his body a mystery of night. He was a creature so far beyond human understanding, that *demon* was the only name I could give him that made sense, the only definition that encompassed all that was strange and dangerous—and beautiful.

We had met only a handful of times. I had feared him in the beginning. Part of me still did. But each encounter had revealed a little more, more and more, until now it was a strange comfort seeing him. Oturu had never been caught in the prison veil. He had always been free. Devoted to my bloodline: to my deadly ancestor, who had found him in the Labyrinth and become his friend.

Tendrils of his dark hair spiraled like corkscrews toward

my face, floating close to the scar beneath my ear. I refused to move, but Dek hissed, and Mal slid across my cheek, rising like a cobra.

"So," I said, proud that my voice was steady. "Here we are again."

His mouth curved into a slow smile. "You, Mistress, with your hounds and the hunt at hand. You, Queen, standing ever closer to eternity."

I was too tired to spar. "Where's Tracker?"

Tracker. The man who was this creature's slave, a man who had been betrayed by my ancestor, turned over to Oturu, forced to serve him.

He'd pushed me in front of a bus once. I didn't blame him.

"Tracker is unneeded," he said, and his hair lashed out again, all of his hair, reaching for me like a thousand graceful fingers. No time to blink before he surrounded me, his cloak flaring wide like wings. And though Dek and Mal snarled, they did not attack. Tendrils of hair slid up my neck, caressing my skull. I stared into the abyss of his cloak and body, faced with moving shadows that briefly looked like eyes, hands.

I heard nothing but my heartbeat. But deep inside, deep, that coiled presence stirred.

Oturu whispered, "From darkness we are born."

And born again, forever, murmured that soft voice inside my mind.

I closed my eyes, holding still, my fingers grazing spiked hair and pointed ears as Rex, Aaz, and Zee pushed near. "You knew, all along. What I am. Ever since we met."

"Even you do not know what you are." Oturu drew me closer, his hair tightening around my body as Dek and Mal growled. "And you will *not* know . . . none of us will . . . until your last breath. For we change, Hunter. We become.

We transform. Every hunt, born again into something new. Until we can hunt no more."

I looked up, trying to see his eyes. The brim of his hat was in the way, and the shadows beneath were deep. Nonetheless, I felt the weight of his gaze.

"Why *are* you here?" I asked him.

He released me, the tendrils of his hair lingering against my bald head, then the scar below my ear. Zee grabbed my hand, and tugged.

"Memories," he rasped. "Truths you need."

"Truths about our Lady," Oturu said, with reverence, "whose path you follow."

"My ancestor," I said, with dread. "Am I so much like her?"

Oturu tilted his head, the brim of his hat so low it almost shadowed his mouth. Once again, his hair floated toward my face. Such delicate twisted fingers.

He stopped, just before he touched me. "We would know her heart. We would know her soul, no matter where it sung. Just as we knows yours. You are not her, Lady Hunter, except in all the ways that matter. Your heart. Your power."

I listened for the darkness with that inner ear always tuned to my soul. Heard nothing. So quiet I might have imagined I'd never felt occupied, hijacked, possessed: something crawling through me, turning everything I touched to ash.

And me, enjoying it. *Me.* Not just that thing.

Power is its own pleasure, murmured the voice. *But the power over life and death—*

Stop, I told it. *I'm not listening.*

You could save so many. You could do so much. Protect earth from the Aetar. Stop wars. Make peace.

I didn't know if those were my thoughts, or the force inhabiting me, but they hit too close to home.

I rubbed my mouth, wishing I had water to rinse, spit. I tasted the grit of ash between my teeth. "What truths?"

"You have been told that she, our Lady, merely lost her mind. But that is not the whole truth. She did not begin that way. Her intentions were good. As yours would be."

My intentions terrified me. "How did it begin, then?"

"Betrayal," Oturu said, and the boys closed their eyes, as one. "That is what you need to know. She was betrayed, for nothing more than living."

"Because she was feared."

"Because *they* tired of her. Tired of watching. Tired of the possibilities of danger." Oturu twisted, arching backward, his swirling cloak rising until I saw the tips of his dagger feet, floating upon the leaves. "We will show you, Hunter. She would have wanted you to see."

I heard the warning, I felt it, but I was too slow.

A coiled fist of hair snaked out, fast as a whip, and hit the scar below my ear. Pain flashed. White light. I heard thunder and screaming, and a howl like wolves wedded to wind. I fell backward, I fell and fell—

—and bled into an endless river into another world.

No transition. No explanation. I didn't land, I didn't hurt myself, but I felt the movement, and I felt the stillness when I stopped moving.

I opened my eyes. Found myself sprawled on wet grass, hands and feet bound. Mouth gagged.

It was so real. I could smell rain in the air, and smoke. I felt the boys on my skin, raging as I had never felt them rage—with a viciousness and wild hunger that poured through me like my guts were being soaked in bile and acid.

I was surrounded. Three men. One woman.

The woman had wings. She was tall and pale, and reminded me of the Messenger, with her red hair and long neck. A silver torc rested heavily on her jutting collarbone, the braided ends embedded with turquoise. Her wings were the color of pearls.

Beside her towered a man with one enormous eye in the center of his forehead, a man of monstrous height, with hands so large just one of them could have spanned my waist twice around. He crouched, staring at me, his rubbery mouth turned down in a frown. "This is not right."

"This is survival," said the winged woman. "We cannot take the risk."

"The Hunter has done *nothing*. She is our ward. Some call her *friend*. If the others find out—"

"If you tell them, you may join her," snapped the other two men, voices blending together in odd harmony. Twins. Long black beards, rubies embedded in their brows, and dressed in armor that shivered with plates of obsidian. "Or do you prefer to suffer this burden for the rest of our eternal lives?"

"We were given a task—"

"—and we are fulfilling it," said the woman imperiously, her wings flaring. "While the demons cover her skin, she is ever immortal. She will never die in that place we send her. She will never be killed. The prison of her bloodline *will* hold."

"What of us, then?" boomed the giant, forehead wrinkling around his unblinking eye. "What you suggest is not worthy of our hearts. Or our creation. We were not made for this task. Our gods would not permit it. This is damnation."

"And so she is damned to the Wasteland," said the twins, their voices hoarse. "And may we be as well, but it must be done."

The giant turned away, the grind of his boots loud as thunder. "By condemning her, we condemn one of us."

"There can be no comparison. None. You know that."

"If we told the others—"

"No. The secret is ours. Our Aetar Masters put the burden on us to know the truth of what she is. What all those of her bloodline are." The woman crouched, wings sweeping around her like a soft cloak.

I tasted tears, salty and hot, and suffered a sob not my own that rose with furious power. The boys raged.

"Hunter," said the winged woman, her cold beauty like ice. "Hunter, this must be done. You are too dangerous. What you carry on your skin . . . too terrible a threat. If any of your bloodline were to die before bearing a child, if the veil should fall . . ."

The woman looked away, wings dragging through the wet grass. "I *am* sorry, sweetling. More than you know. You will *never* forgive us."

"But at least we will never hear you scream," said the twins; and I watched in horror as they kicked my body, so hard I rolled.

The giant cried out, lunging, but he could not reach me. I fell. I fell. I fell, and darkness swallowed.

And no one heard me scream.

No one. No one heard me.

Until, abruptly, I felt hands stroking my hair.

I tasted pine needles on my tongue and closed my mouth.

I heard twin voices humming in my ears, and when I moved my legs, they were unbound, as were my hands.

"Betrayal," Oturu said, again. I barely heard him.

Zee made a hissing sound. Dek and Mal trembled around my neck. I couldn't see Raw or Aaz, but I felt them close, and heard cracking sounds, like, their knuckles flexing.

I rolled over and sat up, slowly. My head hurt. I was dizzy. The boys held me steady, and I swallowed hard to keep from vomiting.

"What was that?" I asked, hoarse.

"Memories," said Oturu. "Memories our Lady gave us."

"Felt so real." I closed my eyes. "And those others. They were Wardens."

"Created by the Aetar, the Avatars, to serve at their pleasure. And their pleasure was to watch our Lady. Our Lady, who trusted them."

I shivered. "The place they threw her . . ."

I couldn't finish. My skin crawled.

"You know it," Oturu whispered. "You have been inside that winding maze, and walked the dark path. But only you emerged into the light, intact. When *she* stumbled free . . ."

He also stopped. I felt cold, and looked at Zee. "The Wardens threw my ancestor into the Wasteland."

Zee bowed his head, shoulders sagging. "No one knows. Not the Wolf, not anyone. Not even all Wardens. Just some. Bad some."

"And, what? They thought putting her there would . . . take care of the problem? Keep you five from ever breaking free?"

"It might have worked," said Oturu. "She should not have freed herself. Just as you should not have."

"I found a body in that place. I know it was hers."

"That was later." Oturu's hair flared wildly around his body. "She chose her death. To protect her daughter from her madness."

I lay back down, staring at the night sky. Zee crawled close and tucked himself under my arm. So did Raw and Aaz. They smelled like butter, and their claws were greasy.

"She lost parts of herself," whispered Oturu. "Her time in the Wasteland brought her closer to what slept within. Too close, in the end."

"She wanted revenge."

"Justice."

I took a deep breath and let it out, slowly. "She's the reason all the Wardens disappeared. Why there's no one left but our bloodline. She killed them all."

No one denied it, but Raw and Aaz gave each other uncertain looks that made me wonder what else there was to know. I would have asked, but Zee gripped my hand, tugging. "Many feared old mother. But her heart . . . her heart was made of iron and honey."

"She still went crazy. None of you deny that. She hurt people."

"The power was too much. What began as righteousness became something else." Oturu bowed his head, his hair and cloak going very still. "We remained with her, even when the hunt soured. We were her friend. All her secrets, she gave to us. Some will remain with us. But she was afraid that what destroyed her would arise again."

"This thing inside me. She found it by accident. I was born already close to it."

Oturu's hair flared and twisted, writhing upward like black flames.

"As was your mother," he said.

"My mother," I replied, as Raw and Aaz made tiny choking sounds. Zee refused to look at me. Dek and Mal quit purring.

"She summoned us. She had questions about our Lady of the Hunt, about her madness, and those who betrayed her."

I closed my eyes.

"Your mother had just come from the Labyrinth. She was heavy with you."

The darkness stirred beneath my heart. A tremble, a faint heaving. I did not push it down. I floated around that force, cold and calm, observing it with a dispassionate inner eye that was removed from fear and pain, or any human emotion. I existed. So did it. We were together.

I was finally, irrevocably, numb.

Oturu towered over me, immense and stark, his cloak flaring wildly. "Hunter. There is something else."

I did not move. I was going to rest here until I grew roots. Dek and Mal wrapped their tails, loose and warm, around my throat, and hummed a faint riot of Bon Jovi's "Keep the Faith." The other boys pressed against my legs and waist, holding my hands. Brave little soldiers.

I watched a long tendril of Oturu's hair sink into the abyss of his billowing cloak, which was not mere cloth but made of shadows that seemed to be pockets of other spaces—perhaps the void I traveled through when traveling from here to there—or something different: energy and flesh and other dimensions colliding to create Oturu.

He had told me he was the last of his kind. I wanted to know why. Maybe I would have asked, except I looked closer at his cloak and saw faces skimming the surface, fleeting outlines of contorted heads pressing outward from the abyss, mouths open in silent screams.

I saw a face I recognized.

Tracker.

Looking at him reminded me of a horror movie—his face, the abyss molded to his features, slick as oil and crawling down his mouth. I didn't know if he could see me. I reached out, ready to try and pull him free. Zee grabbed my arms, stopping me.

"Leave be," he muttered.

I tried to shake him off, but he refused to let go. I attempted to speak, and my voice broke. On my second try I managed a hoarse, "What are you doing to him?"

Oturu tilted his head, contemplating me. "You feel pity."

"He's in agony. All those people are. You have no right."

"We have every right. There are reasons."

"Reasons—" I began, but Zee's grip tightened, and he gave me a warning look.

"Justice," he said. "Justice and promises."

I shut my mouth.

Oturu's hair slipped free of the churning shadows inside his cloak. Clutched within the dark tendrils was a small stone disc the size of my palm. Simple concentric lines had been etched into its surface, and even in the night, it glimmered with a translucence that burned from within. I stopped breathing when I saw it, my heart lurching like it wanted to tick-tock its way right out of chest, or into my stomach.

Seed ring. A fragment of the Labyrinth, like the armor on my hand. Only, a seed ring stored memories, an imprint of souls: energy, leaving a permanent etching of a life. I had been told this seed ring was small, capable of holding only a year's worth of memories. A year. To capture the essence of an entire existence.

This one had belonged to my mother—and it held her life. She had left it to Jack to pass on if I ever found him. Relying on fate—or perhaps a future she'd already known would come to pass.

I'd found my grandfather. I had used the seed ring to see some of my mother's memories. But I'd been forced to give it to Oturu for safekeeping.

I held out my hand. My fingertips were cold. Homesickness filled me, desperate and overwhelming, until it was hard to breathe. "Thank you for bringing this back to me."

Oturu held back the disc. "You must take care. The last time you held the seed ring, you left this time for another. You traveled where you must not."

Four times now. Four times I'd traveled through time. Four times breathing the same air as women who were dead.

"Nothing happened," I told him. But that was a lie. I had never said much, those few times I had found my mother and grandmother—but maybe I had traveled more than I yet realized.

Maybe my *mother* had known more than I realized about the life I would face. A life still in my future.

A life she had tried to prepare me for.

Oturu still withheld the seed ring. "If you are not careful, you will tear time again. The seed ring has no power, but what you wear on your hand is what you must fear." His hair coiled through the air and brushed against my armored right hand. "Labyrinth-born and hewn," he said softly, his mouth hardly moving. "Crafted from ore mined in the heart of the maze."

"A key to any door, in any time and place," I said, remembering his words, from before.

"A key that reflects the desires of its bearer," Oturu finished, then, even more quietly: "You must be trained to control your thoughts. You cannot be left long with such power. Not with the hunt at hand, or what sleeps within you. Not without control."

"The hunt," I said, ignoring the rest. "Do you know about the demons I encountered?"

"We felt them." Oturu's hair twitched, a violent, lashing motion. "We remember the Mahati when they were free. They do not hunt to become reborn in death but merely to breed pain."

"They want me, as the vessel of the Reaper Kings, to lead them."

The corner of his mouth curved. "Will you be their Queen?"

You already are, said that deep voice, from the darkness.

I shut my eyes. Zee murmured, "Maxine."

Whether you choose to be, whether they are fools not to believe.

Silken hair caressed my brow.

As there were Kings, now there is a Queen.

"The veil is open," Oturu said, in his hushed voice. "And so the dreamer speaks."

"I wish it would shut the fuck up." I rubbed my face, feeling cold, and very alone. "It's ridiculous. Even the idea of it is crazy. I won't lead them."

Oturu's mouth still held that hint of a smile. "Why not?"

Zee hissed at him. I stared. "They'll hurt people."

"When the veil falls, they will do that anyway." Oturu tilted his head. "With the veil now cracked, they will begin. Someone must control them. If not you, then one of their own. Who do you trust more, to be the leader of the hunt?"

I tore my gaze from him, looking down at Zee, Raw, and Aaz. All three demons crouched very still, staring at their feet. Dek and Mal were quiet.

"You five," I whispered. "I still can't believe it."

"Another life, another dream," Zee rasped, closing his eyes. "What entered us, we became. Only because we knew no other dream."

I knelt in front of him. "This thing inside me now . . . entered you? Possessed you?"

"That is too simple," Oturu murmured. "There are no words to describe what inhabits your soul. What inhabited theirs."

I flashed him a hard look. "How come you're the expert?"

He stilled. Zee gave him a mournful look. All the boys did.

"We will not tell you," he said, his voice so faint I could barely hear him. "We will not."

I wished I could see his eyes, but the quieted movements of his hair and cloak told a story, as did the pain in his voice. Enough to make me look away and murmur, "Fair enough."

I extended my hand again. After a brief hesitation, his hair lowered the seed ring into my palm.

I did not disappear. No explosions. Nothing wild. I held the disc in my hand and wondered if this was the same as holding my mother's hand—not that we'd ever done much of that after I turned eight. I still wanted to be a kid again, little, when she was the one bearing the world.

How much did you bear? I wondered silently, thinking of my mother, and what Oturu had said.

I traced those concentric lines with the tip of my finger. The armor tingled. I stayed in control. My finger wound closer to the center of the disc. Zee and the boys did not move.

I touched the center.

Nothing happened.

I wasn't sure why I had assumed something would. Hope, maybe. My mother had left me the seed ring for a reason, and if she had known about the big dark secret of our bloodline, and if she had been in the Labyrinth—then perhaps there was something else I needed to know. Something that could help me.

Or just make me feel better.

I looked at Zee, who shrugged. Raw and Aaz watched with large eyes. At some point they'd managed to pull a giant tub of fried chicken from the shadows and were eating from it with a nervousness that made me want to curl up beside them for a leg.

I tucked the seed ring into my vest pocket. "Last words of advice?"

"There is no saving yourself from what is coming." Oturu drifted close. "We came not to save you. But to ease you."

His cloak flared, and the tangled tendrils of his long black hair flowed around my body like the first threads of a cocoon.

"You are not alone," he whispered.

Not alone. Not alone against an army. Not alone against the expectation that I would somehow hurt the world. Not alone, in living.

I touched my chest and felt my heart beat. Such an ordinary human thing.

The second heartbeat was not so ordinary.

Just out of sync with mine. Quiet, strong.

Grant. I imagined his voice in the wind, and when I closed my eyes, I saw him as silver light, and golden, and the sun, pouring like a river from the night into my chest.

"Ah," Oturu murmured. "Ah, young Queen."

He sounded wistful, and for some reason that saddened me. Maybe it meant I was an idiot, too, but I didn't care. I had broken all the rules I was raised on. I *was* a broken rule.

But I was still me. Maxine Kiss. No horns on my head. No fire on my breath. I'd wake up tomorrow and still love music from the eighties, and hot chocolate, and the rain. I'd love cowboy boots and Clint Eastwood movies, and steaks so rare they could lumber off the plate. I would still miss my mother, and I would still love the boys, and I would find some way to make a life with the man living so strong in my heart.

You're naïve, I told myself. *You're fucked.*

All the way, replied another part of me. *I wasn't raised to stop living.*

I reached for a strand of Oturu's floating hair, wrapped it around my fist, and kissed it.

He froze. I said, "Thank you, friend."

"Always," he murmured, bowing his head. "Forever."

CHAPTER 15

I had walked for hours to reach the spot in the pine forest. I didn't want to wait that long to get back to the farmhouse. I tapped my right fist against my chest and slipped into the void.

I found myself, moments later, beside my mother's grave. Grant was there, seated in the grass. I couldn't see his face, just his back. His clothes were rumpled. No one else around. Clear sky, stars, and the oak leaves whispering in the breeze. I saw lights on in the house, and Zee, the others, huddled together to stare at the grave.

Grant was singing, very softly. I didn't recognize the melody, but it rose and fell with the wind, and seemed to scatter light like falling stars when I closed my eyes to listen.

Raw and Aaz hugged his stretched legs, resting their cheeks upon his knees. He leaned forward and patted their heads.

I watched that, and I watched him. Imagining myself as

the woman I had been yesterday, before the blood and pain, and those terrible truths. Remembering pie, and laughter, and candles burning.

I felt unsteady as I walked to Grant. I sat carefully beside him on the grass. He finally looked at me, and stopped singing—last note hanging in the air. We stared at each other a long time. I searched his face for fear, but his only signs of stress were a deepening of the lines in his brow, and around his mouth, which made him look grim.

"Small part of me was afraid you weren't coming back," he said.

"I shouldn't have." My fingers dug into my jeans. "I hope you haven't been out here all this time."

He didn't say anything. Just leaned over to slide his hand around my neck, and kissed me. It should have been awkward. His mouth didn't land exactly where it should, but his lips found mine, and it felt so natural to kiss him back, so warm, like I was coming out of a snowy night into a golden home.

Grant pulled away, just a little, his breathing rough as mine. I wanted to speak but couldn't. No words. No voice.

"You don't remember that, do you?" he said. "Me . . . kissing you."

I brushed my lips over the corner of his mouth, savoring his scent: cinnamon and sunlight, and everything warm. I glanced down, at his hands. Strong-looking, with long, lean fingers. I wanted to hold his hands, and soothe them, and touch his wrists and arms. I wanted to lean against his chest and listen to him breathe. I remembered those things, but they seemed very far away and new—a thousand years, another life.

My mouth twitched. "What I don't remember is how that first kiss in your stairwell ever convinced me to stick around."

Grant stilled, staring. "Really. You don't remember that."

"Not at all," I said. "And I don't remember that danger-ous duet we planned at your piano—"

"A sonata," he interrupted.

"—or that magic line of yours—"

"I want to take you to my bed." His voice was low, strained, and an ache roared through me from my heart down, as he kissed me with impossible gentleness, barely a touch on the lips that I felt in my toes.

"You remember," he said, against my mouth.

"Some things." I closed my eyes, stroking my lips over his jaw, trailing my fingers down his strong, lean throat. "More and more."

He hauled me into his lap and buried his face in the crook of my neck. His arms were incredibly strong, but tremors rolled through him, and the sound of his breathing was occasionally rough.

He held me like that, saying nothing—saying every-thing—for a very long time.

⊰⊱

THE farmhouse was quiet. I didn't see the Messenger, but Jack sat in the kitchen, at the table, staring at the blood-stain on the floor. I couldn't breathe when I saw that and fumbled for Grant's hand. He pulled me close, then led me back outside to the porch.

I had to lean against the rail. "I can't hate him. No matter what I hear, no matter what he holds back from me . . . all those secrets, all the things he's done . . . I still love him."

"He loves you," Grant said. "I can't begin to understand his kind, but he loves you, Maxine. He loved your mother. He loved your grandmother."

I pressed my face against the old wood column, flakes of peeling paint floating down to the porch boards. Dek chirped, licking the back of my ear. "Of all the Hunters in my bloodline, why Jean Kiss? Why did he fall in love with her?"

"You're not all the same, you know." Grant leaned close, his chest warm against my back. "Maybe you look similar, but you're different women."

I thought of Jack, sitting in the kitchen, staring at the spot where his daughter had died. "He'll outlive us all. It'll be the blink of an eye, compared to the rest of his life."

"No, it won't. Not a blink." Grant covered my hand with his, winding our fingers together. "Time is relative. And relative to a million, ten million years, what he had and lost with your mother, grandmother, and you, will last much longer."

"He's alone," I said. "Out of all of us, he's the most alone."

Grant sighed. "Come on. Let's walk."

"Where's the Messenger?"

"Upstairs in a bedroom, last I checked. Staring at the walls."

"You left her alone with Jack."

"She's not going to hurt him. Or take him." Grant rubbed the back of his neck, looking uncomfortable. "She's engaging in a period of self-reflection."

"Right," I said slowly. "What does that mean, exactly?"

"Free will." Grant tugged me into the yard. "Let's go."

I allowed myself to be pulled toward the barn. "You act like you live here."

"I listen when you talk. And you've talked so little about this place, I listened very hard when you did. Plus, I had time to look around. I was curious about where you grew up."

"I didn't grow up here."

He glanced at me. "You tell people you're from Texas. Must feel a little like home."

"I was born here. In that house." I watched Raw and Aaz tumble through the shadows ahead of us. "Zee delivered me."

Grant stumbled a little. "Wow."

"I know."

The barn hadn't held an animal larger than a cat or mouse in over a hundred years, and my mother had always kept it swept and clean. The old station wagon was parked inside.

I ached when I saw it. Trailed my hands down the dusty brown hood and stared through the windshield at the front seat. I could almost see my mother behind the wheel, and me, beside her, in pigtails and overalls, and my little red cowboy boots. Ghosts, in my mind.

Even the boys were reverent, licking the metal and pressing their cheeks against the doors. Dek and Mal sang the melody to "I'm So Lonesome I Could Cry," and Grant joined in counterpoint, his voice soft, sad.

The doors were locked, but Aaz flitted through the shadows and opened the car from the inside. A musty leather and plastic smell wafted out. I thought about sliding into the driver's seat, but stopped at the last moment and climbed into the back. I slid over to make room for Grant. Paper crunched underfoot. It was dark inside the car, but my eyesight was good at night, and I glimpsed maps, hotel pamphlets, loose-leaf drawings made with crayon and markers. Old memories. We had stopped driving this car when I was ten and parked it here. My mom and I had never cleaned it out.

I picked up one of the drawings and smoothed out the paper on my leg.

"I'm putting that on the refrigerator," Grant said.

I smiled, tracing my finger over five sharp splotches with red eyes, set in the middle of oversized purple flowers that were almost as tall as the stick figure with long black hair that had "mommy" written underneath and towered over the second figure, which was just a head and legs and two jutting arms with hearts for hands. I'd written "me" to the side.

Dek and Mal slithered down my arms to examine the drawing. I let them give it a good long look, then leaned forward to place it carefully on the front seat. I glimpsed old cassette tapes, more papers, a knife or two—and then slid back to sit beside Grant.

"This was home," he said.

"For most of my childhood. We'd sleep in the back sometimes. I was little. Mom made it fun, and the boys always brought me things." Zee poked his head from the shadows at my feet, and I stroked his spiky hair. "I think that's when they got into teddy bears."

"Soft and huggable," Zee rasped, and fled back into the shadows. Grant laid his arm over my shoulders and pulled me close. It was strange, sitting in this car with him. But it felt right, too. Even though my memories still seemed far away, even though it was impossible to catalog our two years all at once, it was enough that I felt the weight of that history between us. Anchoring me.

"I saw Oturu," I said, quietly, and told him everything. About my mother, my ancestor. I unburdened myself, and he didn't say a word until I was done.

"That's a lot to take in," Grant said.

"I don't think I've processed it. I'm not certain I believe."

"You believe. The difference is that you know yourself, the parts that matter. You're strong. You love the boys. What

Jack and those demons told you is superficial compared to that."

"Superficial," I echoed, with a bitter smile. "Reaper Kings. End of the world."

"Superficial," he said again, with particular gentleness, and poked Zee with his foot. The little demon was eaves-dropping on the floor. All the boys were in the car. I smelled popcorn and beer, and listened to Raw and Aaz behind us, chewing loudly.

"What do you think?" Grant asked Zee. "Seeing as how you're the other half of this."

"Other half of light," Zee whispered.

The other side of dreaming, added that lithe voice in my mind, each word making the darkness stir and uncoil a little more beneath my skin. A chill rolled through me. My sight wavered. All I could see, for a moment, was my dream of being inside the belly of the wyrm, surrounded by swallowed stars.

But there are things we have never known.

"Maxine," Grant said.

I blinked, and the world returned. I just wasn't certain *I* was still in the world. One foot out of it, maybe. Everything felt so distant.

"I'm tired," I told him, which wasn't exactly a lie. The moment I said the words, I suffered a weariness that was soul-deep, destructive. I wondered what it would feel like finally to give up, to just lie down and die. I wasn't certain I had the energy for anything else.

Grant's jaw tightened, and he pulled me into his lap, holding me close. I leaned against him, my cheek pressed to his chest, breathing in the scent of cinnamon, soaking in his heat. Dek and Mal purred.

"Come on," he said roughly, kissing the top of my bald head. "Don't hurt."

I thought of my ancestor, with ropes around her ankles and hands. Thrown into a hole, like garbage, to spend an eternity buried alive. My mother, pregnant and on her own. If she had dealt with this same darkness that was inside me, never speaking a word . . .

I buried my face even tighter against Grant's chest.

"You're scared," he breathed. "Maxine."

"I'm scared of being alone," I told him, hardly able to get the words out. Unable to hold them in.

His arms tightened. "That's nothing to be ashamed of."

"It is. You don't understand."

He laughed, but it was a coarse, wet sound, verging on grief. "I was never lonely until I met you, Maxine. I wasn't lonely until I realized what life would be like without you."

My fingers dug into his shirt. "Don't say that."

He stilled, staring at me. Silent such a long time I felt uneasy.

"Zee," he said finally, softly. "Get the hell out of here. Take the others with you."

Zee didn't argue. He snapped his claws. Dek and Mal chirped, licked my ears, and faded into the shadows. A deep silence replaced Raw and Aaz's chewing.

"Now, listen," I said, but Grant shook his head, jaw tight, eyes glittering with that odd golden light.

"*You* listen," he said, and kissed me hard on the mouth.

Heat burst through my chest, wildness rising inside me, filled with dizzying hunger. I twisted Grant's shirt in my hands, pressed so tightly against him I could feel every hard line of his body. Felt like years, a lifetime, since I had been so close to him; and there was a small part of me that weighed each second and sensation, holding it up against the rest of my life.

Grant broke off the kiss and grabbed my hand to hold

against his chest. I felt his heart pounding beneath my palm, and he smoothed his thumb over my cheek, the corner of my mouth. Both of us, trembling. "Listen to me. Listen to how much I need you. And don't you dare . . . don't you dare, Maxine, tell me I shouldn't say how much I love you."

He kissed me again, gently. When he pulled away, I followed, sensing words on his tongue. I kissed him hard, afraid of what he would say, and he sighed against my mouth and held me so tightly I couldn't breathe. So tight that if the world fell, he'd still be holding me.

I wanted to hold him that tightly. I wanted to show him the heartache he eased, how full I felt, simply being in his arms. I wanted him to know he was my home. It seemed more important than ever that he know that—because I hadn't known it. I had forgotten. And the enormity of that loss stole my breath away.

Grant pushed me down on the car seat, tossing his cane on the floor. I forced my hands to unclench from his shirt, sliding them down his hard stomach to the waist of his jeans. His skin was hot. Muscles tight.

Grant made a small sound, his hands touching me in fleeting motions that felt as breathless as he sounded—and if I died a hundred, thousand years from now, I didn't think I would ever forget the way he looked at me.

"Your eyes," I murmured.

"What about them?" Grant slid his hand under my sweater, resting his large palm on my stomach, then higher, on my breast. I arched into his touch, sighing, and swallowed my words. I couldn't tell him. I couldn't tell him how it made me feel, to be looked at with such naked hunger and grace.

Maybe he knew. He slid off my vest and pulled my sweater over my head. I shivered, fumbling with his jeans,

both of us moving faster, urgency making us rough. I
needed him. I needed him so badly.

Clothes off, pushed aside, tangled. His skin was hot and
hard, and we rolled over so that he lay on his back, his bad
leg hanging off the seat. I couldn't think, couldn't speak;
all I could do was touch him, sliding down until my mouth
caressed his inner thighs, and then higher, higher, sucking
gently on the tip of his thick hard shaft, my hands wrapping
tight around him, stroking.

Grant cried out, hips bucking upward, pushing himself deeper into my mouth. His hands slid across my head
and shoulders, and he sat up, breathing raggedly, trying to
reach my breasts. I teased him with my tongue, then slid
up against his body, closing my eyes as his fingers sank
between us, touching me hard, then soft, his mouth never
leaving mine.

I reached between us, too, and guided the tip of him
against me, holding him there, rubbing. Grant strained, his
expression pure agony. I kissed his throat, tasting the salt
of his sweat, suffering the most excruciating pleasure as I
pushed my hips down hard against him. He filled me to the
point of pain, then everything eased, and we began moving
against each other hard and fast.

Somehow, we rolled over so that he was on top of me,
half-kneeling off the seat. I hooked my leg around him as
he pushed deeper, harder, driving into me with a relentlessness that made me cry out with every sharp thrust. He
didn't ease up as I came, only clutched me tight in one arm,
still moving inside me as he reached down between us to
touch me, just so, just right. I climaxed again, digging my
nails into his back, and finally he let go with a wordless
shout, his hips jerking so hard, so long against me, I came
one last time.

He collapsed on top of me, and I loved it. I loved feeling him exhausted, and I loved being exhausted, like this: pressed to him, feeling his heartbeat shuddering against mine as something passed between us—light or energy— until the glow I imagined inside my chest burned white-hot, bathing the coiled spirit stirring lazily in its dreams.

"You're my sunrise," Grant murmured against my throat. "Always. No matter what happens, just remember that."

I ran my fingers through his thick hair. "Speaking to the girl who had amnesia."

He groaned. "Don't. I didn't think I could take it. It killed me when you looked at me like I was a stranger."

"I can only imagine that I was trying to protect you." I held his hand against my chest. "Our bond . . . the energy you take from me . . . you realize, don't you, what you're drawing from? The boys said this thing inside me is the worst part of them, and it's going to get free. It's going to change me. And if you're there, too—"

"I love how you always underestimate me."

"Do not."

Grant raised himself up on his elbows and gave me a long, steady look. "You can't make everything right. Sometimes, you just have to let go, and have a little faith that the world will keep spinning, and the sun will rise, and that life will be okay."

"It won't," I said. "It can't."

"Which part?" Grant ran his hand through his hair, tugging hard, a little something wild in his eyes. "I know it wasn't *just* protecting me that made you run. You were afraid of something else. I've never seen you so afraid, inside."

"Because I'll lose you," I said, without thinking. "I love you, and I'll lose you. Nothing keeps. Not in my life. Not *even* my life. And it'll be my fault."

And my life is cheaper than my heart.

I tried to sit up. Grant placed his hand on my shoulder, holding me down. "It's not your fault your mother died."

"She died because of me."

"The boys transferred their protection. If you're going to blame anyone—"

"Don't," I said sharply, feeling tight and cold on the inside. "She could have had more time."

Grant stilled, staring into my eyes with that look he got, sometimes, when he saw too deep.

"More time for you," he said. "More time for you to figure things out."

I looked away, stung. "I never appreciated her. I loved her, but I was angry with her so much. I hated our life. I hated it so much that we never had a home. I hated this car we lived in. I hated that I never could be alone. I hated all the violence and knowing . . . knowing I didn't have a choice because *that's the way things were*. I hated it all; and then she died." I forced myself to meet his gaze. "I didn't have time to tell her I loved her. I couldn't even tell her thank you for being my mother. I didn't understand. I thought I did, but I didn't. I didn't understand what she'd gone through, everything she protected me from, until it was *me*."

"She knows you loved her. She *knows*, Maxine."

I drew in a deep, shuddering breath. "Everything I have here . . . everything about you . . . is all I ever wanted. But that was . . . I had those dreams before she died. After that . . . I stopped wanting. I stopped. I just . . . did what I was supposed to. And I told myself it was what I wanted."

Grant wrapped his arms around me, pulling me gently against his chest. His warmth soaked through my muscles, like I was drowning in sunlight; and he hummed a brief note that soared and rumbled into my chest, in the pulse that matched my own heart.

"You never told me any of this," he murmured.

I wiped my nose on the back of my hand, but the tears still flowed. "I didn't let myself think about it."

He was silent a moment. "There's nothing I can tell you to make it better, Maxine. Except that things change. You can't . . . let what happened make you believe that what you want is wrong."

I covered his hand, stroking his warm fingers. "You always have an answer for everything."

"You love that about me."

"Big ego, too."

"Humble as pie. Sensibilities of a lamb."

I grabbed his ear, dragging his head toward mine. Grant cupped my throat with his large hand.

"If you had forgotten *and* left me," he began, but I stopped him with a deep kiss. Grant stretched on top of me. I loved the weight of him. I loved the heat of his hands cupping my face, then my hip, spanning my waist, and his thumb brushing the bottom of my breast. My eyes and cheeks felt sticky with tears, but he didn't seem to mind.

He was kissing my breast—and I was enjoying it *very* much—when Zee appeared in the front seat, red eyes glowing with agitation.

I froze. So did Grant.

"Maxine," Zee rasped. "Trouble."

CHAPTER 16

I heard the shouts all the way to the barn. I ran, Grant behind me, with the boys racing like wolves through the shadows around us.

I burst through the front door and saw Jack first. Alive, seemingly unharmed.

And then I looked past him, at the Messenger.

She stood in the center of the room, tall and pale, all sharp angles that were male and female, and alien. Her cheeks were wet, splotchy—her eyes bloodshot. She had been crying. Tears still leaked from her eyes. Naked, piercing, grief.

She had lifted the raw hem of her silken shirt. Long white scars covered her torso, and a razor-thin cord was wrapped around her waist, its very tip locked inside a slim handle—which she touched, carefully. The tip slid free, and the cord fell away from her body with a hiss. It looked as though it was made from crystal, and resembled a very short whip—until she flicked her wrist and the cord snapped into a needle-thin blade. Happened in the blink of an eye.

I grabbed my grandfather, intent on pulling him away, but he dug in his heels—his gaze never leaving the Messenger.

"Little bird," Jack pleaded, with utter heartbreak in his eyes. "Please, don't."

I thought she was going to attack him. I was certain of it, ready to tell the boys to kill her—but the Messenger bowed her head, steadied her grip on the weapon—and angled the blade over her own heart.

"No," Grant snapped, behind me. The Messenger looked at him—then settled her stricken, miserable gaze on Jack.

"Praise be your light," she whispered, and pushed the blade into her chest.

Unsuccessfully.

Her muscles strained. Everything about her, committed to running that blade through her body. But the tip pierced her clothing, and no farther.

Jack sighed. The woman shot him a desperate look.

"I must die," she breathed.

"No," Jack said, gently. "Your Maker built a command into your mind. You are incapable of suicide or self-harm."

She made an anguished sound and tried again. I edged past my grandfather, feeling Zee and Raw in the shadows on my right. Aaz prowled to my left, while Dek and Mal were quiet on my shoulders. Ready. Waiting.

"Stop," I said, feeling a disturbed sort of awe at the violent shift of her emotions. What I was seeing now ran closer to the woman I had first encountered in the loft—but a far cry from the robot who had stood earlier in this room, staring at walls. Something had snapped since then. All that self-reflection.

She looked at me—really looked—and hate flickered

through her eyes, a loathing that saddened me more than it frightened. She raised the blade in her hands, trembling, looking ready to drive it through my chest. I held up my hands—but not at her. Just to the boys, waiting so close, red eyes burning.

"Why are you doing this?" I asked her.

Her hand trembled violently, the blade glinting like ice. "Nothing is as it should be. Not even me."

I edged closer. "And how should things be?"

The Messenger made a strangled sound and swung the blade toward my face. Dek and Mal rose up like hissing cobras, shielding me—and the crystal shattered against their heads. Raw and Aaz swarmed around my feet, growling, and the woman gazed down at them and bared her teeth.

"Kill me," she said. "You tried before. I will not save myself this time."

"Don't," I told the boys, and looked the Messenger dead in the eyes. "I'm a contrary woman. Tend to do the opposite of what people want. You say death, I may just force you to live."

The Messenger stared at me with a look on her face that reminded me of the woman at the gas station—the woman with the pink sweater—who had looked so miserable, like someone had ground her down, destroyed her world. Uncanny, how much the two reminded me of each other.

"I opened the prison veil," she whispered. "I was careless, and misused the power given me by my Aetar Masters. That alone is a crime. But what I feel here"—she stopped, and touched her head—"is equally terrible. I have been compromised by doubt. I am worthless, now."

"No," Grant said, but I held up my hand and walked to the woman, so close I had to tilt back my head to look into her eyes.

"You *should* be compromised by doubt," I said. "You

should be afraid, and sick, and shaking with the enormity of the uncertainties in your world. But you should also be burning up with a desire to learn what is true. Because that's why you were sent here, isn't it? *To learn the truth.* And the truth, lady, is that a war is coming, the war is here."

The hunt, said that voice inside my head. *The hunt is at hand.*

I swallowed hard. "If you're so loyal to your Aetar Masters, then you'll stop being a coward who wants to die, and you'll suck it up and fight. Because those demons in the veil, after they're done with this world, they'll go looking for the ones who locked them up. And you *don't* want to know what they do to the Aetar you love so much."

The Messenger trembled. "You are one of them. You are worse. There are stories about you. I did not believe you could be the same woman, but it must be so. Covered in the bodies of our enemies. Wearing the key. You, who traveled the crossroads—yesterday on some worlds, and a million years ago on others. Time passes so oddly in the quantum rose. But she *also* killed the Aetar."

She gazed past me at Grant. "And you. I have hunted the wild ones, and watched the Makers steal their mouths and throw their skins in chains. But you . . . you are different. I saw the emblem on the old woman, and if you came from the Labyrinth with her, and others . . ."

She stopped, looking like she was going to be sick. "Your bloodline is tainted with the lives of many Aetar. Your family led *armies* against the gods."

She swung around, staring at me. "So, who is the real enemy? Who should I fight?"

I smiled. "Fight me, I'll kill you—and you'll save no one. Fight the demons, those demons in the veil, and you'll save billions, maybe more. *And* you might die. Since you're so eager for it."

I turned my back on her and walked to Grant and Jack, both of whom stared at me. I made a face at them. Dek and Mal began humming Elton John's "The Bitch is Back." I reached up and thwacked them gently on the heads.

Air moved against my scalp, gentle and soft. I glanced over my shoulder.

The Messenger was gone.

I let out a breath I hadn't known I was holding, but the tension only tightened in my shoulders. Grant leaned hard on his cane.

"I could have lived without that," Jack said, very softly.

"Do we need to go after her?"

"Not yet. She feels lost, and just *slightly* homicidal. But only toward the both of us." Grant raised his brow at me. "What was that, anyway? Tough-love therapy from hell?"

"Did *you* want to stand around all night trying to make her feel better?" I poked his chest. "Mr. 'I-opened-her-eyes' to a brave new world?"

Grant scowled. Jack rubbed his face. "It was my fault. She wanted to know why I was here, why I tolerated the both of you. When I tried to tell her the truth, that I was not a god, she . . ."

"Reacted badly," Grant finished. "You know, Jack, I'm all for truth. But for a man of your extremely advanced years, you show incredibly poor judgment sometimes.

"Or maybe," he added thoughtfully, studying Jack with an intensity that meant he was looking deep, very deep, "it's personal with you and her."

Unease flickered in Jack's eyes. Zee scratched his claws over his arms, then the floor, making new gouge marks beside the old ones that covered the wooden boards.

"Guilt rots, Meddling Man," he rasped. "How many hearts did you squeeze?"

Jack gave Zee a sharp look. "How many did you?"

Zee bared his teeth in a terrible smile. "Call *us* World Reapers, but you did same, with chains."

"I saved as many as I could," Jack whispered, and rubbed his brow. But his hands lingered, and he stood like that, shoulders hunched, not breathing, hiding his face.

"We run, and we run," he murmured, "but never far enough."

Zee closed his eyes. "The Labyrinth remembers."

Jack shuddered. I moved closer to Grant, and he moved closer to me, and our arms brushed, and though our hands did not touch, I felt like he was holding me up as much as I was holding him. It was good to have someone at my side. It was good.

"I remember *her*," Jack said, still hiding his face. "Our army had come to fight the Lightbringers, for no reason more than that they could kill us. They could kill us and keep us from the human population we so desperately wanted.

"So we threw made-men at them, waves and waves of men who had no hearts, no brains, nothing for the Lightbringers to grasp with their powers—and we did this for months, for years, until those poor guardians had drained the lives of their bondmates, then their own people, until there was no one left . . . and so they used their own lives to stand against us, and died for their efforts. I remember how black the skies were, how thick the mud, and how their voices raged in symphonies that burned the air. It was beautiful and awful, and we killed them. And then we stole their children."

Jack swayed. "Some I saved. There were nurses, soldiers. I gave them babies and sent them into the Labyrinth. I covered their trails. But I was watched. All of us watched each other. In one of the last battles, a baby girl was captured. The Messenger is her descendent."

I watched him, listening to everything he wasn't saying. "You were the one who had to turn that baby over."

He finally removed his hands from his face and looked at Grant, not me. His eyes were red-rimmed, his skin mottled.

"Yes," he said.

Grant stood very still, but there was a coiled quality to his posture even though he leaned hard on his cane. Gaze dark, cold, assessing. This couldn't be a surprise—we'd heard the watered-down version before—but it was one subject I always stayed away from. Partially for my own sake.

But Grant didn't say a word. Not to Jack. He released his breath and gave me a long, hard look.

"We need to close the hole in the veil."

Jack's mouth thinned into a grim line. "Lad—"

"You didn't say it was impossible," Grant interrupted sharply; then he took a breath, and, with strained calm, added: "We don't have a choice. Unless you want Maxine to turn into some . . . Reaper Queen."

"Sounds like a band," I said, trying not to let on how much it rattled me that he used that name. "I could start one with the boys. Like Jem and the Holograms, only better."

Raw and Aaz strummed some air guitar. Grant shook his head, rubbing his jaw. "Jack. It was done before, it can be done again. You manipulated energy, didn't you? That must be what the veil is made of, or else the Messenger wouldn't have been able to tear it open." Grant leaned close: focused, intense. "You can teach me. You can teach *her*. The Messenger. "

"Even if I could," said my grandfather hoarsely, "even if you understood the complexities . . . the power you would need is tremendous. Beyond anyone's reckoning."

Grant flexed his jaw, expression severe. And then, very

deliberately, he looked at me. I knew what he was thinking and shook my head.

"Too dangerous," I said. "No, you can't."

"What are the alternatives?" He grabbed my arm, not hard enough to hurt—but I felt his desperation, and anger. "You want to lead any army? You think you can *fight* one? If that's what you want, Maxine, I'll be there. But I'd rather find another way."

Another way to light, murmured the voice inside my mind. *Paths we have never traveled.*

I wanted to punch myself, as if that would stop the voice in my head. But instead I opened my eyes and found Grant watching me, so grim.

"We'll have to make a stand," he said, quietly. "Now or later. Pick your poison."

"No," Jack said.

I pressed my hand against my chest, feeling the weight inside, the coil. "You'll have what you need, Grant. Even if you don't, you're right. We have to try."

Jack clenched his fingers together, twisting them. "This has risks."

Grant placed his hand on my shoulder. "I'll take my chances with Maxine."

My grandfather pinched the bridge of his nose. "Fine. But I'll need something before we can start."

"Anything," I said.

"One of my bones," Jack replied.

❖

FROM the void, into a room filled with golden lamplight, the smell of coffee and chocolate chip cookies; the shine of the hardwood floor, and the thousands of books that lined the loft walls. The piano. The motorcycle. The Turkish rugs, scattered, along with teddy bears and knives, and empty bags of M&Ms.

The world had not fallen down. I was still standing.

So was home. So were the people I loved.

I took my pleasures where I could get them.

Jack's corpse was gone. Rex was down on his hands and knees, scrubbing the floor. Mary perched on the kitchen counter, still wearing my clothing—holding those butcher knives in her hands. I smelled bleach.

I was surprised to see the zombie. That, and the wildness of his aura took me off guard—frayed at the edges, fluttering as though a thousand little hearts were straining to break free. It was like seeing a demon suffer palpitations—or an imminent nervous breakdown.

Rex straightened quickly when we appeared in the room. He watched me, not the others.

I spread my hands. "Boo."

He did not relax. "Fuck you."

"Get in line," I said. "You know about the veil, don't you?"

Rex's aura flared wildly, then shriveled down to hug his human skin. "We all felt it. We felt *them.*"

"And yet you're cleaning blood off a floor instead of running."

Rex settled back on his heels and looked from me to Grant, who was standing quietly, watching us both. Mary joined him, her gaze fierce as she twisted her hands in an idle, graceful motion that made the knife blades reflect a lethal light.

Not a Lightbringer, but a soldier for them. Loyal to Grant's mother. The Erl-King had called the old woman an assassin. I remembered all of that when I looked at her.

"Safer around you both," Rex said gruffly, drawing my attention back to him. "And that skinner corpse was stinking up the place."

"He just doesn't want to admit that he likes us," Grant said. "Where's the body?"

"I'm a demon. I know people."

Grant stared at him. Rex said, "Fine. I stashed him in the tub."

Grant continued to stare. "We use that tub, you know."

"Good thing you're practically family." Rex glanced back at Jack. "I hope you appreciate this."

"I don't," said my grandfather, who walked through his dried blood toward the bedroom.

I followed him, watching the boys scatter, tumbling under the bed and through the shadows to drag out toys and food. Dek and Mal cheered when they saw the life-sized cardboard cutout of Bon Jovi.

But Zee sat on the bed, claws clasped, legs swinging as he stared at the bathroom. Solemn, thoughtful. A little uncertain.

Jack was already in the bathroom. The air smelled bad—like death. I glimpsed a wrinkled waxen hand hanging over the rim of the tub, and that was it. I stayed just beyond the door, standing at an angle that let me see the mirror—and Jack's reflection as he stared down at his former body.

"Life is too short," he said. "I liked that skin."

"I liked it, too," I told him, unable to speak above a strained whisper. I cleared my throat, and did a little better when I added, "You could have . . . made it immortal. Like you did Byron."

Jack sighed, leaning against the sink. "Byron was a mistake. And making skins immortal is a mistake. It's a peculiar prison, my dear. The Erl-King . . . he wore human bodies like new sets of clothing, and the ones he wanted to keep he placed on ice so they wouldn't rot without a life to keep them going. But even he didn't make them immortal. No one wants the same thing forever. Even my kind . . . change."

Jack gestured toward the tub. "If I wanted to move on with my life, what would I do with this skin if it never died? I took it from the womb. I am . . . him. Without me, there would be no mind, no will. He would exist in a comatose state. A long sleep, forever."

"Sleeping Beauty," I said.

My grandfather bent down and disappeared from the mirror's reflection.

I said, "You've never explained Byron. How he came to be."

"There were extenuating circumstances."

"Like what?"

"Like the boy was going to die. I saved his life."

Behind me, Raw snorted. I glanced at him and found the little demon watching Jack with narrowed eyes.

"I found him living in a cardboard box, Old Wolf. He's scared of men. I think he turned tricks to stay alive. Sounds to me like his immortal existence—which he *doesn't* recall—has been pretty miserable. If I were in his shoes, I think I might have preferred death."

"You weren't there. And hindsight is cruel. I did my best."

"And have you always slipped into Byron's skin after dying somewhere else?"

Jack did not say a word. Raw scratched himself, watching the bathroom. Zee still hadn't moved.

I edged closer and saw my grandfather's reflection in the mirror. He stood still, staring at his hands—an expression of incredible sadness on his face.

I wondered how many regrets he lived with. How many were too many, before the burden became too much to bear.

"Your kind fear going insane," I said softly. "You fear it so much. What *does* it feel like, being nothing but energy?

Do you think you'll just . . . fly apart . . . if you're not in-side a body?"

Jack said nothing. I leaned against the wall, pressing my forehead against the cool smooth surface. "You made yourself a way station, someone to go to between death and rebirth. That's what Byron is. What he's been, all these thousands of years. *Temporary* living."

Deep silence radiated from the bathroom. Until, in a very soft voice, Jack said, "That was never my intention. But there are some things that cannot be altered once done, no matter how much we wish otherwise."

Zee hopped off the bed and ventured closer to the bath-room, staring—I presumed—at the corpse in the tub.

"I remember," Zee rasped, rubbing his head. "I remem-ber killing."

I bowed my head, grieved. I couldn't see Jack anymore, but I heard his voice.

"It was to be expected," he said, gently. "You were pro-tecting her from me."

"Old Mother told us to," said the little demon, leaning hard against my legs. I stroked his head. "Protect the good heart."

"For it is the heart that leads," Jack murmured.

I heard the sounds of clothing being ripped. I started toward the bathroom door, and stopped. I really didn't want to know what was going on in there.

Grant peered into the bedroom. "Visiting hours?"

I heard a thump, followed by a low curse. Grant raised his brow, and limped close. "Do I want to know?"

"I'm not that brave. Are you?"

"That's what I have you for."

"I'm terrified," I replied, and heard a wet sucking sound inside the bathroom.

Grant winced. "That can't be good."

I walked to the door, Zee loping ahead of me. For a moment all I saw was the slender back of a teenage boy—sitting on the edge of the tub—and then I looked a little harder and saw that boy digging his fingers into the forearm of a corpse, trying to pull bone free from flesh. A sheet, thankfully, had been tossed over the rest of the body.

Which smelled. Really, really smelled.

I must have made a sound. Jack looked up—froze—and said, "This isn't what it looks like."

"It looks like you're mangling a dead man."

"Technically, I *am* the dead man, so I'm merely mangling myself." Jack grimaced. "I could use some help, though."

"In more ways than one." I walked into the bathroom. "Oh, God."

"Don't say it."

"Is that—"

"Yes. It's what I need."

I gritted my teeth, studying the bone tattoo that had been, literally, embedded in the old man's arm. I had seen it once before. It was the symbol of Father Lawrence's cult, it was the symbol that Jack used to signify my bloodline, it was a symbol of some future apocalypse—and it looked *exactly* like the scar beneath my ear.

"Why?" I managed, afraid I would vomit.

"Because I forget things," he said enigmatically.

Grant entered the bathroom. He didn't say anything. Neither did I. I turned around, pushed past him and Zee, and walked into the bedroom. I didn't stop there. I entered the living room, ignored Rex and Mary, and headed for the stairs that led to the rooftop garden.

It had stopped raining, but only just. I sloshed through puddles, past the giant planters filled with roses, and stood at the edge of the roof. Downtown Seattle glittered within the low-lying clouds, a concrete citadel of gray hearts. I could see the pallor, I could feel the gathering shadow, and it was everywhere, like the rain, or the ghosts in my breath every time I exhaled.

The winds were strong. My head felt cold. I'd forgotten, again, that I was bald. But almost as soon as I had the thought, Dek and Mal slithered over my scalp, gripping my ears and eyebrows—blocking the chill air. My little demon helmet.

Zee leapt onto the waist-high wall that lined the roof's edge. His eyes glowed, and the spikes of his hair rose and fell, gently, with each breath. I touched his hand, then kissed his brow.

"Would you know if any Mahati have come through the veil?" I asked him.

"None have flown," he answered, after a moment. "But feel them straining. Boil-like, with pus. Ha'an will not hold them long."

"You know him. You remember."

"Good honor." Zee thumped his chest. "Good fighter."

Dek and Mal chirped, as though in agreement. I patted their heads. "Why would you need to fight? What could possibly have stood against any of you? Maybe the Avatars could make creatures that put up a struggle, but—"

"Universe, large," he interrupted. "Labyrinth, larger. Armies not born with swords. Armies got to form. For a bigger need. Badder enemy."

I studied his eyes. "So what would scare a Reaper King?"

Zee stiffened. Dek and Mal shrank against my skull and, seconds later, trembled.

Inside me, deep, the darkness stirred. Lazy eye opening in my mind. I gripped the edge of the wall, trying to push it down—but the spirit, the creature, whatever it was, rose into my throat to rest upon my tongue.

"Some pain does not ease," it said, through me. *"Memories do not cease of what was lost."*

Zee glanced sideways, sharply. "Mistakes made. Too many. Like you."

"We gave what was asked."

"Took more. Stole."

"Saved you."

I clawed at my throat, feeling as though my head were made of glass, ready to break.

Zee grabbed my arm. "Give her, free."

"Let her make me."

Fuck it. I clenched my right hand into a fist and slammed it against my chest. White-hot light burst from the armor, sending a shock wave down to the bone, and beyond. I went blind, but in my head saw the vastness of night and listened to the rub of scales, and a hiss that was a sigh as great as the wind, and cold as some vast track of space beyond the light of stars.

We are beyond the stars, whispered the darkness, but it shuddered away into that nook within my soul, leaving me my voice, and control.

I sank to my knees. Zee crowded close, and Aaz was there, and Raw. Dek and Mal licked the backs of ears, but their purrs were ragged, weak.

"What," I asked slowly, "was that about?"

"History," Zee muttered. "Bad things."

"You fought another war before your conflict with the Aetar." I rubbed my throat. "This thing possessed you five. You weren't born with it. You let it in, because you thought you needed it."

Zee said nothing, but looked at the other boys. All of them, with their large eyes. Raw started sucking his claws—stopped—then started again.

"What was so terrible?" I whispered. "Who was the enemy?"

"Don't ask," Zee muttered. "Gone now. Gone."

I wanted to know. I needed to. But there was such pain in their faces, and loss. I couldn't bring myself to keep hammering them.

"Okay," I said. "So why doesn't this . . . force . . . just take me over, fully? Make me lead the army? Make me do whatever the hell it wants?"

"Not like that," Zee rasped helplessly. "Power *is*."

"Is what?" I wanted to shake him. *"Zee."*

"Told you," he said, with misery in his voice. "Choice."

I blew out my breath. "Right. Just like that."

"Always," Zee said. "Even us, we choose. Choose wrong, choose right, choose to hold our mothers, bright. We changed. Choices changed."

"Even with this . . . thing . . . inside you?"

Zee pressed his claws over my heart. "Takes as much you give."

I covered his hand. "What the fuck is it?"

Raw sucked his claws a little harder. Aaz closed his eyes. Dek, Mal, rested their chins against my ears and began massaging my scalp with their tiny claws.

"Old," Zee breathed.

Old. Powerful. Inside me.

I covered my face. "I need a drink."

Moments later, Aaz tapped my shoulder and pushed a cup into my hand. Not hot chocolate, this time. Hot cider, instead. Burned my mouth, but I sipped it down, trying not to shake.

Remember who you are, I told myself. *You're Maxine.*

I heard footsteps echoing up the stairs, all the way from the other side of the roof. The steady click of a cane accompanied that heavy tread.

Grant faltered when he saw me, but only in his gaze—deepening with that raw glint I knew so well: intense, thoughtful, not at all gentle. I recalled what it felt like to see that expression fresh, as a stranger would. Surreal sensation. Grant, I tended to forget, was an intimidating man.

"Hey," he rumbled. "What scared you?"

"Not even going to pretend?"

He grunted and settled down beside me with a wince. I handed him my hot cider, pulled his bad leg into my lap, and began massaging his thigh just above the knee. Raw scooted close to work on his calf, long claws searching out pressure points. Dek and Mal began humming Billy Joel's "She's Got a Way."

"This thing inside me," I said, slowly, "has a mind of its own."

Zee gave me a quick look. All the boys did. I pretended not to notice. There was more I could tell Grant, but not now. Not until I had time to think.

He knew I was holding back, though. I wasn't subtle. Instead of pressuring me, he leaned back against the wall, watching my face, sipping cider.

"It's wet down here," he said, with all the mildness of a man trying very hard not to be an ass.

"Rain," I replied. "What's up with Jack?"

His eyes narrowed. "Extraction completed. Raw helped, before disappearing."

He set down the cider and pulled out his mother's amulet. "Jack returned this."

I removed the seed ring from my vest pocket and held it up beside the amulet. The designs were different, but both objects blurred my vision, as though I was looking at 3-D art—only, without the glasses.

"Huh," Grant said.

"Want to take bets that the thing inside Mary—*and*

the bone that Jack removed from his arm—are also seed rings?"

He frowned, cradling the amulet in his hands. "I don't know how I feel about that. Memories are sacred. So are thoughts. I see them all the time. Sometimes . . . it'd be nice if I didn't. But if this is a seed ring, and some part of my mother, or someone else, is stored within . . ." He stopped and slipped the amulet's chain over his head. "How did our lives get so complicated?"

Just because, I wanted to say, but silence felt better. I looked back at the door to the stairs, and the golden light spilling out from the apartment below. "I would love to run away."

"We should go to Paris, or Vienna."

"Egypt. I'd have an excuse to cover my arms."

"I know Rome like the back of my hand."

I smiled. "You ever think about handing the homeless shelter over to someone else?"

"More and more frequently."

"What would you do with your time?"

"Be a better man."

"Not possible. You're perfect."

Grant kissed my cheek. "Come on. Let's find out what's so important about Jack's arm."

We held hands as we walked across the roof. I thought about Paris, Rome.

And the cut in the prison veil.

You should be there, part of me thought. *Standing guard.*

But guarding the break wouldn't do any good, either. Not long term, not when some fragment of an army waited on the other side, ready to fall down upon this world.

This world, where no one believed in magic. Those demons would descend, and with them, chaos. I didn't know if they could be stopped with guns. Maybe. But there wouldn't be enough guns—or people trained to use them—to keep humanity safe.

Soccer moms and their kids, rounded up by Mahati. Hospitals and schools and shopping malls. I tried to imagine Lord Ha'an leading his scarred, hungry Mahati through downtown Seattle, and it was both ridiculous and terrifying.

And so close. It could happen at any moment.

We have to close the veil, I thought. *We have to.*

Downstairs, the windows had been thrown open, but the air still smelled like bleach. I didn't see Rex, but Jack sat cross-legged on the couch. Mary was on the floor in front of him, butcher knives lying neatly aside. Aaz already sat near her, holding a ball of purple yarn in his claws. Somewhere, somehow, Mary had found knitting needles and seemed to be making a little demon-sized scarf.

My grandfather held a bone in his hands: the bone that was a mirror to my scar. There should have flesh clinging to its underside, but it looked clean, white—even, I thought, old. I wondered how many bodies it had been dug from over the years.

Jack's eyes were closed. He seemed to be meditating. If he was sleeping, I didn't want to know what his dreams were like. Maybe Grant knew. He studied him with a particular aloofness, like there were Jack-cooties in the air, on his aura, that he didn't want to touch.

"Jack," I muttered.

My grandfather sucked in a deep breath and opened his eyes. He didn't see me at first. He looked through me, focused on some mystery, far away.

"Jack," I said again.

"My dear girl," he replied, voice cracking. "What day is it?"

I shared a quick look with Grant. "It's only been thirty minutes or so since you pulled that bone out of your . . . old arm."

"Mmm." He closed his eyes again, rolled his shoulders, and clutched the bone to his chest. "This may take rather longer than I thought."

"What are you even doing?"

"Searching for threads." His eye cracked open. "Despite appearances, this object is a book. Layered with . . . the patterns . . . I used as a High Lord of the Divine Organic."

"So it *is* like a seed ring."

"Not quite, but close enough." Jack frowned, closing his eyes and settling deeper into the couch cushions. "Maybe you should take a walk."

"Maybe you should hurry up."

His mouth quirked. "My dear, I did not rush the baking of your birthday pies, and I will *not* be rushed in recalling the secrets of how to save the world."

"Seems like you would have bookmarked it," Grant said.

Jack's frown deepened. I crouched beside Aaz and patted his head. He gave me a toothy grin and showed me his ball of yarn.

"Nice," I said. "Stay here, buddy, if you can. Keep an eye on Mary and the Old Wolf."

"Keep an eye on the eye," Mary said to me, her knitting needles a blur. "Weeping blood in the sky."

Grant pulled me up. "Mary, we'll be back soon."

The old woman smiled at him but didn't stop knitting—not even when she focused her brittle gaze on Jack. She was still watching the old man—fingers and needles flying—when we shut the apartment door behind us.

CHAPTER 17

THREE months after I moved to Seattle, and three months before I met my grandfather and the trouble began, Grant and I drove north to Vancouver, Canada, to spend the weekend sightseeing. I'd been a tourist all my life but, after a certain age, had stopped enjoying the experience. One city was like any other. Always a zombie that needed exorcising. Always some wrong that needed to be righted.

We were seated on a bench in Stanley Park when I finally asked him for the exact details of how he'd hurt his leg.

"I walked into it," he said, tossing bits of bread at the wandering geese. "There was a man, a schizophrenic. He'd been in and out of institutions and was violent, frighteningly so. But only to himself. He wouldn't take medications, he wouldn't sit long enough to talk to social workers. None of the other shelters in the city would take him. But I was cocky. I had superpowers. So I tried it my way. Except I tried too much."

Grant tossed out the rest of the bread and finally looked me in the eyes. "Everything I knew about manipulating energy was self-taught, instinctual, based on a lifetime of observing people and seeing how personalities matched up with . . . patterns.

"I assumed those patterns would apply to someone with a mental illness, but they didn't. It was more complex than that. Something I didn't understand until I started . . . fixing things I had no business fixing. I didn't just attempt a tweak. I went too far. I made him worse."

"He came after you."

"I was looking for him, down in the basement. Still cocky. Not believing how bad it could get. And you know all those tools we have down there." Grant patted his leg. "He found a sledgehammer. Crushed the bone. Took his time with the blows. He kept telling me I needed to . . . stay out of his head."

He spoke so softly I could barely hear him. Grim, very grim.

I touched his hand. "How did you escape?"

"He dropped the sledgehammer and ran. I managed to drag myself to the stairs and shout for help." Grant rubbed his knee, but it seemed more like a habitual gesture, as though he needed something to occupy his hands. "But all of that . . . the attack, the surgeries . . . that wasn't the bad part. The bad part was realizing how arrogant I'd become. It crept up on me. I didn't even know. I hurt that man, Maxine. I hurt him because I was self-righteous, because I thought I knew best."

"Except that didn't stop you."

"You can't stop power. You can only control it. Choose how to use it. Choose how to use yourself." Grant's hand stilled against his knee. "This is what I think of every time I use my gift. I think of him. I think of his desperation. I remember to be afraid—of myself, for what I'm capable of. Sometimes you have to cross lines. Sometimes there's a greater good that demands it. But you do so knowing that for every act, even the most inconsequential, there will be consequences. Good, or bad. Immediate, or delayed."

"What happened to that man?"

"He shot himself," Grant said. "In his note, he blamed me."

❈

THE homeless shelter was so quiet. The halls smelled like smoke. We were the only ones inside.

Made it eerie. Gave it a sense of war. A battle had happened here, I wanted to say. Soldiers cometh, enemies slain. Battered, but victorious.

But, no. The fire was just the beginning of where it had all gone wrong.

We made our way to the burned-out section, stopping at the edge of the fire department's tape. Red eyes blinked on the other side. Metal groaned, followed by chewing sounds.

The armor tingled when we drew close, its surface shimmering with a faint glow

"She ripped a hole in the Labyrinth to get here," I said, studying my right hand. "Could it still be weak? Enough to just . . . fall through?

"You'd think she would have left the same way, then, instead of taking Jack into those woods."

I leaned against the wall, staring at the charred shell. It had begun to rain again, and without a roof in this section, the floor around us was getting wet. So was my face. "Those people. The ones she drained. We don't know who they are, or where she found them. She could have bonded herself to others, since then."

"I know," he said, grim. "But what were we going to do? No prison here on earth can hold her. We could have killed her, but she's been bred into slavery, brainwashed from birth. Taking her life feels wrong."

"Us or her, I'll choose us."

"We're not there yet."

We had been there since I'd first laid eyes on her, but I didn't have the stomach for killing, either. "She's dangerous. We need to find her. Especially if we're going to take on the veil, and the Mahati."

Grant looked down, jaw tight. "You believe we can do this?"

For the first time, I heard doubt in his voice. He'd been so fearless through all this. Strong, focused. Me, I always felt like I was falling apart. But not him.

I tried to speak, but couldn't. So I leaned against his back, sliding my arms around his waist—hugging him as tightly as I could. A tremor rode through him. Dek and Mal purred.

"You're my hero," I said. "I believe in you."

He exhaled sharply, but it sounded like a laugh. "I'm a cripple with a talent for manipulating people. I don't know what you ever saw in me."

I kissed his shoulder. "I was falling in love with you even before I remembered us. I saw enough."

Grant covered my hands. "Are we going to grow old together?"

"Yes," I whispered.

He turned his head, enough to see me over his shoulder. "Liar."

I reached up and tweaked his nose. "Don't make me be the optimist in this family."

"Family." He turned in my arms, leaning hard on his cane, while his other hand slid into the back pocket of my jeans. "I like that word."

"Yeah?" My eyes burned, unexpectedly. "Then you think about that. We have things we need to live to see."

Grant sucked in his breath—held my gaze for one long, tremulous moment—then looked away, jaw tight. I stood on my toes and kissed his throat.

"We can do this," I breathed. "Say it. Please."

"We can do this," he whispered. "We have to."

Mal uncoiled from my neck and slithered to Grant's shoulders, draping over him like a snake. His little furred head rested on his ear, making himself comfortable.

Grant frowned, reaching up to tentatively stroke Mal's tail. A purr erupted. Dek chirped at his brother.

I smiled and patted Grant's chest. "You have a body-guard."

He shook his head. "You need Mal."

"Grant," I said, my smile slipping just a little. "Who's going to hurt me?"

His gaze turned severe. "Maxine—"

I didn't give him a chance to finish. I grabbed his shirt, clenched my right hand into a fist, and thought hard about the Messenger.

The homeless shelter shattered into the void.

And inside the void, as I hung there, lost, the darkness stirred within me, opening its eye to stare.

You are frightened here, it said softly. *You do not like the dark.*

Go back to sleep, I replied. *I don't want you.*

You need us. Just as the Reapers needed us.

No, I said, but only to myself.

Because I *did* need *it*. Something, anyway, more than what I had.

Grant and I stepped from the void into an inferno of red rock and golden sand.

Sun white-hot, blinding. Cloudless sky. We stood on a high plateau. Beneath us, more sand and rock, and the outline of a faint road that led in a straight line toward a horizon ridged with yet more plateaus and jagged stone mounds.

It didn't matter much to me where we were. It was day in this part of the world—night in Seattle—assuming we hadn't traveled through time. The boys were heavy on my skin, heavy everywhere, even on my head. I wished that Jack and Mary—and Byron—still had Aaz watching over them.

Grant shielded his eyes against the sun, squinting at me.

"Love the art," he said, as Dek adjusted his tattooed tail across my cheeks and brow, little claws resting over my eyelids. I turned in a slow circle, searching for the Messenger.

Grant stopped in the middle of pulling off his jacket. "I see something. Other side of the rocks. Energy rising up, like a heat wave."

"What does that look like?"

"Muted," he said, tying his coat around his waist and picking up his cane. "She burns at a half-light, as though everything vibrant inside her was drained out."

"You must appear different than what she's used to."

"It's probably unsettling." He didn't say anything else and seemed troubled. I didn't like this any better than he did.

It didn't get easier when I saw her.

We found the Messenger on the other side of the rock

mound, sitting cross-legged in the burning sand as she stared off the cliff at the distant desert plain. Her hands were clasped, her back straight. We weren't quiet in our approach, but she did not look at us, or move. Not until we were almost on top of her.

"You," she said, with a surprising note of weariness in her voice. Weariness, and disappointment, and anger.

She was not alone.

Three men sat slumped on the rocks, heads lolling, eyes half-closed. Not withered, but just out of it. They were dark-haired, bearded, lean, wearing loose shirts over long, checkered wraps tied around their waists. Rifles hung from their shoulders, but none of the men appeared in any shape to fire off a shot.

I walked to them. The Messenger did not stop me.

I checked pulses, and glanced at Grant. "Alive."

"Bonded," he said quietly, and looked at the woman. "Why did you do that?"

"There are no mules here," she said simply. "No good human stock for me to draw upon. And I am not so eager to die as I was earlier."

"Good," he replied. "But I survived many years without . . . drawing from a bond. What you're doing to these men is wrong."

"Wrong," she echoed. "And was it wrong what you did to me, inside my head?"

Grant hesitated. "Maybe. But I'm not sorry."

I had been listening with only half an ear. I couldn't see the bonds that the Messenger had made with the men, but I could taste them, as if they were steel bars on my tongue: cold, sterile.

Break them, if you like, said the darkness. *You already hold the bonds in your mouth. Bite down. Bite. And you'll free them.*

I knew better than to listen—I knew so well—but the temptation was too great. I could do this. I could free them.

So I did. Like cutting a thread with my teeth. My jaw tightened, and I felt inside my mind three vibrating pops that sent a bitter taste flooding my mouth, like blood, raw liquid iron.

The three men jerked violently, eyes rolling back in their heads as they gasped and clawed at their throats. They took great heaving gasps of air, each one making them shudder until I thought their bones would break. I glanced over my shoulder, and found the Messenger clutching her chest like she was having a heart attack.

"Shit," I said.

"Maxine," Grant snapped, pointing. I turned, and found the men fully conscious, fully in control of themselves— staring at me with no small amount of horror and confusion. I had forgotten what I looked like. Even so, if these men didn't remember how they had gotten here—

They fumbled for their guns. I shouted at them, but that only made them move faster, and they shouted back at me, and each other. I didn't understand a word they were saying, but I got the drift. I slammed into the nearest of them, trying to wrench his weapon away. He was strong, wiry, teeth bared in anger and fear.

I head-butted him.

His hands loosened. I yanked the gun away and threw it over the cliff edge. But I was too slow to stop the others. They opened fire—on me—on Grant and the Messenger.

I didn't look, didn't think—I lunged at both men and took us all over the cliff.

I think I screamed. Maybe. The men did, slipping out of my grip almost instantly. I tried to hold on, but they flailed too much.

The world didn't spin. I saw the ground, clear and sharp, every rock outlined in brilliant detail as I hurtled headfirst toward earth.

I could have used the armor to escape, but the men were out of reach. I tried so hard to grab them, but my hands kept slipping away—and I had only seconds. Hundreds of feet, lost in the span of heartbeats.

My head hit first. I felt like an arrow, and at the moment of the impact I had a terrible vision of me lodged in the earth with my feet stuck out.

Instead, I bounced, flipped, spun through the air like a rag doll. Landed hard on my back, skidding across rock and sand. I felt no pain, but I forgot to breathe, and my heart pounded so hard I thought I might have a stroke. Dizzy, lights in my eyes, and the blue sky swallowing me.

I heard my name, screamed. Distant, echoing. I twisted, just enough, and saw Grant—very far away, above me, at the edge of the cliff. I couldn't see much of him, but I raised my hand to wave. It was more difficult than it should have been. Zee and the boys were throbbing against my skin.

I looked left, then right. The men were nearby, very still. I couldn't see much of their heads, but only because their skulls had been crushed into their broken, mangled shoulders

I'm sorry, I thought at them, tears burning my eyes. *I'm sorry.*

Air moved over me. Stone crunched. The Messenger moved into sight—and a moment later, so did Grant.

He fell on his knees beside me, his eyes wild. Blood streamed down his arm, which hung useless at his side. Part of his sleeve had torn away, and the bullet wound was large and messy. I tried to sit up. He held me down, but moving that much made him grunt with pain, and sway.

I pushed his hand away, as gently as I could. "You need a doctor."

Grant bowed his head, jaw tight. "Are *you* hurt?"

I ignored that. The Messenger crouched, graceful. "Lightbringer. Heal yourself."

He gave her a hard, strained look. "I don't know how."

Disdain flickered. "All your power, and you cannot even save your own life."

"So teach him," I snapped.

"Why would I?" The Messenger stood, backing away. "He did something to me that cannot be undone. In my head, in my heart. He . . . twisted me."

"I'm sorry," Grant said through gritted teeth. "I was trying to help you. Truly. I didn't mean to cause you pain."

"That is what the wild ones do. Our powers are too much to go untamed. We cannot be trusted."

"So you put your trust in others," I told her accusingly. "You absolve yourself of responsibility because someone else knows best. Someone who gives you an order you don't have to think about, just follow, without consequences."

"You make me sound like a child."

"I wasn't the one who opened the prison veil."

She gave me a hateful look. Grant snorted with pained, choked laughter, then squeezed shut his eyes.

"Ow," he said.

"Come on," I muttered, prepared to cut us away to a hospital. Except the Messenger grabbed my shoulder.

"How," she asked quietly, "did you break my bonds with those humans?"

Guilt soared through me. "I just did."

"You wasted three lives."

"So you could use them up until they died?"

"Yes," she said, and looked down at Grant. "I can heal you. But I will need a mule—a human—to bond with."

"No. I won't sacrifice someone else."

"They are only human."

"Like us." He fixed his gaze on her. "Just like us."

The Messenger hesitated. Staring at him, her gaze shifting from his face, the air around him, tracking all those strains of color and light that were invisible to my eyes.

Whatever she saw, though, made her shoulders sag.

"I will need to bond to you," she said, quietly.

Hell, no, I thought. But Grant, without hesitation, extended his hand to her—and I was too slow to speak, to stop him—to stop her. She grabbed his wrist.

Grant gasped, squeezing shut his eyes. A terrible pain lanced through my heart, a hooking sensation that was alien and invasive—like a leech, sinking its mouth into me. The darkness stirred, rippling through me with a hiss. I pushed it down with all my strength. Against my skin, the boys shifted—Zee, especially, twisting in his dreams.

The Messenger threw back her head, breath rattling in her throat.

"Lightbringer," she said, and there was a hint of wonder in her voice.

Grant made a strangled sound. My heart tugged—those hooks, pulling painfully outward, toward him. Toward him, through him, to the Messenger. No golden light. Her bond was all pain and taking. Nothing soft.

We could kill her, whispered the darkness. *We do not like her touch.*

Enough, I snapped to it. *You've done enough.*

It was not us who took the bite, it replied smoothly. *Not us who killed.*

The Messenger began to sing, her voice strong, steady—as was her hand as she touched Grant's wounded arm. I watched, struck dumb, as his torn flesh knitted closed. Happened slowly, but steadily; and Grant paled, sweat pouring down his face. I held him up as tremors wracked him, down to the bone.

Until, finally, the wound closed. The Messenger stopped singing and leaned away, still graceful—but slow, careful, each movement measured and small. Sweat also glistened against her face, and her lips had lost all color, fading into her white skin.

No one spoke for a long time until she looked from Grant to me, and her gaze lingered on my face—studying me, but with a troubled thoughtfulness that I bore with my own unblinking stare.

"Your heart is odd," said the Messenger.

"Yes," I replied. "Break the link."

I thought she would say no. Her hand touched her chest, and lingered there as though tasting something warm through her palm. Her gaze was still too thoughtful—and, I thought, a little hungry.

But she closed her eyes, speaking a word that rumbled through me—and moments later the hook in my heart was gone. My relief was immediate and physical—I had to bend over, my fingers digging into my chest as my heart pounded harder than was healthy—harder than fear, harder than sickness.

Grant's breathing was ragged. His face red, eyes squeezed shut. I held him tight against me, pressing my lips into his hair, then against his ear.

"I'm here," I murmured.

The Messenger shifted, leaning toward him. "Why did you stop me?"

I looked at her, but she was focused entirely on Grant.

"Your leg," she went on. "You stopped me from fixing the bone."

"You can't heal everything," he whispered tightly, eyes still shut. "Some things have to stay the way they are."

She frowned. "You are against nature."

"Then what are you?"

"Made," she said, straightening. "Created by the hand of my Maker."

"As was I."

"You were not Made. Not like me."

"We each have our own way of being."

"I am a Maker's ward. I do not have *my* way."

"But it is *a* way. Just like mine." Grant cracked open one eye, peering at her. "No one owns you. But the same is true in reverse. You're no better than anyone else, no matter what you can do."

Her eyes narrowed, but she said nothing. Merely stood, backing away. I climbed to my feet and pulled Grant up beside me. He gritted his teeth the entire time, exhaling his breath as one long hiss when I pushed his cane into his hand and his other arm hugged my shoulders. I bore his weight.

I met the Messenger's gaze. "Did you consider what we discussed?"

Her lips thinned into an unpleasant line. "You want me to fight alongside you."

"We need your help closing the prison veil," Grant said.

"The Maker said it cannot be done."

"The Maker was too hasty. We are going to try." Grant leaned forward. "You don't know who you are anymore. You don't know your own worth. But that's only because you've never had a chance to be *you*. To make a decision that is yours. Whatever you decide here will be your choice. Your life."

No power in his voice. No power in anything he'd told her, except for whatever strength lay in the meaning of his words.

Still a bit of a priest, I thought. Made of more than just magic in his voice. If he lost his gift, he would still be Grant

Cooperon. Able to change lives with nothing more than his conviction, and faith.

I wondered who I would be, without demons and the darkness inside. Better or worse—or just a woman with a nine-to-five, doing her best to survive a different kind of life.

Never knowing the other side of light.

The Messenger watched him—then me.

"I will do this," she said slowly. "And then we will see."

"I hope you see a great deal," Grant said.

CHAPTER 18

I never did learn the name of the village the men had been stolen from.

I made the Messenger take me there, with Grant. We took with us two corpses, and one man who was still alive but passed out. We left them by the road, beneath a palm tree on the outskirts of the village, which was filled with large square buildings made of a pale stone that blended with the cliff face rising behind them. A dog barked at us. I heard pop music sung in Arabic, somewhere distant.

Two little girls, dressed in simple green dresses, appeared around the bend in the road. They stopped when they saw us, and cried out.

The Messenger did not cut space. She watched the distraught children, then looked long and hard at the village.

"This reminds me of the place where I was born," she said. "I was not permitted to see much beyond the walls. The desert was vast and stretched across the world."

I stared. So did Grant. The Messenger glanced at us and tilted her head.

"The Labyrinth is vast, as well," she said, and winked out of sight.

I grabbed Grant's hand and followed her.

We fell into the apartment, in Seattle. It was still night. The boys ripped off my body. I gritted my teeth against the pain, squeezing Grant's hand until it was over and the smoke that had been tattoos coalesced into small hard bodies that glinted like obsidian and mercury.

Jack still sat on the couch, but he held a mug in his hands instead of bone. He and Mary were watching the news. Something in their faces filled me with dread: bone-chilling, acidic. Raw and Aaz bounded close to stare at the television screen.

". . . reports are only now coming in that a Greyhound bus traveling from Portland to Seattle was found overturned beside Interstate 5, just outside Astoria. First responders describe the scene as . . . horrific. Every passenger has been declared dead."

I heard screams from the television, wails of grief and disbelief. I heard shouts, and a man saying, in a shaking voice, "Oh, God. Oh, my God."

The sound cut off. Jack put down the remote.

"Dead," he said, looking at me for the first time since my arrival. His haggard gaze skipped over Grant to the Messenger, then back to me. "But someone is lying about the rest."

"Bus accidents happen," I whispered, as Dek settled heavily on my shoulders. I looked for Mal, and found him with Grant, looped around the man's neck.

"Mahati running hunts," Zee rasped, closing his eyes as though listening to something, far away. "One party. Ha'an leads."

I closed my eyes and took a deep breath. "Jack, did you find what you were looking for?"

"Yes," he said quietly.

I fumbled for Grant's hand. "Start teaching them what they need to know."

"It's not that simple."

"Make it simple," I snapped. "We're out of time."

Grant pulled me near, with Mal half-draped down his chest. "What are you doing?"

"Stalling." I squeezed his hand, glancing at the Messenger. No words between us. Just those cool empty eyes, and that set mouth.

I stepped backward into the void, holding Lord Ha'an's image in my mind—

—and found myself in a forest, not unlike the one where the veil had been opened. The air was cool, wet, and the ground was soft underfoot. I heard the roar of a river, but louder than that, singing: a deep voice, chanting words into melodies. Dek joined in, very softly, his voice high and sweet. All around me, the boys hunched close, red eyes glinting. With wistfulness, I realized. Memory.

I could have been in a cathedral, listening to a monk. Below my heart, the darkness stretched, coils rubbing with a spectral hiss that sank into the marrow of my bones. I searched for my bond with Grant and found it instantly, warm, sunlit. I focused on that. I held tight.

Remember there is much, elsewhere, you can have, said the darkness in my mind.

I ignored that voice. Pushed through the trees and found the Mahati.

I counted eight, not including Lord Ha'an. The demons sat in a loose circle, relaxed, a jumble of human limbs piled in front of them. I smelled blood. I heard the crack of bones breaking. Wet, chewing sounds. My stomach rebelled, but I swallowed hard, kept it together.

Ha'an was the only demon not eating—the only one of them who sang—his voice a low rumble that crashed with the distant sounds of river white water. He knelt with his knees spread far apart, his tined fingers resting across muscular silver thighs.

He saw me before the others, but did not stop singing. His eyes tracked my movements and widened ever so slightly when he found the boys.

One by one, the other Mahati stopped eating and looked up. When they saw me, a collective ripple rolled through them. It tasted like fear, which sent a small frisson of pleasure through me.

Me—or the darkness—yawning with jaws that bloomed inside my mouth, that coiled spirit filling me up from my scalp to my toes. Made me feel as though my heart were riding the crest of a monstrous wave, carrying me higher, with power and grace.

Because we are, it whispered. *We are power.*

Power. Power was choice. Choice had consequences.

I repeated that to myself, again and again, as Raw and Aaz pressed close to my legs, growling softly. The spikes of Zee's hair and spine stood on end. His claws dragged through the dirt.

"Ha'an," he rasped. "Been long."

The demon's voice rumbled into silence, and he inclined his head. "Long enough for the strange to take root. You are diminished, as are your brothers. The old one no longer inhabits your skin."

"Power, still," Zee said. "Power enough to kill you."

"Always," he replied, but not with fear, or anger. "And the human vessel? You are bound to her. I felt that, before, but could not understand it."

"Aetar," Zee rasped.

Ha'an nodded thoughtfully. "We will hunt them again, I think. After we are done here." ·

"You're already done," I said, stepping forward. "The lives you took tonight were too much."

"I made my plea. I told you I would not let my people starve."

I pointed at the mangled remains on the ground in front of him. "These were people, too. There are other things you can eat."

"Livestock?" Ha'an said disdainfully. "I think not." ·

"Better than your own arm."

His eyes narrowed, and he glanced down at Zee. "How can she be the vessel and not know what we need?"

"Different times, different needs," Zee answered simply. "She is our Queen."

Ha'an flinched. "But you are still our Kings."

Zee raked his claws through the dirt, spines flexing in agitation. "Yours. Hers. Together."

The Mahati Lord leaned backward, fixing me with his glittering gaze. "I feel the old one breathing beneath her skin. I know, in my mind, she is the Vessel. But without you embracing her body . . . she is too human. The others will not accept her as a Queen."

"Must," Zee told him. "*You* must."

Ha'an gave him a long, unreadable look. And then he did the same to me—his full regard, lifting his chin, challengingly. "You, with fat and meat on your bones. Do you know what it is like to suffer such hunger that you must eat your own flesh to survive?"

"Do you?" I asked coldly. "You look intact."

A terrible stillness stole over him. I almost took a step back, but Raw leaned against my legs, holding me in place. Dek placed a reassuring claw on my ear.

"The hunt," he whispered, "is not just for flesh. That might fill our bellies but not our souls."

"You hunt for pain," I said.

"Pain is a sharp force," Ha'an replied, as though that should explain so much. "If livestock were enough, we would consume those slow beasts. But minds . . . dreaming minds . . . make power, have a taste, infuse every cell, every lick of blood, every crack of bone, with a force we *must* have to be strong."

You have tasted it, said the darkness. *You have ridden the edges of what he speaks. Imagine being bathed in the light of ten thousand minds, crashing to a final death at your feet. Last moments burn strongest in the feast.*

I stared into Ha'an's green eyes, trying not to tremble with the terrible, nameless hunger rising in my throat. "Take what you already found, and no more. Return to the veil."

Ha'an fixed me with a hard, hollow gaze. "If I do not?"

I glanced down at Raw and Aaz, and they hit the nearest Mahati like bullets made of teeth and claws. I forced myself to watch with pure dispassion as Raw swallowed an entire arm, just stuffed it down his throat, before biting it off the screaming Mahati's shoulder. Aaz burrowed through the other demon's chest, nearly chewing him in two.

I didn't move. I didn't flinch. Screaming on the inside, but there was stone in my heart because there had to be. Ruthless, because it was the only way to keep the people I loved alive.

I looked at Ha'an. "Get the fuck back in the veil. Now."

He held my gaze a moment longer than was smart, then flicked his long fingers at the other Mahati, who began hastily gathering up the remains of their hunt, and newly dead. I wanted to tell them to stop, leave the human bodies—but I had an instinct for how far I could push, and this was all for time. Time for Grant and Jack to make a miracle happen.

"This is not the end," Ha'an said, looking from me to Zee. "Forgive me, but we *will* hunt. We will hunt to live."

We will hunt with you, murmured the darkness. *We will lead the armies of starlight into the horizon, into the war-fires, into the Labyrinth where the shadow rises—*

I bit my tongue and tasted blood.

"We will hunt," Ha'an said again, as though reassuring himself. "We will survive."

"That remains to be seen," I told him quietly. Ha'an was a giant, towering at least three feet above me, with muscles that made him several times as broad. But I felt larger than him in that moment, full with rippling power, and a certainty that my life was rooted deeper than a mountain, older than stone. I didn't like what gave me that feeling, but it was there, and I used it to hold his gaze and make him back down.

"Queen," Ha'an said, softly, with speculation.

He turned and leapt into the sky. The other Mahati followed him.

I remained very still, watching them until they were out of sight.

"Zee," I breathed.

"Doing as you said," he rasped, clutching my hand.

My knees trembled. I was going to fall.

So I fell backward, to home.

⇥≡⇤

I tried to, anyway. The armor had other ideas.

I stepped from the void into moonlight. A river of moonlight, shining through clouds upon a dark plain.

I heard a woman screaming. I smelled smoke. Zee and the boys gathered close, gripping my hands and legs.

"No," he said, his claws digging so deep into my skin I

thought he would cut me. And then he did, and the touch of my blood made him flinch away from me, eyes large. I reached for him, but he stayed just out of my touch, shaking his head and scratching his arms, his face, his eyes.

I stared at him, helpless; but that woman screamed again, and something about her voice cut through me like a knife. Even the darkness stilled, hushed.

"No." Zee grabbed for my hand when I turned to look for that woman, but this time it was me who slipped away, and I ran.

I ran with all my strength, urgency sweeping over me, and fear. My heart thundered in my throat, and the darkness rocked within me, small, smaller, as though hiding. My bond with Grant felt faint, pale, the thread holding us together so thin it might snap if I breathed wrong. I held my armored hand over my chest, as if that would hold us together.

But I didn't stop running. Boys, chasing me like wolves, skipping through the shadows with their red eyes blazing.

I skidded to a stop at the crest of a small hill and looked down at the smoking remains of what had been a small village. I couldn't tell what it had looked like before its destruction, but the fires had long burned out.

The woman had fallen silent, but I found her sitting in the moonlight, hunched over a limp, broken body.

Oturu stood beside them both. His cloak and hair drifted against the wind, graceful, soaking in the silver light. Head bowed, the brim of his black hat swept low.

He looked up and saw me. But did not say a word.

I was afraid to look at him. More afraid to look at the woman. She sat up for a brief moment. Stole my breath, made me ache.

My mother, I thought. She was pregnant, not hugely, but enough to strain the front of her clothing.

But then I looked closer, and I knew I was wrong. Not my mother. The face might be similar, the right age, but there was a subtle difference no one but me would have known. Like listening to the same song played by two masters and hearing the difference only in the tone.

That, and this woman's entire right arm was made of silver.

My ancestor. Five thousand years in the past. Might as well have been another world. Me, a ghost in time.

She screamed again, her voice breaking into a sob so torn, so cut with grief, I wanted to sink to my knees and hold my heart. Something in that sound was too familiar, too close for comfort. I forced myself to study the person she wept over, the person she touched with hesitant hands that clutched and fluttered, and curled into fists that she pressed against her heaving chest.

A woman. I couldn't see her face, but I saw the long dark hair, and the shape of the still body—and I knew. I just knew.

Mother. Her mother.

Red eyes glinted in the shadows near both women. Blinking, staring up the hill at me and my boys. She hadn't noticed us, and I wanted to keep it that way. I backed up, slowly, listening to her sob. Struggling not to weep with her. My mother's body had fallen on the kitchen floor just like that. I had crouched over her, screaming—also, just like that. I could still feel those screams in my throat.

So could the boys. Raw and Aaz shuddered against my legs. Zee stumbled through the grass, while Dek raised a mournful cry. My boys. Monsters. Kings of an army that destroyed worlds.

Like fucking hell.

I turned and came face-to-face with a dark cloak, and tangled hair that moved through the air around me like some aura of night. I suffered a jolt, but only because I couldn't remember Oturu after seeing my ancestor, and her mother. The world could have dropped away, and I would have seen nothing else.

"Lady Hunter," he said. "You should not be here, in this moment. It is not your time."

I closed my eyes, swaying, and the tendrils of his hair reached around my body, holding me up, holding me to him. "Who killed her mother?"

Zee made a small wailing sound, deep in his throat. Oturu hesitated.

"She did," he said.

I flinched, shaking my head. "No."

"It was fast," he went on. "An accident. A rush of temper. Her mother—"

"Stop." I pushed against him, but my hands sank into his cloak, sank deep without touching anything except unimaginable cold. Raw and Aaz grabbed my waist and pulled me away, quick. My hands felt burned when they left his body, but only with ice. I could barely bend my fingers. Zee gripped them in his claws, blowing gently. His warm breath soothed over my skin.

"She lost her mind," I whispered. I could still hear her sobs, drifting over the hill. Gut-wrenching. So alone.

Horrified me. Not just for my ancestor, but myself. If she could do this, no matter the reason . . . if she could just snap . . .

It was not us, said the darkness. *Not us.*

But you cut her mind with power. You made her insane.

She was damaged, it murmured. *Already damaged.*

I tugged on Zee's hand, needing to hold something, anything, to anchor me away from that voice inside my head. I spoke aloud, determined to drown out the voice. To find answers to the unanswerable. "Her mother should have died long before this. You were already bonded to her daughter's skin when she was thrown into the Wasteland. But down there, she has the armor, she's *pregnant*. Must have been years. And her mother was alive all that time? How? Demons should have killed her."

Killed her, like my mother was killed. Like my grandmother. Like all the others before us.

"Different, then," Zee rasped, so softly I could barely hear him. "Wardens around, mothers lasted longer. No bad bargains."

I heard growls, behind me. Zee stiffened. I turned to look, but Oturu touched me again, held me still.

"Do not," he said. "Your wards are not the wards of the past."

"No Zee would ever hurt me."

His mouth tightened. "You must go, young Queen."

I wished I could see his eyes. "How do you know me? We won't meet for another five thousand years."

"Time," he breathed. "Time means nothing, between us."

His hair wrapped around my right hand.

"Go," he said. "Remember us, as we remember you."

Behind me, Zee snarled. Raw and Aaz leaned against my legs, claws out, teeth bared. Dek hissed into my ear. On the other side of the hill, my ancestor wailed like she was dying.

I shut my eyes, focused on Grant—

   on my mother

—Grant—

—home—

Take me away, I thought. *Take me.*

The armor tingled against my skin. I slipped into the void.

But I could still hear her screams.

CHAPTER 19

I walked from the past into a quiet apartment. So quiet, so hushed, I knew without looking around that I was the only one there. Zee confirmed it for me, moments later. Raw and Aaz prowled. I didn't let myself panic. There were no signs of violence. No blood.

I found a note on the kitchen counter.

Jack's place. Love, Grant.

I frowned, glad that Mal had stayed with him. I almost left then, but took a moment to check out the room, drinking in the familiarity of it, the warmth. Not as warm without Grant, but I felt the good echoes.

And the bad, when I glanced down at the floor and saw bloodstains.

Dek hummed "Let's Stay Together." I scratched his head and walked to the piano bench, where the shoulder rig filled with my mother's knives was still draped. Since seeing Jack's body, I hadn't wanted to even think about the blades, but I reached out to stroke the steel—

—and got a good look at my right hand.

My palm was still flesh, but that was all. That fluid, organic metal covered everything else: my fingers, the back of my hand. Couple more jumps, and all of it would be gone. For my ancestor to have lost her entire arm and shoulder meant that she had been even busier.

I shut out my thoughts of her. Pushed them away, down where I put all the distasteful things in my life. I wasn't sure I sympathized with, or hated, that woman. Maybe both. Maybe I felt the same way about myself.

No, murmured that deep voice in my mind. *Your hearts are not the same.*

But you still want to manipulate me, I told it. *There are things you want me to do.*

I received no response to that.

I grabbed the shoulder rig and shrugged it on. The sheathed knives fit snugly against my ribs. I slid into my mother's leather coat. It still smelled like her, after all these years. Made me feel as though I wore another kind of armor.

Outside the apartment, on the stairs, I heard footsteps, humming. Mary. It made sense they hadn't taken her along, especially if the Messenger was with them. Fire and oil. Explosive.

The doorknob rattled.

I had thought about driving to Jack's apartment, just to save me some skin. The idea lasted for all of two seconds.

Five more after that, I stood in a dark alley.

I was disoriented at first, until I realized I was behind Jack's building. It was drizzling, and the air was cold against my head. Dek hugged my scalp. Red eyes blinked in the shadows.

A low voice said, "Dear girl."

I turned. Saw a slender figure leaning on the wall beside a propped-open door. Dark hair, pale skin, those familiar eyes that were too old. I half expected him to be smoking a cigarette.

"Old Wolf," I said. "I was worried when I got back to the apartment."

"I couldn't concentrate there. I still can't. I needed air." He pushed off the wall, studying my face. "What happened with the Mahati?"

"I played tough." I joined him, not minding the rain as I stood and watched my grandfather just as intently as he did me. I soaked him in. "Bunch of pussycats when you get right down to it."

"That so?" Jack's brow lifted. "I can think of several other words to describe them."

I shrugged. "So, no progress?"

He gave me a tired smile. "My kind are made of infinitely complex threads of energy. Brains without flesh, you might say. It's the reason we're capable of understanding—and actualizing—certain . . . elusive concepts."

I smiled back. "Like building an interdimensional prison out of a rift in space-time that's capable of housing a demonic army."

My grandfather inclined his head. "Something like that."

"So we're not smart enough to close the veil? Is that what you're saying?"

"I'm saying that *no one* has the wiring necessary to understand what we did. Even I have trouble with it, and I was one of the designers."

"Right," I said slowly, filled with a hundred different things I wanted to say to him, and ask—nothing that couldn't keep, a little while longer. "How are you teaching them?"

Jack tapped his head. "We've been on the surface of each other's thoughts. If I were even a little bit nosy, I'd be having a field day."

"Groovy." I leaned against the wall, turning my face up to the rain. "I'll stick with intimidating the Mahati."

He sighed, maybe with laughter, or sadness. "Maxine—"

"She killed her own mother," I said. "My ancestor."

I hadn't known I was going to say that until the words were done, gone. Speaking them felt wrong—not the act, but the words themselves, the meaning of them, the truth. I felt ugly for giving them up.

Jack's mouth clicked shut.

"You said you wanted to do things differently this time. You just ignored her before, is that it? Let her run wild until it was too late?" I met his gaze, unable to stop talking. "Did you know that some of the Wardens threw her into the Wasteland?"

Zee had said that Jack didn't know. I needed to see it for myself. I wasn't disappointed. Shock moved through my grandfather's face, a trembling disbelief that made him shake his head and back up a step.

"Never," he said.

"I saw it," I told him. "Straight from memories she gave Oturu. One of them was a woman with wings, and there were twins with rubies in their foreheads—"

Jack's breath caught.

"—and a giant with one eye, a cyclops. He was against the others. Too slow to stop it, though."

"No," he murmured, but his gaze was distant, like he was talking to himself. "Oh, oh, no."

"The Wasteland fucked her up, Old Wolf. The Wasteland ripped open the hole to that sleeping shit inside her. But it started with *them*."

Jack sagged against the wall, shutting his eyes. Even in

the body of a teen, I could see the old man. He looked frail, and I felt bad for telling him. I could have made it easier. Tried to, anyway.

I heard heavy footsteps on the other side of the door. A cane. I straightened and touched Jack's bony shoulder. "Come on. Let's go in."

But he shook his head and gave me a look so pained, so miserable, I stopped breathing.

"I didn't know," he whispered.

"I know that," I said. "I know, Jack."

"She was so angry," he went on, as the door beside us pushed open. "The things she did to them, I never understood."

Grant peered out, Mal draped over his shoulders. He looked at me with relief, and a deep warmth that was all in his eyes and not the grim line of his mouth. I had a feeling he had been listening a long time. Our voices would have drifted easily through that open door.

I shook my head at him, just as Jack shuddered violently and rubbed his chest, like it hurt.

"I will make this right," he said, closing his eyes. "I was a coward then, but not now. I will fix this."

I frowned. "Jack?"

He looked me dead in the eyes. "I love you, my dear. I love you, always."

"No," Grant said, alarmed. He lunged forward. "Jack—"

My grandfather's eyes rolled back, his mouth going slack. He collapsed, boneless, but I caught him before he hit the ground. All the boys bounded from the shadows, red eyes glowing.

I gritted my teeth. "Jack."

"That's Byron again," Grant said, grim. "Jack's not inside him anymore."

I touched the boy's face. His skin was warm, but not feverish. Pale, though, and hollow. His mouth began moving, but I couldn't hear what he was saying.

I picked him up in my arms. Staggered a little, but managed his weight. Grant stayed close, his hand lightly gripping Byron's ankle. His gaze was distant. I heard him humming.

I carried Byron inside and skirted boxes and old dusty furniture, searching out the stairs. Up and up, until we reached Jack's apartment. The door stood open.

No lights burned inside, but I heard shuffling sounds and a lamp switched on. Dek's tongue was hot on my ear, and both he and Mal sang a brief snatch of Gladys Knight's "Walk Softly."

Grant said, "There's a rip inside him. It's bleeding."

I gave him a sharp look. He added, "In his spirit, not his body."

I hefted Byron higher in my arms and tried to navigate the narrow maze of books. I knocked quite a few down, Grant faltered behind me, trying to walk over them. I apologized silently but didn't stop or look at the Messenger, who sat at the kitchen table and watched me pass with a growing expression of alarm.

"The Maker," she said.

I shook my head at her and carried the boy to the bedroom. It was a small, closed space—bed unmade, clothes on the floor, along with more books. I didn't get the feeling that Jack had spent much time in here. Even for an immortal, too much to see and do. He gave lectures on archaeology, sometimes. I wished, now, that I had attended more of them.

Byron stirred when I set him down. He was still mumbling. I leaned close, letting my ear hover over his mouth.

"Knock," he said, so softly I could barely understand him. And even so, I thought I misheard everything.

"Knock once for light, knock twice for death, knock three times to find the world all dead . . . and four, always, to *raise* the dead." Byron twisted, lines of pain and fear etched in his brow. "No, don't touch me. Please. Please, don't . . ."

We would not, said the darkness.

His face crumpled, and he started sobbing. I crawled onto the bed and pulled him tight against me.

Grant laid his hand on Bryon's head. Closed his eyes, his hum taking shape, strength, his voice rumbling like a rolling explosion deep underground, so deep all I could feel was the shaking beneath my feet. I watched him, and when I blinked—in those flashes between blinks—I could almost see the threads between us, golden and hot. Pulsing together like one heartbeat.

I smoothed back Byron's wet hair. The teen stirred again, eyes flickering open.

He saw me first. Maybe. He seemed so dazed he might as well have been blind. Hs looked at me, past me, around me—wildly—before focusing on my face again.

He stared. I tried to smile. "Hey."

"Maxine," Grant said. Byron looked at him, then me—quick, still wild—and his face crumpled again. This time with a trace of fear.

"Who are you?" he said.

I sat back, breathless. "Byron. It's me."

He shook his head, and I had the most terrible feeling that this was my punishment for forgetting Grant. I had spent my whole life being a stranger, an unknown, but for this boy to look at me like that . . .

It terrified me. More than demons. More than the end of the world.

Grant's hand clasped my shoulder. I steeled myself. "You don't remember anything?"

I don't—" Byron stopped and touched his head. "I don't know. It's all a blur."

"You've been sick," Grant said, his voice flowing with reassurance and power. "We've been taking care of you."

I blinked hard and slid off the bed. "Rest, kid. You've had a tough couple days."

Byron's gaze was piercing, sharp. I thought he would argue. Maybe even try to run.

But Grant started humming again, and the teen had trouble keeping his eyes open. He frowned, rubbing them, then swayed back down on the bed. He still watched us, though, uneasy and pale.

Hollow, I thought again. His eyes, so old.

"I don't know you," he murmured.

"That's okay," I said softly, and tried my hardest to smile. "Just rest."

Grant's voice rumbled to a deeper pitch. My skin tingled. Red eyes blinked in the shadows. Raw stared down at him with sorrow, memories in his gaze. The boys had known Byron in another life. Never spoken of it, except in snatches that were always pained.

Byron's eyes drifted shut. His body relaxed.

Grant touched my elbow. We left the room, and I closed the door. Leaned against it, bending over, covering my face. Grant kissed my head. I was aware of the Messenger standing close, watching us.

"Sit down," he said.

I shook my head. "Bad enough it was me. At least I still remembered some things." I reached for his hand, holding it tight. "Can you help him?"

"I don't know," he said, hoarse. "I'm not sure I should try. I've never seen this before. It's as though Jack's possession, and departure, punched open a hole inside the boy's spirit. I can see into that hole, but it's like looking inside a body for the first time if you know nothing about medicine. You see the parts, but that doesn't tell you how they go together or what they do."

"He is right," said the Messenger, staring at the bedroom door. "There will be complications."

Grant gave her a grim look. "We have to assume this has happened before, and Byron always survived. But it looks wrong. I don't know what Jack did to him all those years ago."

And where did Jack go? I asked myself, desperately afraid of the answer. I glanced down at Zee. "Can you find him?"

"She can," said the little demon, pointing at the Messenger.

The woman fingered the iron collar sitting so heavily around her neck and stared at Zee, then me. "Yes. I can track him."

I matched her stare, studying those narrow eyes, which were far more thoughtful now than when we had first met— trying to kill each other, with her sent to abduct Jack.

She might still take him. I didn't trust her. Not with my grandfather, not with Grant.

"Please," I said.

The Messenger looked away, her expression unreadable. "I will try."

And just like that, she vanished. Papers blew loose onto the floor in her wake. My ears popped.

"Sometimes I think I'm losing my mind," Grant said.

"Race you," I muttered. "What are we going to do about Byron?"

He sat down hard in one of the chairs at the kitchen table and stretched out his leg with a wince. "I don't feel comfortable trying to bring back his memories. I might make him worse. You know that's a possibility."

We could fix the boy, murmured the darkness, rolling beneath my skin. *We could find what was lost.*

I closed my eyes. Grant said, "What?"

I tapped my head. "The thing inside me has an opinion. It thinks it can heal the boy. But it's also the same genius that suggested I break the Messenger's bonds with those men."

"You couldn't have predicted their reactions."

"I could have imagined there would be consequences. Nothing is free, nothing is cheap. You taught me that."

"You knew it before we met."

"Whatever. I can't take that risk with Byron."

"You know," Grant said, "when you couldn't remember me, I was just about desperate enough to try anything. If I could have gone into your mind, I would have."

"I trust you more than I trust myself."

"Don't," he replied.

"You've got too much faith in me."

"No more than you. You wouldn't have stayed in this town, otherwise. You believed in something, Maxine, and it wasn't just us."

I sat down beside him. The bone fragment was near my hand. I almost touched it, but remembered where it had come from, and stopped.

"Tell me," I said. "Tell me what I believed in."

Grant leaned over, and his lips brushed mine. Heat rode down my throat, into my heart, spreading beneath my skin. I closed my eyes.

"Possibilities," he whispered. "You believed in possibilities. You still do."

I took a deep breath. Grant picked up my right hand and traced the armor with his fingers. "I felt you go very far away from me. Jack complained that I couldn't concentrate, but that was why. I thought we would break."

I shivered, hunching deeper into myself. "I saw something terrible. I saw what I could become."

Grant slid his hand beneath Dek to rest his large warm palm on the back of my neck. Mal lounged across his shoulders. Both boys purring.

"Look at me," he said softly.

I looked. Brown eyes, intense, thoughtful. I loved his eyes.

"It's going to be okay," he said.

I touched his cheek. I wanted to speak, but my voice wouldn't work. My voice wasn't enough to tell him what I needed to say.

"I know," he said.

I frowned.

"I know that, too," he added.

I poked his chest, and he captured my hand, leaning in to kiss me hard on the mouth. I climbed into his lap, and he broke away just enough to bury his face in the crook of my neck.

"I couldn't do it," he said tightly, as something hot and wet touched my skin. "Jack tried to teach me. I could see the surface of the pattern in my head, but it was impossible to hold on to."

"You tried."

"That's not good enough."

"We'll find another way." I tightened my arms around him. "I hope Jack doesn't do anything stupid."

"Like closing the veil on his own?" Grant pulled back to look into my eyes. "I could tell he was considering it, even before you came back."

Dek licked my ear. I bowed my head and met three sets of red eyes, peering up at me from under the table. "He's going to kill himself if he tries that." My voice broke when

I said those words. "I have to stop him. If that's why he left here—"

"Maxine," Zee rasped, crawling close. He held the seed ring. I hadn't felt him take it from me, but he pushed it into my hands. He grabbed Grant's hand, too, and placed it over mine.

Grant and I shared a quick look.

"Zee," I said, but he backed away, taking Raw and Aaz with him. Dek and Mal stopped purring.

"I wonder—" Grant began, but never finished.

The world began to burn around us.

⊰⧓⊱

LAVA. We were in lava.

Or something that reminded me of it: liquid fire, viscous, thick as quicksand, burning bright and golden hot. Buried in it, over our heads. I could not see Grant, but I knew he was there, wrapped around me. Just as I was wrapped around him, so close together we were in one body.

My mother was beside us, bald and naked, covered in tattoos. No mouth, no nose, no eyes—the boys forming a solid cocoon.

Just a vision, I told myself. Grant and I weren't really there.

But her memories felt real.

I didn't know how long she had been inside the lava, but her hands moved, and she clawed upward until her head broke the surface. She was on the outer edge of an entire lake filled with lava. The air shimmered with heat. Thunderous gray clouds roiled overhead, and the shore was nothing but shining black rock, cracked with fire.

I saw movement, far away. Tiny figures riding creatures that could have been horses—except with six legs and armor that made them look like black armadillos. My mother watched them. No eyes, no mouth—nothing to indicate her thoughts—but I knew she was afraid.

She had been hiding.

My vision blurred, flashing into deserts, mountains, cities floating on clouds—jungles where the skies were purple—plateaus where reptilian humanoids lounged on stone platforms beneath two blazing suns—until, finally, I found myself with Grant in a room full of books and shadows, stone pillars shimmering like pearls, and my mother buried in soft blankets. I smelled roses. Birds trilled. She had hair, but it was very short. Her face so young. Younger than me. Covered in tattoos.

"You will carry my heart when you leave me," said a low, strong voice. "The heart of the Labyrinth. Unto you, and no other. I have never loved another as I love you."

"Then let me stay," said my mother. Her voice was shocking. I had never heard her sound so soft, so full of need. It embarrassed me. I wanted to see who she was speaking to. I was desperate to see, but no matter how much I struggled, the vision did not change. All I could see was my mother, but even she became indistinct, as though trapped behind a blurred lens.

"I wish you could stay," that deep voice murmured. "But I cannot stop the future I see. You *must* go."

The room faded a little more. I glimpsed the man, moving like a ghost. I could barely see my mother—little more than a tattooed figure shrouded in shadows.

But I saw the seed ring that was pressed into her hand.

"You know how to use this," he said, quietly. "I have already imprinted the things she will need to know."

My mother grabbed his arm. "I can't do it without you. I don't know how to be a mother. I can't protect her."

"You can shape her," said the man. "She will do the rest."

My mother faded away. But not the man.

I still could not see him—not clearly—but for one chilling moment I felt as though he could see me, searching through time, and whatever space separated us, to stare into my eyes.

"Reborn in blood," he said. "Remember, *both of you*, that thoughts become things. For all that exist with a will, this is true. But for you both, especially. You, born from the heart of the quantum rose."

He stretched out his hand—in it, a dagger.

Which he threw at our heads.

The blade sank through my skull. Grant's skull. Both of our minds, locked together. The steel burned through my brain like fire, carrying flashes of golden threads, starlight, sunlight, lightning bolts braided into long ropes that wove through the sky—

—and then, nothing.

I opened my eyes and saw the Messenger.

I stared, not really seeing her, and tilted my head sideways. Grant lay beside me. Both of us in a tangled heap on the floor. Dek and Mal sprawled on top of us. Zee, Raw, and Aaz crouched at our heads, red eyes large with concern.

Grant made a small groaning sound and rubbed his eyes. I didn't move. All I could think of was my mother, and that mysterious man.

Your father, said the darkness. *Your father, who looked into our eyes and did not flinch.*

Just like your man of light.

Zee grabbed my shoulders and pushed me up. Raw and Aaz did the same for Grant. My palm hurt. I looked down and found my hand clenched tight around the seed ring. The Messenger also looked at it, with displeasure.

"Our Aetar Master," she said slowly, "has been taken."

Her words were cold and went right through me. A roaring sound filled my blood, my ears.

"Taken," I echoed dumbly.

"The demons," she said, and a heavy weariness entered her voice. She stood very straight, her hands clasped together in a tight, bone-breaking grip. "I tracked the quantum fire of our Aetar Master and arrived at the mouth of the veil, in time to see his light borne up into the prison."

Jack. My grandfather. Inside the prison veil.

"Shit," I said.

CHAPTER 20

MY mother had raised me on myths and fairy tales, on riddles based in keys of three—three daughters, three sons—always the third path, the third charm. In hindsight, I sometimes wondered if she hadn't done so in order to prepare me for my grandfather, upon whose shoulders rested Odin, Merlin, Puck—every wise man, every trickster, every old god and meddler. And even if none of it was true, and my grandfather had passed through history as nothing more than an anonymous witness—that was the *possibility* of Jack. Jack could be anything, anyone. Magic was the same as the man.

And I wasn't going to let him rot in hell.

Grant grabbed my arm as we stood. "You're not going without me."

I covered his hand with mine. "We don't know how to close the veil. Someone has to stay here in case things get bad. You'll be needed."

Needed to fight if those Mahati decided to bust ranks and tear through the world. More likely than not, even if I managed to scare them again.

Or you can lead them, murmured the darkness. *Lead them on the hunt you want, preserving the lives you want. That is your right.*

"Maxine," Grant said, covering my hand that held the seed ring. "I know what to do."

Pain spiked through my skull. Like a dagger, sinking into my brain. "What do you mean?"

There was a look in Grant's eyes that was sharp, so grim it made me afraid. "Whatever hit us at the end of that . . . vision . . . left something in my mind. I know how to close the veil."

"What do you speak of?" asked the Messenger. "What vision?"

I didn't know how to answer her. All I could do was hold Grant's gaze, watching determination sink into every line of his face. Whatever he had seen, he believed.

"Thoughts become things," he said, softly. Dek chirped, licking the back of my ear. Mal did the same to Grant. The other boys scattered around us, quiet. I looked around Jack's home, feeling dazed, and focused on the closed bedroom door. I imagined the boy sleeping on the other side, in the dark.

"Call Killy," I said. "We'll need her to watch Byron."

He didn't argue. Just reached inside his back pocket and pulled out a cell phone. He limped away, leaning hard on his cane. I watched him, then stared again at Jack's home, at the maze of piled books, and the paintings on the walls—the lovely mess that was chaos and a perfect tumble of words and cozy charm. I had eaten birthday pie at this battered table. I had blown out candles and made a wish.

Everyone safe. Everyone happy. Forever, and ever.

The Messenger stood still, her eyes closed. Meditating, conserving her strength.

"How did they capture him?" I asked her. "He's nothing but energy."

"The demons developed devices during the war," she said, unmoving. "They had many ways of hurting our Aetar Masters."

"Like what?"

She finally opened her eyes. "I do not know. The Makers do not speak often of the war. Too many were lost."

"And no one worries the veil will fall and that it will begin again?"

"I am not privy to such thoughts," she replied coldly, and shut her eyes a second time. "I require a mule if I am to fight."

"Take a demon," I told her. "One of the Mahati."

She frowned. I slipped the seed ring into my pocket and walked to the bedroom to check on Byron. Zee, Raw, and Aaz came with me, pouring through the shadows. I left the door open and felt the Messenger follow as I sat on the bed beside the boy. He was deeply asleep.

I couldn't see human auras or holes in spirits, but I know what that furrow between his eyes meant, even while unconscious—and I recognized the way he clutched his covers with his fists. I wanted to ruffle his hair but was afraid of waking him.

His memories are buried in layers, murmured that sinuous voice. *His time with you is close to the surface, but if you wait, it will be more difficult.*

I'd rather him forget me than be hurt.

We will not harm him.

I wanted to believe that. It was so tempting. I could feel my need on the tip of my tongue, another kind of hunger:

to explore the limits of the power inside me. For one good cause. Helping Byron.

"You wish to act," said the Messenger.

"I don't want him to forget me. I know it's selfish."

She studied the boy. "We are trained to forget attachments. Attachments interfere with our ability to serve our Aetar Masters."

Something in her voice, the way she said it, made me search her gaze. "You remember, though. You remember someone."

The Messenger's jaw tightened, and her hand twitched toward the boy's foot. "I will attempt to retrieve his memories."

I hesitated—expecting her to say something else—but all she did was hum, and narrow her eyes as she stared at Byron. The teen stirred in his sleep, clutching his blanket a little tighter. Her voice took on an odd sound—

—and she stopped, abruptly. I didn't like the way she looked at him. Like something startling, unexpected, had just flashed her. And not in a good way.

"I can do nothing more," she said.

"What happened?"

She stood gracefully, towering over the bed. "He is a complicated child."

Raw, perched nearby, made a mournful sound. Inside my head, that deep voice said, *Just one touch.*

I put my hands in my lap. Below us, down in the art gallery, I heard the faint chime of the doorbell. Not much insulation in these floors. Zee reached out from beneath the bed, grabbed my ankle, and tugged.

"Needed," he rasped quietly.

I stroked his head and leaned over to study Byron's sleeping face. I had known him for a year and a half, and in that time he had gone from being a kid I was just helping, to someone who made me feel . . . like a mother.

He should have looked older, but he was the same fifteen-year-old I had first met in a dark, wet alley. Brave, good kid. I wanted to wake him up to see if he would say my name, but that was pathetic and made my heart break a little more.

I stood and left the room. The Messenger had already slipped away, but she stood at the kitchen table, studying the bone fragment. Ignoring me with such intensity I felt the skin prickle on the back of my neck as I wound through the maze of books to the apartment door.

A woman's voice drifted up the stairs. Not Killy. But familiar.

I found Blood Mama standing with Grant, alone in the art gallery's shadows, a good ten foot distance between them. Mal had looped himself over Grant's head, hissing. I looked for anyone else—inside, or on the sidewalk outside the gallery—but the hush and feeling of empty air was complete. She had come alone.

Same human skin. Same coiffed appearance, with her perfect legs and red hair. But her aura did not thunder, and her human face was hollow with pain and fear. Raw and Aaz clung to my legs. Zee sidled near, watching Blood Mama with fire in his eyes. She could not look at him. She could not look at me.

For all her arrogance, she had been afraid of the veil's breaking, of the other demons finding their freedom. Her worst nightmare, maybe, as much as it was mine. For different reasons. I remembered the Mahati eating her children. I remembered what Ha'an had called her, which was the same name the darkness had given her in Killy's bar.

Lady Whore.

I almost felt sorry for her. Almost. Except for the fact that she had arranged my mother's murder.

"Where's the entourage?" I asked.

"Don't," she said. "Don't enjoy this."

I was silent a moment, feeling tired and cold. "There's nothing I enjoy less."

Her aura shuddered, collapsing around her shoulders before flaring, once, as though in defiance. "Do what Lord Ha'an asked."

"Lead the hunt." I drew in a deep breath. "No."

"No," she whispered. "I knew this day would come. I made my bargains, I extracted promises from your blood-line. But none of that means a thing without your protection from the Lords of the prison."

I walked closer, Zee and the boys gathered close like wolves. "Did you think the veil would break, and somehow I'd be a different woman? Overcome? You thought I would give in that easily?"

Her eyes glittered. "The power inside you is immense, and thoughtful. And it loves only one thing. Death."

You do not know us, said the darkness, rising thick and hard into my throat.

"Do not presume," I said, a moment later, those words emerging on their own, without my control. Grant shifted, watching me. Zee touched my knee.

Blood Mama shuddered, lowering her head. "Lead them. It is the only way to stop them. You will never kill them all, no matter how strong you are. The Mahati are only the beginning. Ha'an is a strong Lord, but still weaker than the others. He thinks too much."

He is loyal, said the deep voice, receding from my throat. *He does not connive like her. Or the others.*

Stand-up guy. Who still wanted to eat humans.

I glanced at Grant, but he studied Blood Mama with that inscrutable expression I knew so well: thoughtful, a little cold. But not cruel.

"If you're afraid," he said, "stay outside the veil."

Her disdain was sharp. "And what good will that do me? The veil is open, Lightbringer. You cannot convert all the Mahati."

"But we can close the hole," he told her quietly. "We can lock them up again."

I drilled holes in his head with my gaze. He ignored me, but there was something in his eyes, something I had to trust. I had no choice.

"You're a fool," said Blood Mama warily. "That is impossible."

"You will not make any more children if you do this," Grant went on. "You will not harm humans. You will not scheme. You will not live on pain."

"Otherwise, get the hell out," I told her. "I'll be sure to bring your name up to Lord Ha'an. I'll be seeing him soon."

Fear flickered, and she went very still. "Do not."

I smiled. "My ancestors may have been stupid enough to promise you your life, but I don't think anyone ever said they wouldn't *talk* about you. That right, Zee?"

"Right," he rasped, dragging his claws against the floor.

My smile widened. "Ha'an is going to *love* you, when I'm done."

Blood Mama swore at me, her aura flaring wildly. "How do I know this is not a trick?"

"We're not asking much," Grant replied, "for a demon desperate to live."

She pointed at him, her finger making a hooking motion. Mal hissed at her. All the boys growling.

"I promise," she spat out, ignoring them, looking only at him—and then me. "I promise not to connive, not to make children, not to cause pain. I promise on my blood, on my honor as Queen."

"No queens here," Zee rasped. "None but Maxine,"

Blood Mama flinched, giving him a hateful look.

Shadows moved on the sidewalk. Grant opened the door.

Killy clicked her little bootheels into the studio, followed closely by Father Lawrence. He looked human, brown-skinned and round in the stomach. There was a bulge under his black sweater that screamed gun. I'd seen him shoot before. He had good aim—at close range. I suspected, strongly, that he wasn't going to be returning to the priesthood.

Killy didn't talk to me. Or look at me. She faltered when she saw Blood Mama. And then, again, when she saw the Messenger, who had come down to stand silently in the shadows. Listening, watching.

But Killy said nothing. She sucked in a deep breath and brushed past, disappearing up the stairs.

Father Lawrence glanced at us all but settled his gaze on me. "Is it time, Hunter?"

I could only guess what he meant, but the safe answer seemed to be, "Yes."

The priest nodded, with a wistfulness that made my heart hurt—and glanced at Grant. "Take care of her."

"You do the same with Killy and Byron," Grant said.

Blood Mama was already backing away to the door, disgust on her face—and fear. I held out my hand to Grant, and he took it. The Messenger gripped my shoulder. Zee wrapped his claws around my wrist. All the boys gathered close.

I closed my eyes. Focused. The armor tingled. So did the scar beneath my ear.

"Away we go," I whispered.

We entered the forest below the crack in the veil, and it was dark and cold, except for the red seam frozen in the sky. I saw no demons, but that meant little. I smelled blood, and the scent made me hungry, deep inside. The darkness rippled into my throat, spreading beneath my skin. Zee, the boys, stared up and up, their eyes glowing.

"As soon as I have Jack, I'm out of there," I told Grant, hating how breathless I sounded. "If I'm longer than five minutes, start anyway."

"Right," he said. "Of course I will."

"I'm serious. Are you sure you can do this?"

"Not even a little."

"Liar," I said, watching his mouth tick into a faint smile that did nothing to smooth away the grimness of his gaze and set of his jaw. I glanced at the Messenger. "Remember what I said about the Mahati."

She ignored me, staring at the crack in the sky. I refused to look up—if I did, I wasn't certain I would be able to go through with this. It didn't matter that I was supposed to have power. It didn't matter that I had the boys. I felt small and terrified, like a kid in a dark room. Terrified of what I would find, of what would happen to me. Scared to death that I would fail.

I looked once more at Grant, soaking him in. Feeling that second pulse ride against my heart—our bond white-hot.

"Be careful," he whispered.

"You, too," I said, and slammed my armored fist against my chest.

Moments later, I stood within the prison veil.

❦

OF all the nightmares, and all the things I had never let myself imagine that I would have to do, entering the prison veil was surely at the top of the list. I had no concept of what to expect: fire, maybe, burning air, brimstone, acid.

Torment.

Instead, I walked onto a solid stone plain that looked like the first jut of primordial land, pushed from the sea: cracked and steaming, and heavy with the scents of blood and sulfur. Zee, Raw, and Aaz tumbled around me, crouched and staring. Dek clung to my throat, but Mal had stayed with Grant.

Clouds shrouded the sky, rolling golden and crimson, and in the distance I saw statues: immense carved beasts with wings and talons, and long, sharp faces that resembled the Mahati. Beneath those statues were small groups of moving figures, and smoke, and walls. Homes hacked from the rock itself.

From there to where I stood, and all around, were the Mahati. More than I had imagined, more than I could have conceived: thousands upon thousands, hundreds of thousands. I stood in the middle of a city—behind me, more structures hacked from stone: low towers, and narrow lanes, archways covered in rippling flags, torn and stained. I heard singing, the clang of metal, voices garbled in melodic conversations. Small naked figures darted through the crowd—children, I realized with shock—silver hair loose and flowing, and their long fingers sharp as knives.

All the fear I had brought with me faded into a coarse sort of wonderment.

Life in the prison veil. Life, going on.

And it was raw, and beautiful.

No one noticed us at first. Where the boys and I stood, they were too busy dividing up clusters of Blood Mama's parasites, which were filling the air with high-pitched, bloodcurdling screams. Vast nets filled with shadows had been dumped on the stone ground, and the Mahati who waited for them appeared hollow with hunger. The lines were long.

They need more, murmured the darkness. *So much more.*

Not from me, I told it, though I felt a terrible regret. *Not from earth.*

"Jack," rasped Zee, pointing. I looked, and saw a bright light burning just above the heads of a distant Mahati crowd. The light pulsed in one spot like a beacon, locked in place.

Lord Ha'an stood beside that light, taller than the Mahati around him. He gazed across the heads of his people, into my eyes. Others followed suit. A cry rose up, a deafening trumpet of voices raised at once—falling, at once, into a profound hush. Those nearest stopped moving, maybe breathing.

Dek licked the back of my ear. I exhaled, drew in another deep breath, and walked to Ha'an. The first step was the most difficult, but I looked at Jack's light—straining now, toward me—and kept moving. The boys spread out, low to the ground, graceful and quick: sleek as bullets, the spikes in their spines longer, sharper, as though the very air was changing them.

Mahati stepped aside for us, kneeling. All of them, thousands of bodies, rippling downward with shoulders and heads bowed. Maybe they knelt for the boys, and not me—but the sight was still terrifying and struck me numb. It was not supposed to be this way. The veil was hell. I had been raised to fear it, fight it. Kill what waited within.

But my gaze swept over those lowered heads, my own head spinning, and the only eyes that stared back belonged to children—little Mahati—who did not know enough to be frightened, or respectful, or whatever the hell made their parents drop to their knees. They stared with solemn, curious eyes—and as alien as they were, I couldn't think of them as monsters. Not a single one of the thousands of Mahati surrounding me.

A threat, yes. A terrible threat. They would destroy and enslave humanity if I couldn't stop them.

I didn't know how to stop them without killing them. And that seemed just as wrong.

It is wrong. Look how they would worship you, said the darkness, rolling through me with a terrible pleasure: uncoiling high in my throat, stretching every inch of my skin until I felt ripe, ready to crack, split, spill.

Ha'an towered, waiting in silence. When I drew near, he folded his long, tined fingers over his chest, bowing his head at the boys, and me.

Green eyes glittered. "I thought you might come."

I looked at Jack's light: translucent, a white fire pitted with turquoise and purple, seemingly locked within the cradle of a stone pillar. I could see a spike, at this distance, driven up through the middle of him—and sensed a low vibration in the air. His light strained and fluttered in my direction—his soul, consciousness, dreams. My grandfather.

"For the Aetar," I said. "Yes, I came for him."

"Will you save him, too, as you do the humans?" Ha'an turned and swept his fist outward, a sharp, violent gesture. Mahati scrambled to back away, pushing each other, some carrying children. Leaving us alone in a large semicircle—a grant of privacy.

Raw and Aaz sniffed the sand around the pillar, making a full circle before coming back to me. Zee stayed close. Dek was very quiet. Ha'an watched us all, inscrutable.

"How will this end?" he asked.

I looked at him, all around him, at the Mahati—strange and dangerous, with their sharp fingers and missing limbs, and those chains that chimed in the crimson air like silver bells. I looked into their eyes, those shining black eyes that stared at me with fear and hope, and distrust—and a

great heartbreak soared within me, which had nothing to do
with the darkness, though the darkness curled around it as
though nursing a sore.

"I don't want to be your enemy," I told Ha'an. "But I
can't be what you need."

Not yet, breathed the darkness inside me.

Ha'an tilted his head, anger burning the backs of his
eyes, and something else, too: deeper, more thoughtful.
"You are gambling with our lives. Not just our bellies,
but our lives. We, who are locked in the veil, are not one
people. We are different breeds, and there were wars once
between us, for those differences. When we joined together
to survive, when we filled the army with our lives, it was
only the strength of the Reaper Kings that kept us from
each other's throats."

I glanced down at Zee and the boys, who stared at Ha'an
with such regret, such sorrow: memories so strong I could
taste them, feel them, on the tip of my mind, like a dream.

Their memories, our memories, your memories, said the
darkness. *So desperate, to open our door—to summon us
for our power—and we came to the Reapers with a will
and a hunger. Helping them gather the clans, forcing them
to bond before the war spread, and all those lives were lost
to the shadow.*

And the price? I asked, wondering what war, what enemy, could be so terrible to frighten my boys, the boys I
knew now. Not the Avatars, surely. *What did you want?*

It did not answer. I shivered, and listened to Ha'an say,
"The veil is weakening, everywhere, all the walls that di-
vide the Mahati from the Shurik, and the Yor'ana from the
Osul. I told you before . . . my people are too weak to stand
against them. They will enslave us."

He crouched before Zee, dragging his long fingers
against the stone. "You understand. Perhaps you are not

the Vessel any longer, but you and your brothers are still Kings. Our Kings."

"Different life," Zee rasped. "Different dream."

I crouched, too, dragging my own fingers against the stone, my silver, armored fingers, which glimmered in the red light as though soaked in metallic blood.

"There are other lives at stake," I told him. "Lives I'm responsible for."

Responsible for people who do not know, or care, that you exist. Billions of humans who cannot conceive of the power you wield, or what you sacrifice. But the Mahati care.

I ignored the voice. Ha'an stared at me. "Humans are worthless except as slaves and food."

"You're wrong."

"Wrong or not, we are starving. Look at them. All but the very young are missing limbs, and flesh. We have been forced to desecrate the dead."

"Like you said," I told him, "it's not just flesh you want, but pain. You want the *hunt*, not the meal. And until that changes, *I can't help you*."

Ha'an's jaw tightened, and he looked down at Zee. "You agree with this?"

I held my breath when Zee hesitated, but the little demon finally said, "Yes."

"We have reached an impasse, then," he said, with disappointment and weariness. "I cannot kill you. And while you could kill me, kill us all, I suspect you would have done that by now if that were your true desire."

I had been raised on violence, witnessed violence—all my life—but I had no stomach for it. I glanced at Jack— his burning light—and felt another light inside me, shining beneath the coils of the darkness.

But more than that, I felt *me*, my own self, running

even deeper than the darkness and the light. I felt my own
roots inside my soul, roots I had been born with, roots my
mother had grown—and when I thought about killing all of
the Mahati, when I thought about letting them kill, every
fiber of my being said, *NO*.

So lead them, breathed the darkness. *That is the only
way. No one else can be trusted. You could do such good.*

My vision wavered. I reached for Zee, needing his shoulder to stay upright. I felt as though I were being pulled into
the void, but it was just my mind, my sight swept sideways
with dizzy speed. Images shimmered in front of me, inside
me, spreading over the coiled scales of the darkness like
some movie screen.

I smelled smoke. Fires flickered. I found myself in a different place, even though part of me was firmly aware that
my body still crouched on stone, inside the prison veil.

But in my mind, I peered through the leaning trunks of
palm trees and wild undergrowth. I heard human women
screaming. Human men laughing, swaggering into sight,
armed with rifles and machetes—dragging those women
over the ground, most of them already naked. I couldn't
move to help them. Not with all my will.

This is now, said the voice.

The scene faded, replaced by other, more terrible, vi-
sions. Glimpses of terror, suffering, every profound
humiliation—and the voice said, *This is now, somewhere
now*, and on it went, with me unable to look away, even for
a moment, until it felt as though I were being ripped apart
from the roots of my soul to my skin. I wanted to scream. I
wanted to tear myself apart for all those men, women, and
children who right now *at this moment* were being raped
and murdered and forgotten. Everywhere, around me, below me, outside the veil.

See what you are responsible for. You, Hunter. You could

change this. You could fix this, with a word. You already decide who lives or dies. You, killer. You, who have murdered demon and human. This is no different. Lead the hunt.

Do not give up an army that could change the world.

Do not give up an army that needs you. The same atrocities will happen to the Mahati if you walk away. Now or later, they will be ravaged. Can you live with that?

"No," I whispered, breaking on the inside—breaking. A scream boiled in my chest—rising higher and higher—burning through me, killing me. What I wanted I couldn't have. Not both. Not both, without sacrificing something terrible. All that power, gone wrong. Power always went wrong. That was the price of having it.

A woman screamed inside my mind, but the voice was familiar. I was in moonlight again, watching my ancestor sob over her dead mother. Lost in those sobs.

So lost. I felt the boys pull on me, grabbing my arms, but their touch only made the sensation worse, like I was going to rip out of my skin. I was going to. I could feel it. I wanted it. Just to stop. Everything. To stop.

No, said a little voice inside my head. Not the darkness. Something even deeper.

No, it said again.

No, it whispered. *No, baby. There's always a way. Always.*

The scream building inside me broke into a sob, and an immense hand wrapped around the back of my neck—a spider's touch, each finger long as my forearm. My eyes flew open, just as Ha'an kissed me hard on the mouth. I was too shocked to move—and it was that shock that brought me crashing down. I could think again. I remembered myself.

Ha'an tasted like blood, and his mouth was huge. Darkness rose up through my throat and touched his lips. The Mahati Lord shuddered, and broke away.

I wiped my mouth, trembling. "Why did you do that?"

He gave me a haunted look. "To understand something. Now I do."

Zee stabbed his claws into the stone. "You see the other side, Ha'an. In her mind. Humans, us, together. Hearts, bleeding, together."

I leaned hard on my elbow, rubbing my face—still unsure about what had just happened. I stared past Ha'an at Jack's wavering light, imagining for a moment that I could see an imprint of his face, there and gone, in an instant.

"War is coming," I said, still staring at my grandfather. "With the Aetar. It's only a matter of time."

Ha'an followed my gaze. "But he is not your enemy."

"No," I said.

He made a small, thoughtful sound. "Fighting the Aetar was a simple thing compared to the war we left behind."

I wanted to know more, but now was not the time to ask. "I can't afford a war. Too many innocent people will get hurt."

"And you are alone."

"No." I touched my chest, suffering a strange twist in my heart, that I could say that out loud and mean it. "I'm not alone. Just outnumbered."

"As are the Mahati." Ha'an leaned back, surveying the surrounding demons. "We are not your kind, but you are part of us. You feel it. Not just because of the thing inside you."

I feel it, I want it, I thought, as though I had slid on a glove worn some hundred years past, only to find the fit was still just right. Forgotten, but familiar.

Give in, said the darkness. *Choose. Let us hunt.*

I tasted blood in my mouth. *No.*

Yours, said the darkness. *Your army, your people, your responsibility.*

No, I said again, struggling with the need heating my veins. But another part of me, shivering, said: *Yes. I want this.*

This. Not just power. But the Mahati themselves. Their lives.

They need you. They could do such good if led.

Lead them, Hunter. Bind them. Be the heart that guides them.

I looked at Ha'an and found him studying me with those cold green eyes. Alien, but not. My threshold for the strange was becoming ever more tolerant. Dek purred against my ear. Raw and Aaz prowled, while Zee watched me: solemn, thoughtful.

"Here, now, we must make a decision," Ha'an said. "Especially as you plan to close the veil."

I flinched. Ha'an touched his mouth with those impossibly long fingers. "I saw many things inside your mind."

"Too much," I said.

"Enough," he replied. "I see now that each of us is bound by different needs, but one is the same. To protect. To save."

"Always, that," Zee muttered to himself, looking at Raw and Aaz.

"Yes," Ha'an said gravely. "It was why you brought the clans together."

I closed my eyes, unable to imagine that life, that history. My boys, as they must have been.

Magnificent, said the darkness, and I glimpsed five hulking shadows bearing down on a stone city, shadows large as the city, each step, each coiled slither, shaking the ground with lethal violence.

Then, nothing. I sagged forward, covering my eyes. The armor throbbed against my hand.

"I'm going to need an army," I said, before I could stop myself. The words sparked a cold, heavy dread inside me. I had held that thought for a long time, I realized. Ever since my encounter with the Erl-King, and the knowledge that the Avatars—the Aetar—would be coming. I just hadn't wanted to admit it.

"And we will need to be led," Ha'an said. "Perhaps not now, but soon. I do not trust the other High Lords. I am not certain I trust you. But them"—he pointed at Zee and the boys—"them I would follow, back into the inferno."

Zee touched my hand, his sharp black claws a stark contrast to my frail human skin. Raw and Aaz laid their claws on top of his, and Dek coiled even more tightly around my throat. All of us, family. Jack, with his light. Grant. Byron. I had been raised to believe that was something I could never have. But I had made the choice to do something different. Led by my heart, not my head.

Be relentless in the things you do, my mother had once said. *Make a choice, don't look back.*

"Okay," I whispered to myself. "Okay."

I looked up and stared into Ha'an's eyes. "The parasites, Blood Mama's children, have been slipping through cracks in the veil for thousands of years. Use them to get a message to me if there's trouble here."

"It will be the Shurik," he said, leaning forward. "The wall between us is thin."

I didn't know who the Shurik were, or what they were capable of, and it didn't matter. "If there's trouble, I will find a way to return here. I'll stand with you."

"You will bind their High Lord?"

"Yes," I said, with no clue what I was promising—just that I had to. "I promise."

Ha'an stilled. And then, with an odd gleam in his eyes, said something unexpected.

"I heard your name, inside your head," he told me. "Maxine."

I frowned, unsure where this was going or what it had to do with anything I had just promised. "Yes."

He regarded me with that terrible thoughtfulness. "The Reapers went by another name, before the war. They are the last five of their breed. The rest of them, murdered. An entire world, exterminated." He glanced down at Zee, who shifted uncomfortably. "What was your race called, my King?"

"Kiss," Zee said, so softly I could barely hear him. "Born from, bled from."

"Maxine Kiss. Hunter Kiss." The Mahati Lord smiled faintly, while I sat, stunned. "That will do, young Queen of the Kiss. I find your promise acceptable. We will wait to hunt until you lead us. In return, you will protect us." His smile twisted into something wry. "We will try not to be a burden."

I swallowed hard, but my voice was still hoarse. "Thank you."

He inclined his head, then leaned in, close. "My people are still starving, and they will riot if they know the veil is closing against them. They will feel it. It has already taken all my power to keep them from breaking free and hunting, wild. So I must fight you. I must hunt you, I must try to kill you, or else my people will not respect me. I must try to break through the veil, or I will not live to see another hour. I must do this, with all my power, and throw the lives of my people on your sword, so that when it is time for you to be what we need, I will still be here as your ally and not some memory of a fool who risked his race on the mystery of a strange and powerful Queen."

"I think I like you," I said.

The corner of his mouth softened. "Then do not kill me when I hit you."

I blinked. And then found myself slammed backward, Raw and Aaz taking me to the ground as Ha'an leveled a blow at my face that most certainly would have left his fingers buried in my eyes. Zee snarled at him.

"Fuck," I said, scrambling to my feet. Ha'an threw back his head, a rattling roar tearing from his throat. All the Mahati leapt to their feet. I turned and ran like hell toward the stone pillar, and Jack. The darkness burned beneath my skin.

You are strong against us, it said. *Will you stay strong?*

You don't own me, I told it, heart thundering. *You never will.*

We are in your blood, Hunter. I could taste its smile. *We own each other.*

Hair cracked through the air like bright whips. My right hand glowed white-hot, and seconds later my fingers gripped the hilt of a sword. I swung it hard, vision blurred, unable to look at the faces of the Mahati I struck. My skin was vulnerable, but Dek protected my neck and head, and Raw carved a path of guts and bone between Jack and me. Thick layers of gore covered the little demon's body, his grinning mouth frothing red. He and Aaz held spikes in their clawed hands, and they tore through the Mahati, ripping flesh like butter.

I reached the pillar. Zee was already there. I glanced over my shoulder, but there were too many Mahati to see more than bared teeth, silver skin, and the flash of those delicate chains. I saw Ha'an, behind his people, watching me. Regret in his eyes.

I didn't know how to free Jack, but I felt the stone vibrating with a hum that sank into my bones. Zee reached the top, and jammed his claws against the spike that rose up into Jack's light. He snapped it.

Jack exploded upward—a fireball, wings, a glimpse of sunlight—and then shot down with the same speed to shimmer over my shoulders like a cape of pure warm light.

My dear, he said, inside my mind. *My lovely girl.*

The Mahati closed in, snarling. I called out for the boys, thought of Grant—

We winked out, slammed into the void, and in that moment of stillness I felt my heart beat and my blood roar, and sensed a great weight bear down upon my soul, as though I were the door holding back a heavy storm that railed against me, howling in my ear.

And then the void spat us out into the forest.

It was raining. Winds strong and cold. Jack spilled away from my shoulders. I collapsed on my knees. Hands slid around me. Grant.

I shuddered, gripping his arm, noticing as though from a great distance that my hand was covered in blood. "Close the veil. Now."

"They are coming," said the Messenger.

I looked up. Bodies poured free of the veil, falling toward us. More than I had expected.

"Zee," I said, hoarse. "Can Ha'an be trusted?"

"Yes," he said, but with concern. I looked for Grant, and found him behind me, on the ground, eyes closed, mouth set in a determined line. Rain dripped from his hair, down his face. He was soaked.

When I began to stand, he grabbed my wrist.

"I need you with me," he said.

"I will fight," said the Messenger, flexing her hands. Claws pushed through her fingertips, and her skin seemed to glow. "Attend to the veil."

I barely heard her. Grant had begun to sing.

His voice rolled from his throat with the same power as a thousand monks chanting, ten thousand, countless thousands of voices rolled into his one. Overwhelming, inhuman, a primeval *om* that could have been the hum of a star burning, or blood in the veins—the sound of the spark that was the difference between the living and the dead.

Mahati slammed into the ground around us. Zee and the boys pressed against our sides. I glimpsed the Messenger, her head thrown back, mouth opening in a scream I could not hear, but that made one Mahati warrior stagger into stillness, staring at her with horror. And then, with that same horror, he turned and began attacking his own kind. I looked for Jack, but did not see him. The scar beneath my ear tingled. More bodies poured from the veil.

I closed my eyes. I couldn't watch. I had to trust we would be safe. It was all I could do to stay upright as Grant's voice sank into my bones, gaining strength. Golden light strained beneath my eyelids, threads of light, and I imagined that light burning brighter and brighter inside my chest, even as the darkness grew larger, spreading through my body until I thought I would burst at the seams and flood the world with shadow.

The darkness fed the light, and the light fed the darkness. I could see it, feel it, working inside me with every heartbeat, every breath, music and blood flowing together in terrible harmony.

I felt myself begin to change. It was not a subtle thing. My joints ached, and my muscles stretched, and the world seemed to grow infinitesimally small—my flesh fire. I burned with power. A killing, wild power that made death and life seem insignificant against the abyss yawning beneath my glowing, golden heart.

My eyes flew open, and the world was red, my skin shimmering with moving shadows that twisted like snakes. I turned my head to Grant, slowly, with effort. Rain sizzled against him, steaming, and his eyes were black—black, all the way through—obsidian veins pulsing against his throat and through his temple.

Awful, monstrous, beautiful. I couldn't hear his voice anymore, but the air around him vibrated in waves of heat.

The ground shook, sending some Mahati to their knees. Others lunged at us, driving sharp fingers toward our hearts. I expected Dek and Mal to stop them, but the little demons didn't move—and the Mahati turned to ash before they touched us. Grant threw back his head, shuddering. His skin split, bleeding—and so did mine, all along my hands.

Stop, I said, inside my mind.

You wanted this, replied that voice. *This, which is nothing to what I can give you.*

Voices filled my head, a screaming howl. I shut my eyes, focusing on my bond with Grant, wrapping my soul around it, and him. Trying to protect him from the darkness inside me.

Don't change, I told him, hoping he could hear me. *Don't lose yourself to this.*

Not like me.

My right hand burned. Against the backdrop of darkness and light, I suddenly found myself within the memory of the seed ring—the tower, the books, the scent of roses. An oasis. Grant stood with me, shivering.

The man—my father—was there. I could not see his face.

"This is what you must do," he said, pointing to the dagger in his hands. The blade shimmered with engravings so intricate, so dizzying, I wanted to be sick.

He shoved that dagger into Grant's head. I felt the blow, and screamed as threads of tangled radiance fell over me, and cut.

"Make this, and you will close the veil," said the man, somewhere beyond my sight. *"See it. Will it."*

And the darkness whispered, *So be it.*

I opened my eyes. The Mahati had stopped fighting. Their silence was immense, deafening. Some stared at us—others, the sky.

The veil had begun to close. I watched the red seam fade.

The Mahati howled. Most leapt into the sky, racing to return to the prison. To family, to friends, I didn't know or care. Others were too slow, and Zee, Raw, and Aaz killed them quickly, without mercy, their bodies moving like bullets through the shadows, quick as thought. Covered in gore.

The Messenger fought alongside them—her, and one Mahati. She was also covered in blood, nicked with wounds, but she looked over her shoulder at Grant and me, and there was something in her eyes that was made of fear, awe.

The darkness swelled. I closed my eyes, focusing on the light inside me, the burning light. My light. Grant's light.

You can't have him, I told the darkness. *You can't have me.*

We already do, it said.

No, I said, and another strange power rose from deep inside me, a tidal wave of resolve that was desperate and felt like love.

No, I said again, and slid my soul beneath, and around, the darkness. *No. You can't change us. You can do many things, but you're not that strong.*

I forced the darkness away from Grant. I tore it loose and shoved it down, deep into the well where it had always slept.

It stayed there. Grant made a choked, breathless sound, between a gasp and a sob.

And the veil closed, becoming stars and sky.

CHAPTER 21

OVER the years, I'd come to believe that my mother had known when she was going to die. Zee had never said a word about her murder—the boys didn't talk about the deaths of those mothers who had come before—but I had a feeling.

We went fishing the day before her death. It was going to be my birthday, and if there was one thing we hadn't done, ever, it was tie a line to a hook and dangle it in water.

East Texas summer. Humid as a wool blanket soaked in boiling water. Suffocating, even in the shade where we had spread a blanket over the coarse grass at river's edge, listening to the wind in the leaves and watching the brown water glitter.

I didn't catch any fish. Neither did my mother. Mostly we just sat, and drank lemonade, and were quiet in each other's company.

"I wish we'd had more days like this," said my mother.

I had never heard her sound wistful, but it was there, on her tongue, in the air, in the way she drank her lemonade, in how she so carefully did not look at me.

"Me, too," I said.

My mother stared up at the leaves and the glittering sun. "Sometimes I made you hate me. Sometimes I frightened you."

I drank my lemonade. My mother was wearing jeans and a tight sleeveless shirt. She had left her weapons at home, except for a pistol that lay on the blanket between us. Her arms glimmered with mercury and quicksilver, embedded amongst the black scales and twisting knots of muscle, the curve of claws and spikes that looked so real I had spent hours as a young child touching her arms, marveling that I did not cut myself when I ran a finger over her skin.

"Baby," she said. "I'm proud of you."

I think I blushed, or buried my face in that glass of lemonade. "I haven't done anything."

"You will." She said it like she meant it, punctuated with a mysterious smile. My mother rarely smiled. Usually it was just a twitch of her mouth, a certain warmth in her eyes. When I was little, I'd told myself that watching her bake—on those rare days when we had a kitchen—was like seeing her smile.

"I'm proud of you," she said again, looking me in the eyes. "You're not much with a knife or gun, and you've never had hard fists. But that doesn't matter. You've got it there." My mother pointed at my chest. "You've got the good heart, baby. Never forget that. Not when the world falls down, not when the worst happens. The worst always happens. But you'll be fine."

My mother's smile faded, but not the warmth, not the intensity. "You'll show them, baby. You'll show them what matters, and it won't be power, and it won't be how hard you crush, or how easy you kill. None of that lasts. None of that has meaning. Just this. Hold on to *this*, and you'll never break. You'll never lose yourself. Never. Not my baby."

Her eyes were bright, but she pulled me into a hug before I could wonder if those were tears. Her arms were strong. The boys, warm, between us.

"I love you," she whispered. "I believe in you."

I believed in her, too. I believed in her more than myself.

The next day I watched her die.

After that, I stopped believing in much at all.

But everything always changes.

⋙⋘

ACCORDING to the news—both local and national—several farms north of Seattle experienced mysterious and devastating thefts over the course of one night. Livestock disappeared—whole herds of cattle, horses, pigs—large animals that should have been difficult to transport, gone in hours. No one could explain it. No one had seen anything—no one that the police deemed reliable—though one elderly dairy farmer, leaning out his window to smoke a cigarette, had claimed to witness "damned flying men" making off with his Holsteins.

The UFO enthusiasts loved that.

Several days later, newscasters reported that each of those farms had received sizable donations from an anonymous source—more than enough money to cover all losses. Tragedy, turning into a triumph of the human spirit.

Or something like that. It sounded good. If nothing else, the farmers were happy—if on guard—and the police kept scratching their heads.

The stolen livestock were never recovered.

━━◆━━

WE went to Texas that same night we closed the veil.

Stayed in Seattle just long enough to get Byron, who still slept, guarded by a werewolf with a pistol and a psychic in red cowboy boots who took one look at Grant and suffered a migraine.

We didn't talk about why we couldn't go back to the apartment. Felt too close, maybe, with too many memories of violence. Blood still on the floor. A body in the bathroom that needed to be interred before someone followed the smell and accused us of murder. Lots of reasons.

But mostly, we just wanted to run away and didn't know where else to go.

It was an hour, maybe two, before dawn. I settled Byron on the old couch. He didn't stir, not even a little. Concerned me, but there wasn't anything I could do.

Grant sat in the kitchen, watching us. He was bleeding. His hands, his face, long cuts where his skin had split. His eyes scared me the most, though: bloodshot, crimson, through and through. He tried to smile for me when I sat down beside him, but a deep breath accompanied the attempt, and he began coughing. Blood flecked his lips, then his palm.

Raw disappeared into the shadows and came back with a first-aid kit, still wrapped in plastic. Little thief. I pulled my chair snug against Grant's and tried to open the kit. It was hard to see. My eyes burned, and every muscle in my body felt like jelly. I fumbled the case, almost dropping it, and Grant placed his hand over mine.

"I'll keep," he said.

I shook my head, but the tears had started. He pulled me close, a tremor rolling through us both that started with me and ended with him, until our teeth chattered, and we clung to each other not just for reassurance but because we were cold.

"I almost lost myself," he said. "I never thought it could happen, but that power felt so good. I could have done anything in that moment, Maxine. It showed me."

Sounded too familiar. My fingers curled against his rain-soaked shirt. "Like getting rid of all the bad people in the world."

"Changing them. Demons, too. No crime, no abuse. Peace on earth."

"The one thing that could tempt you."

"It said if I did that, I could keep you safe. That you wouldn't die young." His voice shook. "If it hadn't let go of me when it did . . ."

I kissed him, both of us desperate, lost, clinging to each other with all our strength. I didn't let myself think about what we had done, how close we'd come. To what, I didn't know exactly, just that we had stood on the edge of something terrible, a transformation that would not have left us human. Not in our bodies, maybe not in our hearts.

I heard a groan behind us, in the living room. I tried to pull away from Grant, but Dek and Mal knotted themselves together, binding us, and their purrs were deafening. Grant kissed the tip of my nose, then my eyes. He wasn't shivering anymore. Neither was I.

I heard movement, accompanied by another soft groan. Grant shut his eyes, shaking his head, and patted Mal. Both boys chirped at us and untangled their bodies so that we could shift apart. Not far. I couldn't bear the idea of being far from him. My heart felt too raw.

Byron was sitting up, holding his head. Except, there was something in his posture—

"Jack," Grant said.

I sighed. My grandfather squinted at us, like his eyes

hurt. When he tried to stand, his knees buckled, and he fell back on the couch. I looked for Zee but didn't see him—or Raw and Aaz, for that matter.

Grant's cane was on the floor. I pushed it into his hands. Both of us still bled, but it had slowed to an ooze. We had to cling to each other when we stood. Legs wobbly. Progress slow, as we hobbled to the couch. Jack watched us, a faint smile touching his mouth.

"The both of you," he began, and shook his head. "You fill me with such hope. And terror."

I ignored that. "Are you okay?"

"Yes," Jack said, but with a hollow tone in his voice that made me think he might be lying. He rubbed his hands together, white-knuckled. "You both look terrible."

Grant and I studied each other.

"I still think you're cute," he said, rubbing my bald head.

"You look fresh from the fight," I told him. "Very hot."

Dek and Mal began singing Bonnie Tyler's "Holding Out for a Hero." Grant kissed my cheek and sighed.

Jack said, "Maxine. In the veil . . ."

He stopped, as if he couldn't say the words. He looked at Grant with the same consternation. "And you. What you did, lad—"

"Impossible," Grant interrupted quietly. "I know."

"No, you don't." Jack twisted his hands even more. "What you did, the pattern of it . . . I've never seen anything like it. I couldn't have helped you erect it even had I tried. It's not something the Aetar would have designed. It's not even close to what I attempted to teach you. In fact . . . I would say it's . . . superior."

Grant stilled. So did I. I felt the seed ring, in my pocket— heavy.

"Lad," Jack said again, more urgently—but he was

interrupted—and we were saved from answering—by the front door opening.

It was the Messenger. She had been sporting injuries earlier, but those were gone, her skin flawless and pale.

"You should come," she said.

We followed her outside. It was still dark, but I felt the sunrise, close, like someone breathing in the night.

"Where's the Mahati?" I asked her.

The Messenger pointed. I looked, and saw a tall figure standing beside the barn. He was missing his left arm, chunks of flesh from his thighs, but his spine was straight, his silver braids long, and the chains that dangled from his ears to his nose chimed with a soft music. He watched us, and I felt his rage quiver like a living thing.

"You know," I said, "call me a hypocrite, but when I told you to bond to a Mahati, I didn't really mean that you should keep him."

Alive, I didn't add.

"He is strong," said the Messenger, in a crisp voice. "Stronger than any mule. See how he still retains his mind even though I control his body? I can do much with him."

She fixed me a hard look. "And I must, as it was made clear to me that humans are not to be bonded with."

"It's . . . still wrong," I said, sounding lame. Grant tweaked my hip and shook his head.

"Does that mean you're staying?" he asked her.

The Messenger touched her collar. "For now. There are things . . . I think I should learn."

I looked to see if Jack had anything to add, but he was staring at something behind me. I turned, and saw the hill where my mother was buried. My eyesight was good, even in the dark. I sensed movement. Small bodies. Dirt flying.

I took a step, alarmed. Grant grabbed my arm. "No, it's not what you think."

"How do you know?"

"It's in their auras," he said.

"They're burying me," Jack said, in a heavy voice.

I didn't know what to say. I touched his shoulder, took Grant's hand—

—and we stepped from the void onto the hill.

Jack's sheet-wrapped body had already been placed in a deep hole, set beside my mother's grave. Raw and Aaz teetered on the edge, their bodies covered in dirt. They clutched teddy bears to their chests. Zee crouched on top of a massive stone slab that looked as though it had been torn fresh from the earth. He was scratching a message into it.

Kings, I thought. *Kings and children. And friends.*

Jack walked to the stone. I joined him.

"Jack Meddle," I read, over Zee's shoulder. "Meddling Man. Father. Grandfather."

"Loved," Jack finished. He looked at Zee and the boys. "This is a tremendous gift."

Zee shrugged, not quite meeting his gaze. Raw and Aaz tossed their teddy bears into the hole, on top of the body. Dek and Mal hummed some strains from "Good Morning Heartache," doing their best Gladys Knight impression.

"Any words?" Grant asked Jack.

My grandfather stared down into the hole for a long time, then looked at my mother's grave.

"Your mother made me forget I was immortal," he said, voice soft. "As did you, Jolene, when I knew you.

"And you." Jack looked at me, his eyes full of shadows and pain. "There is no higher compliment."

He turned away from me and kicked dirt into the grave. I touched his shoulder. "Let me."

Jack stood aside, watching as I buried his old body. It was hard for me. I kept wanting to cry, which was silly, because everything that mattered stood beside me.

But I was going to miss that face.

Zee helped, in the end. So did Raw and Aaz, and Grant, though I made him sit down in the grass when he started coughing.

Until, finally, it was done. Buried and done. The boys pushed the stone over the soft dirt, and I brushed it clean with my hand. The armor glimmered. I had lost a little more palm to the metal and didn't care. I listened to the oak leaves stir, and a bird sing, somewhere close, in anticipation of dawn.

"I should go," Jack said. "The boy needs his body back."

"His memories," I said. "Let Byron keep them."

Jack hesitated. "I did that once. It was a mistake."

"Not this time." I wiped my eyes with the back of my hand. "He has a family now."

Jack said nothing. Just stood there, as though he was drinking me in, or seeing the past, or thinking something that sent a careful, thoughtful warmth into his eyes.

"Your mother was right," he said. "My good, sweet girl."

"Jack," I said.

He held up his hand. "Look for strangers with glints in their eyes, and devilish smiles. Look for me soon, my dear. You make an old man want to live again."

I reached for him—but all I caught was Byron, collapsing to his knees. Jack, gone—and I hadn't even seen his light fade.

I held the boy to me, stroking his hair. Grant limped close, as did Zee and the others. Dek and Mal crooned a lullaby.

Byron stirred, burying his face in my neck.

"Hey," I breathed.

"Maxine?" He sounded tired, confused, and tried pulling away. I wouldn't let him go. "What happened?"

"Nothing." I kissed his head, holding him tight. "Nothing you need to worry about."

⋯⟐⋯

THE kid had questions, but he was also exhausted. So tired that I had trouble getting him back to the house. I didn't see the Messenger or the Mahati—which was fine because I didn't want Byron to see them.

I put him in my old room. It was strange, being there. The wallpaper with its little painted horses was peeling, and the old wooden bed frame was more battered than I remembered. I opened the window to let in air, and while the boy was in the bathroom, Raw and Aaz brought clean sheets, blankets, and pillows for the bed, along with a bag of clothes that still had the tags attached.

I tucked Byron in. He was asleep before I pulled the covers over him.

It wasn't quite dawn when I started walking back to the hill, but the eastern horizon was turning a lighter shade of blue, and the stars were fading. The boys bounded alongside me. The air was sweet.

My scar tingled. Soft tendrils of hair stroked the back of my head.

"Worlds change," said a silken voice, behind me, "and what was, takes new forms, and is reborn again."

I turned, but no one was there. I looked up, glimpsed a shadow in the sky, then that disappeared, as well. A falling star, made of night.

I found Grant where I had left him, sitting beside my mother's grave.

"You're here more often than I am," I said, falling down beside him. He held his mother's amulet in one hand.

He gave me a weary smile, the cuts in his face making it

look crooked. "Seems like a good place to think. About all the little mysteries."

So many mysteries. Nothing as I had expected. Not the prison veil, not the Mahati, not the bargain I'd made. Not my mother, the Labyrinth, or the man there, who had imbued the seed ring with the knowledge of how to close the veil. A man who had known that it would fall not just into my possession, but Grant's.

It was my father who helped us, I wanted to say, but the words wouldn't come to me. I found Grant watching me, though, and there was a look in his eyes.

"Mysteries," I said. "Like us."

He placed his battered hand over my heart, and I held it there, listening to my body, something deeper than my body, feeling the pulse of my link to Grant—and beyond that, the slow, coiled darkness resting, waiting, dreaming.

Scared me, but not like it had before.

I might not know *it*, but I knew *myself*.

Raw and Aaz crawled into our laps. Zee shuffled close, but he was watching the east, and the dawn sky.

"Miss the sun," he said.

I had forgotten the sunrises in Texas. I'd lived in Seattle for so long, I'd almost forgotten the sun. I missed it, too, but not like the boys. I pulled Zee close and kissed his forehead. Dek and Mal hummed to themselves.

Grant shifted slightly and took my right hand. He pressed something small against my palm. I frowned, and looked.

It was a ring. Small, delicate, made of pure soft gold. No gems.

Zee and the boys stilled. So did I.

Grant tried to speak, but the words wouldn't come out. He tried again, and I covered his mouth with my hand, staring into his eyes.

I stared, and stared, then extended my left hand.

Grant took a breath, and picked up the ring from my other hand. He slid it carefully onto my trembling finger.

Zee laid his head on my knee and closed his eyes with a faint smile. Raw and Aaz covered their mouths, rocking. Dek and Mal purred.

"With this ring, I thee wed," he whispered.

"Until death do us part," I said.

31901050670506